THE BELL

ALEC HUTCHINSON

ISBN:1539717492
ISBN-13:9781539717492

DEDICATION

To my parents – I feel this one's probably good enough.

'Everybody's youth is a dream, a form of chemical madness.'

- F. Scott Fitzgerald, *The Diamond as Big as the Ritz*

The following stories take place in
Auckland, New Zealand, circa 2011…

F12

The lockdown bell was marked by being both broken and continuous. It rang for three seconds, then stopped for exactly one, and then rang for three more seconds, and this would repeat until the all clear was given – until the practice was over or until the police had cleared the intruder from the school. When the alarm sounded in F12, Mr Blasco's twenty-three Year 12 English students had been engaged in a discussion about the nature of the American Dream. They had been studying *Death of a Salesman*. During the previous lesson, Willy Loman had killed himself for insurance money and been buried in the epilogue.

Akaash, who was sitting in his usual spot near the door, had been wondering why it was relevant. He wasn't a salesman, and he wasn't American, and this wasn't the nineteen fifties. Maybe Willy just needed an online presence. 'If he'd had a YouTube account he could've networked better and said goodbye to all that door-to-door shit.'

'That's an interesting idea, Akaash. But do you think any of his fundamental challenges would've changed? How is selling yourself online any different to doing it face to face?'

'You can do it at home. You can spend more time with your wife and family instead of having affairs with secretaries in Massachusetts or whatever.'

'Where's Massachusetts?' Penelope asked.

'Think more about the process, Akaash,' Blasco continued. 'Yes, Willy is selling a product, but in order to do that he also has to sell himself. He has to portray himself as a big man and a success, otherwise people won't do business with him. And because he's not a big man, he has to fake it. He has to puff himself up. Eventually he starts believing his own lies. He becomes a victim of his own propaganda...' He broke off for a moment and wrote his last sentence on the whiteboard before lurching back to his train of thought. 'If Willy were doing business online, he'd still have to sell himself, still have to pitch himself as a success...What about the fact that he's a salesman? What's Miller trying to say there? Anyone?' As with any question asked by Blasco, the class was quiet for a period, most doing their best not to draw too much attention to themselves. As per normal, Sean's hand went up first, although Blasco chose to wait a little longer and let things linger. Sean's answers tended to be perceptive and sharp, their depth rescinding any need for the others to respond. 'Akaash? You got anything for this? Why did Miller make him a salesman instead of a tow truck driver or a beautician?'

Akaash shrugged, already content with his level of

involvement for the day.

'Okay. Sean?'

'It's like a metaphor. Like, we're all salesman under capitalism, and we're all selling ourselves, so Willy's just a symbol of someone who's being beaten at it.'

'Good.'

'And the American Dream is all about having the freedom to sell yourself and become a big shot, but that's what Miller is critiquing, right. He's saying that in this system, where we all have the opportunity to be winners, a large chunk of us still have to be losers for that to be possible.'

'Any of you write that down?' Blasco asked. No one had.

'But it's still just American shit,' said Akaash, feeling he had something to add again. 'We've been talking about this American Dream stuff for a while and…'

'You don't think it applies?

'Yeah.'

'Doesn't it?'

'My dad said Arthur Miller was a communist.' This came from Wendy, who'd been sitting near the window and discreetly trying to send text messages to her boyfriend in a science class on the other side of the school. Token involvement in discussion meant Blasco would ignore her indiscretion.

'Interesting. Did he say it from the side of his mouth as if it were a dirty thing to be, or was it kind of celebratory?'

'The first one.'

'What's a communist?' asked Penelope.

'Can you do me a favour and ask your dad who he voted for in the last election?'

'Yup,' Wendy said. She pushed send on a message made solely of emoticons.

'I think that's important,' Sean said, 'because the play is clearly attacking the ideological status quo, which was, and is, capitalism. Like, Miller's a humanist–'

'Sean.'

'Like, he doesn't hate Willy–'

'Sean.'

'He feels sorry for him, and if Willy's a symbol of–'

'Seany Sean.'

'The average man, then Miller really feels sorry for everyone. We're all losers.'

'Brilliant, buddy – write all of that down – but hand up next time. When you race ahead like that it frightens the natives.'

Instinctively, Sean looked around and back at the rest of the class. Monique was chewing a pencil and looking out the window; Jun was drawing penises on his desk; Brayden looked as if he had had a long night and might well be asleep. 'They don't look frightened.'

'They express it with resignation and boredom.'

'You haven't answered my question,' said Akaash. 'This always fuckin' happens in this class.'

'And I thank you for keeping us on track. So, is the American Dream, as projected and critiqued by a nineteen fifties Arthur Miller, relevant to us sixty years into the future and stuck on a clumpy archipelago at the bottom of the world?'

'What's an archipe–'

'A chain of islands, Penelope. And Massachusetts is a state in the North-Eastern U.S., and communism is a political and economic system where wealth and resources are meant to be distributed evenly amongst the people.'

4

'That sounds nice.'

'It does sound nice, although its application is a lot more complex than its earnest intent, and history has—'

'Sir, it's happening again.'

'Sorry, Akaash. Is it relevant? Let's answer your question with more questions, yeah?'

'Fuck, sir.'

'Indeed. Now, I imagine that the ear piece you have in your left ear is connected to a digital device of some sort, and that device is filled with music you like to listen to? Where does most of that music come from?'

'Yup.'

'My guess is it's not filled with Ethiopian jazz or gypsy folk music.'

'Nope.'

'And the last, let's say, five movies you watched. Where were they from?'

'One was from India.'

'Bollywood is growing. And the last five TV shows you saw?'

'I get it, sir.'

'And all the Xbox you play—'

'I don't play Xbox; I just like to read the plays of Arthur Miller—'

'Where are all the most popular games developed, and who are always pitched as the good guys in first person shooters?'

'Stop it, sir.'

But the lockdown bell stopped Blasco before he had a chance to stop himself. Brayden began to stir on his desk; Jun looked up from his drawings. Sean asked if the class should shut the windows and close the curtains, but Penelope was already up and doing it. Blasco couldn't recall if this was a practice run or not. They tended to happen once a year, and in the weeks leading up to a drill the senior management would have sent out an email or mentioned it during staff briefing. But Blasco never checked his emails, and he was frequently too late to catch the briefing. He tried to remember whether they'd already had the drill. The last time around it had been a hot day like today. He'd been wearing short sleeves, and a tie to foster the illusion of formality. It could have been the beginning of this year...or it could have been the end of last. Things start to run together when you've been in once place for too long.

The students were asking questions. Drill? Sir? Aren't we supposed to be under the desks? Won't that just make you an easier target for a shooter? Akaash was standing near the door, his bag already on his back. Aberrance in the school day was always an excellent chance to skip out. 'How long is this meant to go on for?' Penelope asked. Ten minutes if it's a drill. Ten minutes of ringing, three seconds on, one off. Wendy checked her new message: just a question mark. Blasco moved over to his computer to check his emails and hunt out an indication. Brayden got up and stretched his arms, yawned, moved to the windows and poked his head through the curtains.

TOM & DAVE

I could do it, Dave said.

Bullshit, Tom said.

The two boys were sitting in the Midway House – an abandoned bungalow five minutes' walk from the school. They were both Year 12, both in their school uniforms, both smoking. The house was down a hill and around a short dirty track, surrounded by the camouflage of tall bamboo. Empty beer bottles clanged on the floor as they kicked them. The rear window looked out on the harbour, its glass long since smashed.

I don't think it'd be anywhere near as hard as movies and shit make it out. You just do it, Dave said.

What about the consequences? I mean, even if you could get over the guilt side of things, there's the consequences. You've got to know you're going to get caught, and then they arrest you and you have to stand in those weird blue jumpsuits in the court dock and cover your face up so the reporters don't get a good shot of you.

I'd own that shit. I'd flash gang signs at the motherfuckers, just jump up onto a table and shout shit.

Pleading insanity? Tom said.

Nah, Dave said. Nobody buys that anymore. You gotta own it and seem like a psycho so when they chuck you in remand you've already got a rep and no one will fuck with you.

Or they'll see it as a challenge and totally fuck with you. You'd be shanked the first night – piece of glass in your kidney. Nah, the way to go is to just lose it completely when you're done with the shooting. Strip naked and start eating your own shit or something.

I'm not eating my own shit, Dave said.

Would you prefer life in prison?

I wouldn't want to eat my shit and then have the defence fail and end up in prison anyway. Then I would've eaten it for nothing.

I don't know why we're talking about shit-eating anyway, Tom said. You wouldn't be able to do it in the first place. Even if we took away the consequences, like a hypothetical, and you were in a room with your worst enemy and you had a gun and you had free rein to pull the trigger and just walk out of there, you wouldn't be able to do it.

I totally would.

Bullshit.

I totally would.

Nope, said Tom, stubbing his cigarette into the wall. You'd get in there and look him in the eye and see this sad pleading face and you'd fold. You'd suddenly find that you were staring back at yourself, you know? A human mirror. And then you'd start crying, drool coming out of your mouth and everything, and then you'd get down on your knees and just hug him. And then you two would just be sitting there, holding each other and rocking back and forth until the sun went down.

Why does it have to be a guy? Fuck you can be a gay sometimes.

You'd rather shoot a girl in the face?

Maybe, Dave said. You wanna hear a joke?

Is it gonna suck?

Nah, it's good.

It's gonna suck.

Stick with me. So they're looking to hire a new special-ops guy, like a new James Bond or Jason Bourne.

Who's *they*?

I don't know, some government agency.

Are we in the States or England or what?

I don't know, does it matter?

It matters to me, Tom said. I need context.

Fine, it's fucking America. And this government agency is looking to recruit a new guy for their super special-ops, black-ops undercover hard-core unit for like the nastiest most brutal jobs, like assassinations and stuff.

I don't know if units like that actually exist. I mean, even if they did–

Just shut up and listen to the joke. Suspend disbelief for a second. Anyway, so they have to recruit someone new, so naturally they go through who they have in the army and the marines and all the navy seals and find the best of the best, and then whittle it down to three candidates and set up some interviews. The interviews take place in this steel room underground at the Pentagon, and in the room there are some generals and some high up political types, and there's a gun on a table in the centre.

You're telling this really well by the way.

And the first candidate comes in and sits down, and the generals tell him that they want him for this position. But they don't tell him a whole heap about it. They just say that it's an important role, that it's vital, and that he'll be doing his country an enormous duty. But they need a certain kind of person, and in order to prove that he can be the kind of person that puts his country above everything else, he'll have to complete a task. The candidate's like, yeah, I'm in, and then the generals point to a door at the back of the room. They say, behind that door we have your wife. She's tied up. If you want this job, you have to pick up that gun, go in there, and shoot her in the head.

Heavy.

Yeah. So this first candidate, he thinks about it for all of a second and he's like no, I can't kill my wife. And then he thanks the generals for the opportunity and leaves.

He thanks them for the opportunity to shoot his wife?

The second candidate comes in and sits down and the generals give him the same shit about how the role is about duty and doing a service for his country, and then they tell him the same thing: your wife is tied up in the other room, if you want the job then you're going to have to pick up this gun, go in there and shoot her in the head. This second guy doesn't back away. He picks up the gun and feels its weight in his hand and then gets up and goes into the room with his wife.

That's a nice detail, about the weight.

The generals wait outside and listen and everything, and the guy's in the room for quite a while, but eventually the door opens again and he comes out and puts the gun down, and he's like, I'm sorry, I really thought about it, but I can't kill my wife.

Again, him apologising seems unnecessary.

Well, he's a nationalist, you know. He's a patriot.

Good word.

Anyway, he leaves, and then in comes the third guy. He sits down and the generals tell him about the importance of the role and how crucial it is to national security and defending the homeland and stuff. And then they point to the door at the back of the room and tell him—

That his wife's in there and if he wants the job then yeah yeah—

But before they even really finish saying it this guy's picked up the gun and kicked open the door, which is left swinging from the force, and then the generals hear all this screaming and smashing, like agonising shit, and when he comes back out he's panting and covered in blood, and the generals ask what happened in there? And the guy says, well the gun you gave me wasn't loaded so I had to beat the bitch to death with a chair.

ALi

Ali was born in the Horn of Africa, the Cradle of Civilization, and when he was seven years old he watched a man have his left leg and right arm severed with a machete. The memory was dusty now, but sometimes it came back to him in flashes: a ring of onlookers, a pile of rocks, his view obscured by the legs and hips of adults. The images faded in and out; blood on white teeth, blood in the dirt. The man had stolen something and this was his punishment.

By the time he was ten, his family had become refugees and had left Somalia behind. For nearly two years they lived in a camp in Ethiopia: his mother and father, his younger sister, and a much broader familial clan of aunts and uncles and cousins. He received limited schooling and gained a skeletal knowledge of French and shredded fragments of English, although most of the time it was simply waiting, because the lists were long, and resettlement was a nuanced process. And of course there was a difficultly with resettling Somalis: it was important to keep wider family networks together. It was impossible to send one branch of the family to Germany and another to England. It had to be a single target country in order to ensure immersion and minimise the paralysis of culture shock. The bonds of family, the research suggested, were essential to success once grounded in a host state.

Ali knew nothing about New Zealand, except that two of his uncles and one of his aunts were already there with children in tow – cousins Ali had never met. In a letter they had said it was green – all green – and that it was cold, and then Ali was on a plane – his first – and he was looking out over the sea, and then over the mangroves that led into the runway at Auckland Airport. The letters hadn't lied. It was green, and the sky was thick and grey and somehow wet without there being any rain.

His house had everything. It had carpet and wallpaper. It had running water that came from taps and a shower that produced hot water whenever he wanted it. It had couches and a TV and he had his own bed in a room with his sister. It even had grass outside – rich grass, that was thick to touch and moist if you put it in your mouth. And his cousins lived only a short walk away, so he could see them whenever he liked.

And he liked his cousins, so he saw them a lot. In that first month after resettlement he would walk to see them when they had finished school and sit in their house with them and listen to whatever they talked about. When they were around each other none of them spoke English, so it was easy for Ali to keep up, but his cousins were older than he was, so he didn't like to interrupt. Most of them had been in the country for nearly a year already, so to Ali they seemed urbane and sophisticated. They listened to aggressive rap, wore puffer jackets and jeans and had shoes with colours on them. He knew immediately that he had to get some for himself. But it was too early for him to ask his parents for something other than trackpants. They had only just moved, after all. They needed time to settle. Both of them were already taking English classes, but whenever they got home his dad would fall back into Somali. It had more complexity. It could explain more. His mother tried her best to use English, but it didn't sound right and Ali could see the pain of confusion on her face whenever she was using it. And when she finally surrendered, she told Ali that he was the best hope for English in the family. 'You will start school next week,' she said. 'You will speak English every day. It's much easier for young people to learn new languages, and it's important that you do.'

Ali was excited about school. He would meet new people and make new friends – ones with different coloured skin and different coloured eyes – and he would learn things and make his parents proud. Except that his cousins had made him nervous, because where he was excited, they seemed oddly reticent. Maybe, he thought, it's because, for them, the newness has worn off. Maybe for them it's just what they do. 'What's school like?' he'd asked. His cousins had looked around at each other – Odawaa at his brother Tarabi, Tarabi at his cousin Nasir – like they were measuring something.

'School is school,' Nasir had said. 'It is what it is.' Ali wasn't sure what that meant. 'Just stick with your family and everything will be fine.'

But Ali didn't want to stick with his family. He wanted to learn English and make friends and be like the TV. On the TV people were friends and it was fun, and he could tell this in spite of only understanding a quarter of the conversations. He often watched shows with his dad, who understood things even less than he did, but in order to help his son learn – and partly out of his own desire to catch fragments of narrative – he made Ali try to translate what was being said. 'I think the doctor is saying that the patient will die,' Ali would say.

'What is he dying of? He looks fine to me?'

'It's hard to say. I think the doctor said he has eaten too much ice and he is positive.'

'Ate ice? Are you sure? Was the ice infected with something?'

'I don't know, dad. I need to listen.'

His worries about his trackpants and oversized jumper became less of a concern when he received his school uniform. His family had been given help with the costs, and now he truly looked like he was destined for success. He had dress pants and a business shirt and a new belt and a school bag, and in the mirror he had the look of someone who was going somewhere, someone who was on their way. His mother hugged him. It was a good day. He was starting school, and a donation meant his family had new furniture, too (second hand, yes, but new to them) *and* a computer. Ali had had to translate for his parents when the man had arrived with it and plugged it in and explained how to use it. This is for documents and this is your connection to the internet and this is how you send an email. His dad had missed most of it. His mum had simply smiled and nodded. She was just happy that the family had something that looked so technical. Before the man had left he'd looked at Ali and smiled and said, 'You look good, kid. You off to school today?'

'Yes, sir,' Ali had replied, air whistling through his front teeth. 'My first day.'

'Knock 'em dead, yeah.' The idiom was confusing.

And frankly, so was school. It was like a million foreign idioms all moving at high speed. First he shook the hand of a man in a suit, then a fat woman in a cardigan gave him a piece of paper filled with numbers and letters and he had to follow her around while she pointed at buildings and said things too quickly and in directions other than his face. Then he was in a classroom with desks and a big whiteboard and a tall man with a tie that might have been the teacher and who'd said Ali's name out loud while Ali looked back at faces that looked at his: too many to take in, all different colours, all moving and smiling and laughing and staring and talking. And the sound: swirling and ubiquitous, like too many TV channels overlapping each other. In the roar of it all he understood nothing. He was given a seat at a desk and then the teacher said something and although Ali didn't know what it was, the students around him began getting out books from their bags – books that Ali didn't have – but right now he was too scared to ask, so he smiled and looked straight ahead and hoped everything would be fine. Which, despite all indication that it wouldn't be, it was, because the person next to him, an Asian boy – the first Ali had seen up close in real life – gave him a piece of paper and a pen and said something quickly, and then the teacher was writing things on the whiteboard and the class was copying, pens moving rapidly across the page, tongues half-poked from mouths, hands bent into academic claws. Ali mimicked them. He leaned in and started to write, looked up to recheck he was copying correctly, then bent back down to his page: Personification – Attributing human qualities to inanimate objects or abstract notions, e.g., This chair hates me. Give your own example... 'What does abstract mean, sir?' – Ali managed to catch the question. He even nearly understood it. He looked up from his writing. The answer, however, meant nothing to him. Rhetorical Question – A question that... And that's as far as he got, because a bell went, and he was worried, of course, that he hadn't finished the other fifteen definitions, but it was too late, because things were moving forward and soon he was in another room with another teacher and there was more he didn't understand, and then a bell went again and it seemed he was meant to walk around the school while other students ate lunch, and then he got lost, and another bell went, and after sitting on a bench for a while, unsure what to do or where to go or who to ask, another overweight white woman shouted at him and told him to go where he was supposed to be, and he understood this, so he went home.

It wasn't all like that though, and after the first week things started to make more sense. Despite what critics say about the unwieldy bureaucracy of public schools, sometimes things do get noticed, and Ali was quickly moved into an ESOL class for all English periods. This once-a-day ESOL hour was an immediate release for him. Vertically streamed, it was a mixture of Chinese students and a handful of Africans, all of whom spoke with heavy accents and broken syntax. It became a safe-house. Regardless of background, people smiled here; they breathed easy and took their time. And best of all, Ali shared the class with his three cousins, Nasir, Odawaa and Tarabi. Now he could talk to them and feel at home and protected, and when lunchtimes came around he could meet them at a pre-organised spot rather than walking in aimless circles through crowds of disinterested faces. It made everything okay. He could speak Somali and laugh and belong. And this was important...

STELLA

Everybody knew that Stella was depressed. Her peers knew it. Her family knew it. The guidance counsellor was well aware of it, and people passing her on the street and who cared to glance could usually figure it out. So she wasn't coming to school much, and when she did, she was late, and most days she left early and walked home and thought about dying.

On Monday Stella's mother left her in bed, and when she finally got up at eleven she immediately got stoned and sat in the garden and stared at the caterpillars chewing on the swan plants. By three she was back asleep and dreaming of a different space.

MS BAKER

Ms Baker had Bloom's Taxonomy gun-stapled to the wall above her desk. The poster had been laminated, and unfortunately that meant light from either side of the class reflected off it, so unless you were sitting directly in front, it was difficult to read. Not that any of her Year 10 Science class had bothered to. They were a lower band, quick to anger and with all the attention span of house pets. To them, words like 'Evaluating' and 'Analysing' might as well have been Chinese symbols on a shop front, unfathomable and hardly worth the effort.

When the lockdown bell began to ring, she had been attempting to break apart the beginnings of a fight. It had been a tough lesson, the kind that stirred her into nervousness even as she was planning it the night before. And she always planned the night before. It was her first year teaching, after all. She didn't have a ready-made supply of lesson plans, or the casual ethos of the senior teachers. Whereas they walked into class and managed to figure out what they were teaching in the time it took to do the roll, she was routinely buried in photocopied hand-outs and the feeling that things were on the verge of going horribly wrong. Not that they really ever had…but they might. She'd had dreams where she'd started bleeding from the nose mid-lesson, dark red spots accumulating on the lab table in front of her as her students began to laugh, at which point she had passed out and woken up, her boyfriend stirring next to her in bed. 'You alright, Steph?' he'd ask.

'Bleeding dream again.'

'Oh.'

She'd asked him what he thought it meant one morning as they were drinking coffee and he was more receptive than usual. 'It's hard to say, you know. It's not like you do an awful lot of cocaine or anything.'

'It just feels like I'm under pressure, like things are out of my control,' she said.

'Then that's probably it. It's *your* dream,' he said, folding the newspaper out in a way that indicated he didn't want to talk about it anymore. 'I'm just a humble I.T. guy, remember. I think—'

'In ones and zeros,' she said, padding out the line. Fuckwit.

Standing in front of the class now she had the vague awareness that her relationship was coming to an end, that it would terminate as soon as one of them had the volition to do it. The details were the problem. They shared a flat. They shared a bank account. They only had one car. And it was an odd thought to have at the time because at that moment there were other things going on, like Eddie Tangaloa holding Corban Roberts by the back of his neck and pushing him hard into the desk. 'Eddie!'

The rest of the students had turned around to watch.

'Eddie! Take your hands off him!'

But Eddie couldn't hear her. He was in the middle of something that required his focus, his worksheet explaining the difference between mitosis and meiosis having fluttered gently to the floor. Ms Baker moved to the back of the class and got between the two boys, forcing Eddie to shift. 'Out!' she said, stern and hard – the practised teacher's voice, designed to command attention – but Eddie was looking around her body, through her, as if she wasn't there.

'Fuckin' little faggot.'

'Out, Eddie. Now!' And then Eddie was gone. The class could hear him smash his hand against the door of another room as he disappeared down the corridor. Some of the kids were laughing; Corban was rubbing his neck.

There was a process for things like this. Ms Baker was supposed to take Eddie aside as she went through her drawers and filled out a form, and then Eddie was meant to go to a designated room for the rest of the lesson where a senior teacher would oversee the work he'd been given and make sure he stayed in line. But the adrenaline of real life meant this rarely happened. Situations arose too quickly, were too violent, and Ms Baker was left shaking and unnerved while the problem kid in question wandered the school grounds.

'Let's get things back on track, shall we.' She stood at the front again and tried to regain her composure. If you pretend to be confident, then you are confident. 'Have a look at your worksheets – you should be about finished by now. Who can explain the difference between mitosis and meiosis?'

'Mitosis is the reproduction of sex cells and meiosis is

the reproduction of body cells,' said Emily.

'Good try. You've got the ingredients there; you just need to put them in a different order.'

'Huh?'

'You've got them mixed up.'

Of the thirty-one kids in the class, only Emily's mum and dad had turned up to parent teacher night, and for this Ms Baker had liked them instantly – two funny little people with thick glasses, limited social skills and an interest in their daughter's future. She wanted to hug them. And maybe as a result she ended up telling them that their daughter was doing better than she really was. But what did it matter? Self-esteem couldn't hurt, and these people needed a little praise. As for the rest of the students, Ms Baker had tried to make the effort to call the parents at home. She'd sat at her kitchen table with the phone and a list of names and numbers while her boyfriend played on his computer in his office.

Corban's parents had assumed he'd done something wrong, and she could hear the shouting begin in the background, and so she'd backtracked at high speed and told his mother lies: 'He's doing wonderfully. He's really engaged. I was just calling to let you know that. And if he can renew his focus then I think he'll be well prepared for—'

'He's not focusing? Jesus!'

'No, no he is…'

Joseph's house. Someone picked up the phone but then chose not to say anything. She could hear music playing somewhere in the background. 'Hello?' She listened for a response, pressed her ear harder into the receiver. The gentle suck and burn of someone dragging on a cigarette. 'I'm calling for the parents of Joseph

Hartnell… Do I have the right number?' And then the line went dead.

Eddie's house. Three rings and then, 'Yup!'

'Hello, this is Stephanie Baker. I'm Eddie's science teacher. I was wondering if I could talk to either of his parents?'

'Yup!' And then the voice turned away from the phone. 'Eddie! Some woman on the phone for you!'

'No, I don't want to talk to Eddie, I need—' But the line had already been abandoned. She heard shuffling, then the turbulence of a hand on the receiver.

'Yup!'

'Hi, Eddie, it's Ms Baker from school.'

'Aw fuck!'

'No, Eddie, everything's fine. I just wanted to talk to one of your parents.'

'Why?'

'I just want to chat to them about your progress. Can you put one of them on the phone?'

'Not home.'

'Are you sure?

'Yup.'

'Well can—'

And another line went dead.

'I told you it was a bad idea,' her boyfriend had said without looking up from his game. 'No one wants to be bothered at dinnertime.' On the screen in front of him two disembodied digital hands were carrying a chainsaw and the chainsaw was gnawing into the body of a woman in a bikini.

And in the classroom a new fight was starting, and whatever Corban had said to Eddie seemed to apply to

Joseph as well, because now Joseph was out of his seat and standing over Corban and staring him down, and Ms Baker knew that this one was going to be bad because Corban was staring back, and even above the noise of the class – who'd given up on their worksheets and were throwing things at each other and burping and making faces at nothing – she could hear the word faggot bounce back and forward like a ping pong ball. It was odd, she thought – a thought on top of a thought – as she moved swiftly toward the back of the room again, that in its own way Bloom's was being put into action. Because Joseph had *remembered* what Corban had said, and he'd *understood* it, and then he'd *applied* it himself, and now the two of them had jumped into the higher-order section: they were *analysing* each other, *evaluating* who would come out on top. All they had left to do was be creative about the violence they inflicted. But before they had a chance, and before Ms Baker had arrived to slide in and separate them, the lockdown bell did it for her.

MiNA & AHMED

The nerve endings on young people are more sensitive. They feel things more. They appreciate chocolate in the way drug addicts appreciate heroin; they can be genuinely and authentically happy; and when the pull of their biology drags them in the direction of the opposite sex, their need to satisfy the urge is almost crippling.

Mina met Ahmed.

They weren't in the same classes, but peer groups overlapped at lunchtimes, and it was one of those rare teenage events where each became the object of the other's affection, regardless of gawkiness or acne. It's hard to say how it actually started – who said what to whom, or how they came to be sitting in the same movie theatre together with their fingers just – just – touching enough to know the other was there. Phone conversations. Text messages. Both of them gradually pulling away from their friends to find corners around the school where they could be furtive and alone. On Tuesdays Mina watched Ahmed during his soccer practices after school; Ahmed waited for her on Wednesdays while she tried her best to play netball – missing catches and running awkwardly, a smile on her face like it didn't matter. He wrote notes for her and slipped them into her belongings when she wasn't looking, and during Biology she would open her exercise book and out they would fall – clumsily written odes full of awful clichés and ugly rhymes that sealed up what it meant to be in love. Every song she listened to related to them, every hopeful cinematic romance bore connections to her own. She took photos of him whenever he wasn't looking and stored them away for herself; she planned futures for them in foreign countries where the backgrounds were a passionate haze and they moved from place to place in obsessive soft focus.

Mina's Year 11 creative writing was an exercise in code. All metaphors and arcane euphemisms, it detailed the weekend she'd lost her virginity in the park behind the movie theatre. While the event itself had been shrouded in darkness and took place closer to a garbage bin than she would've liked, her story transported the reader to a place between clouds where two souls mixed and danced to the harp music of cherubs. Ahmed had to console her when it failed to pass. 'Turgid to the point of being unreadable,' the marker's comment had read. 'This piece would have benefited from an edit in order to increase clarity. Also, be more careful with your punctuation.'

'Fuck them,' Ahmed said to her when she came to him crying. 'They don't know what they're talking about. This is great.' And he found this easy to say because that's what he really thought.

During year-level assemblies the two escaped the allocated seating of their classes and sat with each other, hands cupped together between them while guest speakers talked about the perils of drug use and peer pressure and the best ways to deal with the inevitability of depression. As the amplified voice echoed around the hall and berated the audience about the myriad hazards of teen sex, the two of them smiled at each other, swapped looks. They were older than they were; older than everyone else around them. They were committed. When the speaker lectured on the danger of random hook-ups, the message wasn't for them. Nor were the comments about STDs or the emotional risk involved for those who used sex to boost their self-esteem. 'If you're just going out and hooking up all the time,' the speaker had said, 'then your studies are definitely going to suffer.' Not for Mina and Ahmed.

They helped each other with homework in the library after school. Ahmed went through the basics of trigonometry with her; Mina covered supply and demand with him. Because they were going to need money if they wanted to escape and live the way they planned. They needed to stay focused. Ahmed made a point of tucking in his shirt; Mina's uniform was meticulous. They did this for each other, since it was important that nothing got in their way. There had to be no reason, no barrier, to them being with each other. Not again; not like there had been.

Fathers, of course, are protective of daughters, and mothers care about the futures of their sons, and with the intensity of the couple's feelings, neither one of them had been able to keep it secret for long. There had been shouting in the house when Ahmed's mother discovered photos of a girl in her son's wallet (such an old-fashioned way of storing memories). Shouting because his privacy had been invaded; because he was too young for the clearly heavy involvement; because he was growing up;

shouting because his mother had called her father and then the roof had come off completely. Threats had been made about switching schools, about removing Ahmed from the source of his distraction, because this girl was clearly the reason his report had been so bad and that he was preoccupied and late and non-responsive, and during the phone conversation it appeared Mina's father was a mirror to her ire. In the end, it had been Ahmed's dad that had saved them. Quietly, he had been proud of his son's process into maturity, and for the first time as a father he felt he had a role to play. Steeped in religion, he remembered how his own parents had attempted to violently quash his early romantic aspirations. Now, twenty-five years on and living on the other side of the world – a man who kept his bourgeoning atheism a secret from his wife – he saw the chance to rectify things. And so he made the physical trip to the home of his son's clandestine girlfriend and met with her father and mother and shook their hands – Ahmed sheepishly in tow – and he sat with them and explained the story of his adolescence, emphasising with dexterous verbal ability that when his own parents had forbade him from seeing a girl, it only made him try harder, sneaking out whenever he could, lying to them, his schooling suffering badly beneath his desire and rebellion. 'So I ask that we be modern about this,' he said. 'They like each other, and I know my son to be a good boy, and I'm sure your daughter is a fine girl. And if the relationship is to be, it will be. If not, then they will both learn from it.'

With the proviso that the relationship could continue only while the two of them maintained spotless study routines and age-appropriate behaviour, the two fathers shook hands and Ahmed was left sitting in the passenger seat on the ride home. 'Now it's up to you,' his dad said, rolling a filterless cigarette while the palms of his hands conducted the wheel of the car. 'If you mess it up, it'll be on your terms.'

This thought plagued Ahmed. While the intrusion of his parents into his romantic life had left him feeling unmistakably like a child again, his dad had given him the responsibility of an adult. For the first month after the intervention, he adhered strictly to the rules. He worked hard; he helped Mina study; he obeyed the curfews that had been set down around him. But it wasn't long before Mina wanted more. The gate had already opened, after all, and if they could just squeeze in some time and isolation, then why not? 'Just follow me,' Mina had said in a lascivious whisper across the books that lay between them. Her foot was touching his beneath the table. He may have been imagining it, but Ahmed believed he could smell her.

He tracked her through the door and across the field. Beyond them, a junior soccer team was practising. His shoes were getting mud on them. The sky was mottled and cold. He could see the goose bumps on her bare arms.

Before long this was a regular thing, and when it happened outdoors and behind the trees at the back of the field, it meant he had to leave quickly and get home before his mother and scrub the telltale dirt from the knees of his school pants. There was no time for the lover's linger. It had to be brief and abrupt. Not that it could have been anything else at this point. When proximity and age mixed, they fizzed uncontrollably, and neither one could restrain the other from the bites they inflicted. 'It's because you want to eat me,' Mina had said. 'You like my taste.' And Ahmed was disturbed by how much he found this to be true. When the moment struck, he wanted her all, and with

Mina's back against the twigs of the undergrowth he pressed his teeth into her arm, and then into her face, cutting her lip. And after it was over he felt guilty and evil and wanted to apologise, but Mina said it was because he loved her and he shouldn't worry. He was sweet. The boy who wrote her poems and left them in her books.

HENRY

Henry found himself standing in the wrong part of the school when the lockdown bell started to sound, and for a moment he considered whether his planned escape had backfired, whether the gears of fortune had finally begun turning against him.

Because Henry always managed to get away with things. All it required was charm and confidence. You just had to own it. This philosophy had got him in and out of whatever he wanted. When he wanted a cup of coffee, he simply walked into the staffroom and made one. 'How the fuck did you get away with that?' Greg had asked while his friend sat calmly and sipped his free java.

'I just did it. I walked in, the kitchen lady smiled at me; I smiled back and helped myself to a cup.'

'Fuck off.'

'It's true. You just have to believe you belong.'

The following day Greg had attempted the same thing, but his shaking hands and shifty demeanour were instant giveaways, and when it came time to talk his way out, all he could muster were stammers and ums, and instead of a coffee he got a detention.

Lying helped, of course. When Henry wanted a crash mat to make lounging in the sun that much more agreeable, he forged a note from an absent teacher and acquired one. When he was late, a relative had died. When he wanted to leave early, he just got up and left. 'You'd be surprised how little teachers notice,' he'd said. 'I mean, they teach like thirty students each lesson. They're engrossed. And honestly it'd be rude if I interrupted them and tried to come up with an excuse. It's politer to just get up and go.'

Before his escape on the day in question, his Year 12 History class had drifted off the topic of the Cuban Missile Crisis and were instead debating whether or not dictators like Hitler and Stalin would ever come to power again. Through the happy accident of a class seating plan, Henry had been placed next to Leila Grey, and although her long legs, clear skin and low I.Q. meant she was out of his league, Henry enjoyed flirting with her in oblique ways, doing his best to befuddle and confuse her, and hopefully foster that look she got when she didn't get something. Mrs Vanderbilt was selecting from the students with their hands up, facilitating discourse on a topic that she believed to be fruitful. 'Ben, you've had your hand up for a while.'

'It could very much happen again,' Ben said, looking studious and playing with his glasses. 'I mean, just look at the news. We have lots of Middle-Eastern countries with dictators, and they're always prosecuting their people.'

'Persecuting,' someone said.

'Good,' said Vanderbilt. 'Anyone else? Jason.'

'I think people are sheep, and that they want to be led.

33

Just look at history. It's full of examples of it happening, and history repeats itself, you know.'

'Veronica, how about you?'

'I agree with Jason,' she said, and Jason was chuffed.

'Henry?'

'But I don't have my hand up.' Laughter.

'That doesn't mean you can't be an active participant in the discussion.'

'Okay.' Henry cleared his throat theatrically and opened his exercise book. 'Let me just consult my notes on this one… What are we talking about?' Laughter. He looked sideways at Leila and found her trying to stifle a smile.

'Can you foresee dictators like Stalin or Hitler ever coming to power again?'

'Oh, okay. Short answer: no.'

With her age and floral dress, Mrs Vanderbilt was a woman of patience. 'See if you can give us a longer answer, Henry.'

'Well, to tackle both Ben and Jason's responses first up, the dictators in the Middle East tend to be confined to their states and operate where there's an almost total information blackout, so the public don't know what's going on. When that changes, so will the political systems. I know the Arab Spring's not the best example, but give it some space – revolutions take time and the world is complex. As for history repeating itself, it will only do so if the world stays the same, and if you look at the last twenty years, the world we live in now doesn't even vaguely resemble the past. As for a new Hitler or Stalin type figure, I don't see that happening unless the entire world collapses somehow and we all have to start over.'

'Why not?'

'Because we have too much access to information now. Political analysts call it transparency. And these dictators operated on information blackouts and carefully orchestrated propaganda campaigns.' He glanced sideways; Leila was making the face. 'You just couldn't convince a modern public that some massive yet specifically defined enemy likes to cook babies on the ends of their bayonets. They just wouldn't buy it. Besides, today's world is way too networked. Globalisation, you know. If you ask me, the real problem is that history means we always focus on dictators when the modern problem is the guilt-free tyranny of democracy. Like, who's really responsible for the drone strikes against civilians?'

'Good answer,' Mrs Vanderbilt said, and Jason was annoyed, and Leila was confused, and Henry decided not to give any credit to the dinner-table discussions with his father who held a doctorate in political science.

'Um, Mrs Vanderbilt.'

'Yes, Henry.'

'Just one more thing – may I use the toilet?' Laughter. It was time to leave. Better to go out on top than ruin things in the aftermath.

Outside the class it was a clear warm day. Early afternoon. In the distance Henry could hear a lawnmower. Things were good. He stopped for some water at a drinking fountain; the sun had made the water warm and it tasted metallic and bloody. Across the courtyard he saw a Polynesian boy in a Year 10 uniform walking toward the admin block. Kicked out of class, Henry thought. Why force it like that when you can just leave?

With no desire to return to the lesson and only a fictional urge to urinate, he sat on a bench in the sun and closed his eyes and slipped peacefully into fantasies. Most of them involved driving somewhere with a girl – Leila Grey, habitually… and what a ridiculous name she had, the moniker of a comic-book temptress with erotic superpowers – and when he opened his eyes again it was to focus on the problem of not having a driver's licence. A fake I.D. could get him beer, but it couldn't transport him to the beaches and mountainsides of his daydreams. And it could only get him female company for the brief interval it actually took to purchase their R.T.D.s – then they were off to meet older guys with vintage cars. Guys who were already out of school working as apprentice builders and mechanics and who had tattoos and all-year tans. These were the real problems of the age. These were the things that required time and attention.

He walked the school with his hands in his pockets. If he'd had the ability to whistle, he would've. At the weights room he stopped to do chin-ups with a group of Indian boys, talking himself up before managing just one. At the basketball courts he interrupted a game and tried to shoot for three, inevitably missing not only the hoop but the backboard as well. Outside a junior maths class he taunted a kid through the window, making obscene gestures before ducking and running when the kid alerted the teacher. At the window of Mr Blasco's classroom he pulled the finger at Akaash (because he liked him). Akaash gave him the finger back. Blasco simply ignored it. After knocking on the door of Greg's classroom he handed a note to the teacher, who, half-asleep it seemed, read it out loud without thinking: 'Greg, your girls' swimming practice has been moved to tomorrow.'

When the lockdown bell began to sound, he found

himself between activities. He'd memorised Vanderbilt's photocopy code, and he wanted to use it, but he was unsure how. He was considering making a series of flyers that announced a coming-out party for Greg, but for some reason empathy was getting in the way of their production. But now the bell was sounding – three seconds on, one off – and Henry was standing exposed in the school's interior courtyard, and over the bell he found it hard to hear the lawnmower, and he noticed that the seagulls that hung around the bins in the period after lunch had upped and gone, and around him classroom curtains were beginning to close – like they were shutting him out, like he was the problem – and he wondered what to do: to stay, to let it pass, or to return to his room; and for a brief moment – a second to be precise, the exact length of the pause between the sustained electric clang of the bell – he wondered if he really did hear a scream.

DANNY

Very early on, Danny had been identified as *Gifted and Talented*.

Danny also once drank his own piss on a dare.

It was fresh of course. That was part of the deal. Out and in with as little time as possible to let the stuff ferment. It wasn't so bad. All he'd had to do was shoot it into a bottle and throw it down, and as it had passed across his taste buds while the others were watching and sniggering, he'd been struck by the realisation it tasted a lot like cellotape.

He didn't do it for nothing. There were a hundred dollars involved – ten from each member of the audience – and while Danny was aware that he was conducting what amounted to an amateur freak show, he wasn't worried about the social aftermath. People only got picked on if they hesitated or made a deal out of something. If he'd made a face or quavered or thrown up, it would have been tough to live down. But he didn't. He sculled it straight and fast and then howled like a wolf, and by being able and willing to eliminate his dignity, he paradoxically increased it.

It was a skill he had learned rather than something he was, because if he was going to be big – if people were going to recognise him on the street – then it was vital that he could eliminate his ego at will. In the immediate aftermath of the dare, one of his peers had suggested that he do it for the internet and post it on his channel, and for a moment he considered it, but it was important that he kept his channel clean and sold himself as someone worthy of praise rather than disgust. It was a fine line. The video in which he covered his chest in clothes pegs was already borderline, and his attempt to pierce his own nose had been considered by many of the comment makers to be a bloody exercise in dumbness. Piss drinking would tip the scales.

Having been forced into a school play at the tender age of ten, Danny had quickly discovered the joys of attention. It didn't matter that he mangled his lines quite thoroughly, because the audience had started to laugh as he ad-libbed his way through the death scene. While Mrs Keer had been less than pleased, the accolades that poured in afterward – from friends, from slightly tipsy adult members of the audience – had made it worth the telling off. So acting became a thing, but not because he liked acting. For the most part he was terrible at it. When an overly-ambitious intermediate school teacher attempted to stage Brecht's *Threepenny Opera*, Danny's Mack the Knife came off as maudlin and soft rather than brazen and self-assured, although it's hard to expect range from a twelve-year-old. His singing voice, however, was passable, and when the adults who'd been forced to sit through the show were required to make an encouraging comment, they picked his singing to congratulate – the least dreadful aspect of the whole three-hour affair. Danny clung to these comments. 'Not half-bad, buddy,' which to Danny meant: excellent, keep doing it – there's a golden ticket in there somewhere.

In his first year of high school Danny tried out for the school show, a science fiction spin on *Romeo and Juliet* where the Capulets and Montagues were warring alien civilizations, however he was given a minor role and no matter how badly he attempted to mess up his lines, his part was too inconsequential for it to make a difference. To sate his urge for mass attention, he was forced to compete in the Talent Quest, the annual lunchtime competition that catered to the needs of people just like him. Where the rigidity of scripts had left him bottled and claustrophobic, the Quest offered the freedom to be a total buffoon. And it was a better audience, the genteel stoicism of a theatre crowd subbed for a school hall's worth of peers that yearned to be rowdy and offensive. The anarchy was appealing. Yet, despite his best efforts, in his first attempt he was knocked out in the opening round – beaten by a girl with a flute and a kid that could juggle three balls. Maybe, he thought, they weren't ready for his material. Maybe the edginess of sitting down in a chair and staring back at the audience for his allocated three-minute slot was too avant-garde for a crowd of backward suburbanites.

The following year – Year 10 – he took a different tack. Enough time had passed and in the end he'd accepted the audience's criticism; they needed content – stuff – in order to be entertained. So Danny put together a musical number. He even learned three chords on the guitar, and when he sat in the chair on stage and played them in sequence and began to sing, the audience wasn't sure what to think. The lyrics were all about Jesus, although less as a religious icon and more as an erotic symbol. For the first minute the crowd were unusually quiet, and then someone shouted 'fag.' There were ripples of laughter, and then Danny played harder, really getting into the sensuality of the whole thing, and suddenly it was difficult to tell whether they were laughing *at* him or *with* him, the waves of attention washing around his presence. The end of the song came with a hard strum against all the strings at once, and amid the applause he made the snap decision to take off his shirt and try to lick his own nipple.

The performance landed him a meeting between his parents and the year-level Dean. Although a clear audience favourite, he would not be moving on to the second round, and there was a serious discussion about what constituted appropriate behaviour in a school environment.

Blasphemy and nudity were out.

Back in the day-to-day grind of going to class, Danny's Talent Quest endeavour had made him a curious kind of student: while he was now popular – as in, other students liked him and thought he was funny – he also had no close friends. He sat at different desks and next to different kids each lesson, and while he was friendly and talkative with them all, there was the sense that the others were scared of him. His ability to self-efface at any moment put them on guard and made it nearly impossible for them to open up. At lunchtimes he drifted from group to group, chatting and moving, always welcome but never at home, and when the weekends rolled around or the holidays arrived, he was completely and utterly alone.

The sit-down meetings with the Dean continued in Year 11. Danny's subject teachers were finding it hard to conduct lessons around his interruptions and jokes. 'Danny, can you get off the desk, please?'

'But, sir, I find it easier to be educated from this vantage point.'

'Sit down.'

'But my perspective, sir, it's enhanced from up here. I'm not so restricted by the chair.'

'Danny…'

But Danny liked the Dean, so his frequent trips didn't bother him. They could talk about things, like movies and life and stuff – because that was the Dean's style: make the kid feel like a person rather than a cog, talk to them as you might talk to a friend. 'Have you thought about taking up a sport or something, Danny? It might do you good to run around a field and kick a ball.'

'Not my thing, really. Weak arms. Gammy legs. Besides, the show's coming up and I want to try out for the lead.'

'What are they putting on this year?'

'Don't know. Doesn't really matter.'

'You're not going to sabotage it are you?'

'Depends on the part I get.'

'I think you need a hobby,' the Dean said. 'You seem to have a lot of extra energy, and it would be good to have you focus on something.'

On the Dean's advice Danny's parents bought him a video camera for his sixteenth birthday. The idea had been that since Danny apparently liked movies and acting, then just maybe he could dovetail these interests into the constructive pursuit of amateur filmmaking. And for a short time he did. He filmed everything. He filmed his walks home from school; he filmed old women waiting at bus stops; he filmed his next door neighbours bouncing on their trampoline, close up shots of his dog, rain on the pavement, the passing of time, a dead cat that had been run over by a car. There was no method, no direction, just the accumulation of moving images that he streamed back onto a hard-drive until he'd collected a full terabyte and needed more room. He started bringing the camera to school and filming whenever he could. He got in people's faces with it just to record their reaction; he taped every conversation and every interaction and every tiny mundane detail. He filmed himself urinating. And when Mr Jefferies told him to stop recording and put it away, he didn't, just to see what would happen. On playback, the footage ended with the teacher grabbing the camera and finding the off switch, his face red and aggressive as he stared back down the barrel. The device was confiscated, of course, and another meeting with the Dean ensued. 'Come on, Danny. You're a smart kid. What makes you do these things?'

'I dunno, attention.'

'Attention.' The Dean said the word as if they'd made a breakthrough. 'And why do you want the attention?'

'It makes me feel good.'

'Yes, but...don't you think this might be the wrong kind of attention?'

Danny actually thought about this as he sat there in the Dean's little office looking out through the cracks in the venetian blinds. It was a big topic, after all, and if they'd really got into it they might have been there all afternoon. 'Well, Danny, what do you think?'

'I think in the long run it's going to be hard to tell the difference.'

Unwilling to be drawn into what he suspected was

provocation, the Dean redirected the subject. 'Look, the summer's coming. How about we make a deal? I'll give you the camera back now provided it stays at home for the rest of the term, and then over the holidays you try to make something interesting with it. Like a film or something. You know, something people might want to watch.'

'And that's the right kind of attention?'

'Sure.'

The summer began. Danny had no actors, no script, no plot. He filmed a man begging for change. He filmed broken bottles in the car park of the supermarket. He filmed people coming in and out of a public toilet, seagulls pecking though garbage, an irate bus driver, the passing of time, a dead hedgehog. The Dean had been right. He needed structure to his work – an arc or a conflict. His films to date were like sitting in toilets and unspooling the toilet paper; it was counting what had already been counted. So he turned the camera on himself.

It took a long time for him to do considering his interest in being seen, but cameras, it has to be said, are much tougher than live audiences. With real people, Danny knew where he stood, and the boos and applause and laughter were easy indicators that either fed or drained his ability to perform. A camera was a single dead eye looking back at him. It gave him nothing – no smile, no nervous looks away – just a blinking red light to signal that he was being watched. Without the energy of a live audience he found it difficult to do anything, and he wondered where to look – which is why he ended up looking beyond the screen in his first video, past the camera at some indeterminate audience member. He even talked to them as if they were there and simply unwilling to respond, struck dumb by the number of clothes pegs pinched against the skin of Danny's chest. 'You think I can get another? This is pretty sore now. How many is it now? That's twenty-five by my count. Twenty-five? Let's do twenty-six.' He eventually reached one-hundred and fifty, having stolen extra from his neighbour's washing line in the middle of the recording. In the final shot of the video he unclipped them all at high speed, his eyes watering joy as he moaned himself into freedom, each peg leaving its own individual red mark against his torso, the culmination producing what appeared to be a nasty rash.

As the summer progressed, Danny's personalised YouTube channel became what amounted to a friend. It was his window, his marketing agent, his gateway. And the world was full of people who used their channels as a platform for attention and respect. All he had to do was keep uploading and create a base, and the likes he received and the subscribers he obtained were objective proof of his significance. His clothes pegs video, carefully titled *A Stupid Kid Does Something Stupid*, had been an almost instant hit, gaining over a thousand views in its first week, including twenty-three likes and seven dislikes – seven little red thumbs pointing down. But positive or negative, it didn't matter to Danny. In fact, dislikes were crucial. It meant his work was polarising, that it was stimulating a gut reaction in his viewers. He took the time to respond to comments made. 'LOL it looks like you got off on that shit.' – codwarrior238.

'Thnx yeah i did. An erotic high point in my life so far. Highly recommend it. Also, can't wait to lose my virginity.'

Eventually, though, his channel began to look denuded and small. Twenty subscribers was good, and over a thousand views was like gaining the attention of half his school, but when he measured himself against the world of professional vloggers, he was still coming up a long way short. Pretty girls with nose rings who made weak social commentary about trends and issues were clearing two hundred thousand hits in a week. They had audiences and fan bases, and with the number of hits they were getting they were probably even making money. Some guys were managing to swing past a million, simply by ranting about paedophiles and racism and swearing a lot, their videos cut up frenetically as they shouted into the webcam. They weren't doing anything special, just telling the audience what they wanted to hear in a slightly more emphatic voice than the audience could muster themselves, because the audience for these things – according, helpfully, to the analytics and statistics button – was, more often than not, thirteen- to seventeen-year-olds. Stuttering, slow, uncharismatic. Danny's peers. The same ones he entertained in class by doing nothing more complex than being an idiot. For his second video he decided to immortalise his Talent Quest performance, and while his parents quietly watched TV in the lounge, sealed off by Danny's permanently closed bedroom door, he set himself up in front of the camera and played the whole thing out again, this time ramping up its licentious qualities and spending some real time searching for his nipple during the inevitable coda. Titled *Jesus is My Lover*, the clip managed to haul in a wide-ranging audience, amassing close to four thousand hits before plateauing – a clear split down the middle between likes and furious dislikes. Some of the comments were obscene, charged with the unique fervour that religious desecration fuels. 'Fuck u, kid. Ur going to hell.'- davet654

'Thnx for the feedback,' Danny wrote. 'I'm glad you're watching. That does, however, presuppose there is one.'

Heated debates followed, and Danny was surprised that the comment-makers inevitably transcended the video itself and began to engage in religious debate all of their own, leaving him free to watch and count the rising number of views. And he adored these people – these numbers. They were what he was there for, and as the view-count climbed, so did the warm feeling of acceptance and significance. This was what the whole thing had been about. The school shows, the Talent Quest: what was the point? The audiences were too small, the structures inflexible. Here he had the freedom to pirouette and preen, and the more he did it, the more attention he got. 'I love you all,' he posted beneath *Jesus is My Lover*, and he meant it.

TOM & DAVE

I get it, Tom said. He hates his wife, so he has no problem beating the shit out of her. It's a funny joke. Well done.

Yeah, but it's only funny in the rhythm of the joke. Break it apart like that and it kind of loses its kick. Don't do that to my joke.

It's not your joke. You heard it somewhere.

Yeah, but I told it.

Somewhere beyond the broken windows of the Midway House a bird made a loud squawk and took off for the harbour. The two boys were smoking fresh cigarettes. It might have been around noon.

Have you noticed Gavin's getting into Nazi shit? Tom asked.

Fuckin' drain-baby.

And it's not like there's a whole crew of Nazi girls waiting for his dick, so he can't be doing it to get laid.

Don't analyse it, Dave said. Gavin's a retard. But

you're wrong. There are heaps of Nazi chicks, they just don't shave their heads and carve swastikas into their skulls.

Like who?

Andrea's a Nazi. I mean, she's not all like Hitler Hitler Hitler or anything, but you should listen to her spout shit about chinks and coconuts and Arabs and shit.

She's kinda hot, too. That's almost a turn on.

Sick, huh.

Lure of the devil.

Dave kicked an empty beer bottle across the floor then vigorously cleaned his left ear with his index finger. Nazis are played out, he said, inspecting the wax he'd collected. They're in everything. They're boring.

We need fresh icons of genocide. Like the Hutus.

Whose shoes?

Hutus. Rwanda. Death by machete.

Imagine a machete attack. I mean, you see that shit in movies and the arm or the head always comes clean off. In reality the machete would be blunt and rusty and you'd have to hack through the bone and muscle.

Tasty.

You'd end up sweating real bad and there'd be blood on your face and–

And then the Armed Offenders Squad would turn up and take you out from a distance. One to the leg to incapacitate and then some safety rounds into the head as they got up close.

You'd have to take hostages, Dave said. Like take Andrea and hold her close, use her like a human shield and then pull her into a secure room and wait it out. Start negotiating for a plane and–

And eventually get safe passage to Uganda and hope

that Stockholm syndrome has set in by then and mate with her under an African sun–

That wasn't where I was going with that.

Bullshit. And eventually, at the end of your dream, you get her to squeeze out some machete-wielding kids to continue your reign of terror while you make sick racist love with her into old age.

Why Uganda? Dave asked

Dunno, Tom said.

You know you could probably keep your spree going for ages, even if all you had was a machete.

A blunt machete.

I mean, this is New Zealand. We're slow to respond. We're docile.

Good word, Tom said.

You've just gotta catch people by surprise.

ALi

Every afternoon, naked women danced and sang on the TV, and Ali was in love with them all, and it was much easier to watch them and be in love than to attempt the homework he didn't understand. The words that were used to make up each sentence describing what he had to do were too long, and when he looked up their meanings on the internet, their definitions were even more complex and only added to the confusion. In spite of his parents' best efforts, the computer was still a mystery to them, and his sister was too young to make it worthwhile, so it had become Ali's by default. At the behest of his cousins, he had signed up to Facebook, and in the evenings he could sit and type comments to them. He felt guilty communicating in Somali – a different kind of guilt to the one he felt while watching the naked women dance – but guilty all the same. It was a new area of human emotion for him, one he'd only learned to feel since accepting the world of technology.

But the internet was a wonderful thing. When his Social Studies teacher had asked him to write a paragraph describing the Hindenburg Disaster, all he'd really had to do was get close to spelling Hindenburg correctly when he typed it into the search bar and up came the necessary information. Lots of it. Page after page. With his new knowledge, he copied and pasted what he needed into a Word document, typed his name at the bottom, and printed it out. He was pleased. This was the first homework he had managed to complete and he looked forward to showing his teacher how successful he had been.

'Ali, can I see you for a moment?' Mr Gleeson had asked. The other students were already making their way out of the room.

'Yes, sir.'

'Take a seat, pal.' So Ali sat at the chair in front of his teacher's desk. When the last of the students had left, Mr Gleeson handed back Ali's homework. The scribbles in red were difficult to read, however their shapes and density made them look urgent. 'Do you know what plagiarism is?' Ali shook his head vigorously. 'Because this is not your work.'

'Yes,' Ali said. A partial sentence.

'So you know it's not your work?'

'Yes,' Ali said. 'It is my work.'

'No, it's not your work. You've copied it.'

'Yes,' Ali reiterated, moving his whole mouth to form the vowels. 'It is my work. I copied it. See.' Ali pointed to the sheet. 'My name. Ali.'

'I don't think you understand,' Gleeson said. 'You have to put it in your own words. If you simply copy someone else's work, it's cheating.'

'Cheating? So des not good?'

'No.'

Speaking later with his father, Ali tried to explain what had happened, because unexpected disappointments left unexpressed can metastasise into rage. 'Mr Gleeson thinks I cheated.'

'Did you?'

'No, I did what I was asked. I found a paragraph that described the Hindenburg Disaster. And then he called me something I didn't understand.' Ali was clearly getting angry, pacing back and forth in the living room.

'Do you want me to talk to him?' his father asked, but Ali already knew how that would go. He'd seen his dad trying to ask questions at the supermarket.

'No, it's okay.'

'Are you sure?'

'I can work it out for myself. I will ask my ESOL teacher.'

'Good boy,' his dad said. 'Now please, tell me what's happening here. Why does the blonde woman not want to be with the man?'

'He doesn't have enough money.'

'Ah.'

Ali's ESOL teacher explained things more carefully. As he listened to the slow clear explanation, Nasir sat at the back of the class and made jokes in Somali about how studious his younger cousin was. It was hard to concentrate, but he got the gist of things. Copying and pasting was not enough. He had to rewrite all the sentences so that they said the same thing but with the words in a different order – an exercise which seemed rather pointless to Ali, since all the words made perfect sense in the order they were already in. The sum result was the feeling that the wall he had set out to climb was in fact much higher and slipperier than he'd first anticipated. 'Don't worry,' Nasir said. 'You work hard, you will do well. You worry too much.' But it was hard for Ali to take comfort in his cousin's comments, since Nasir had been in the class a year longer than Ali without any noticeable improvement, and regardless of his charisma, he didn't have a single friend that he wasn't loosely related to in some way. Instead of attempting to complete his work when he returned home, Ali switched on the TV and watched the naked women sing and dance. They sang back through the screen and directly to him and assured him everything was going to be okay.

Over the following month Ali's efforts in class began to slide. Where he'd at least attempted to complete the homework before, now he gave in quickly to the pleasures of watching TV, Facebooking, and playing soccer. He'd become acutely conscious of the fact he was ESOL, and in his mainstream classes he sat alone. When group work was required, he was placed in a group by the teacher rather than being selected by other students. And there seemed to be an understanding at times like this that he was going to be unable to help the students he'd been placed with, that his input would invariably only create extra work. Making friends was a whole other thing – a hard, maybe impossible thing – because he watched the other students talk and smile, and he was well aware of the grumbling when a girl was asked to pair up with him for an exercise, and in many respects he felt lucky that he didn't understand the details of her complaints. His only genuine social attention came from Gavin during maths, but Ali suspected there were more levels to it than he understood, because one minute Gavin would be smiling at him, and the next Ali would find himself the target of scrunched up papers or tiny bits of eraser – too small to hurt him, but definitely enough to throw him off task. And when he lobbed them back, there was an argument, and Ali found himself standing chest to chest with someone he didn't understand, and then the teacher had moved him to a desk at the front, far enough away to prevent verbal communication, but not far enough to stop the tiny bits of eraser when the teacher's back was turned.

'You want us to do something about it?' Nasir asked before their afternoon soccer game.

'Like what?'

'You know, hurt him.'

'Yeah,' said Ali. 'I want you to hold him down and flick things at him.'

'You sure?'

It dawned on Ali that his cousin was serious, that there wasn't even the vaguest inkling that it had been a joke.

'No, I don't want you to do anything. I just needed to talk about it.'

'Look,' Nasir said, and he pointed to the group of relatives and hangers on that were already kicking the ball around the school field, passing and calling. Odawaa was smiling with big white teeth and patting Tarabi on the back, having fouled him quite intentionally. 'Any one of these guys will help you. They're your family.'

'Thank you,' Ali said. 'But I am fine. Everything is fine.'

His cousin slapped him the shoulder and laughed and ran onto the field – the school field – where they played most afternoons whether it was raining or sunshine, a continental grouping, a grouping of very dark faces and high cheekbones, slide-tackling and chipping and passing and shooting.

Although Ali's parents found it difficult to decipher the comments in their son's mid-year report card, Ali knew well enough what they meant, and he felt guilty giving them a mistranslation – 'easily distracted' became 'very dedicated' and 'achieving at a low level' became 'working hard to achieve' – but he sensed that it was for the best. After all, the report, a slender strip of cardboard and ink, didn't fairly represent the effort he was putting in. Nor did it take into account future effort, the work he was *going* to do. It was also worth considering the mood in the house at the time; his dad needed good news, because he was still unemployed, and the TV, it seemed, had turned against him. He'd watched a movie about Somalia in which Americans had crashed a helicopter in Mogadishu. Even without a full understanding of the dialogue, memories had returned, and a growing awareness of the codes and conventions of cinema had filled in the rest. 'They celebrated killing our people,' his father had said at the dinner table. 'Hundreds of them, mowed down with machine guns. And we looked like savages. Every few seconds there were more Somalis running at Americans and howling.'

'It's just a movie,' his mother had said, trying to quell her husband. 'Nobody takes that sort of thing seriously.'

'But they do. They see it as truth. How do you think that will affect me when I apply for a job? What if the man interviewing me has just seen this movie, and when he asks where I am from I have to tell him that I am from where they howl and scream and where children shoot white people?'

'Are you forgetting the reasons we left?' his mother asked, and for the first time in years Ali remembered the blood on the man's face and his teeth in the sunlight.

'No,' his father said. 'But I do not want to be associated with those reasons.'

So Ali thought it best to give his Dad positive news. He needed relief. And it was only a partial lie, because Ramadan was coming, and he could easily centre his contrition on becoming the student he was fictionalising himself to be.

'This is good news, Ali,' his Dad said, returning to the happier topic. 'It is important for you to do well. The world is full of misconceptions and lies, and it is your job to correct them.'

'Don't put so much weight on him,' his mother had said. 'Correcting the mistakes of American movies is not his responsibility.'

His Dad finished his food and then looked at his son and his report card, and Ali felt the guilt again.

Ramadan was hard. In class, Ali ducked his head and did his work and ignored the bits of eraser landing around him. And his teachers noticed his renewed diligence. In Social Studies, Mr Gleeson was impressed when Ali wrote an entire page – all his own original words – on what Ramadan meant to his culture, and when he was given an Excellence grade (a grade that ignored the syntax and simplicity and rewarded the sentiment) Ali took it home and showed his parents and explained what it meant, and his mother told her friends who told their sons, and even Nasir was patting him on the back and telling him he was a success. 'That's the highest mark a Somalian's ever got outside ESOL,' he'd said, although Ali chose not to believe him, because if that was a fact, then it was a depressing one.

Without food or water during the day, afternoon soccer became a chore. At first they still played, although the games were slower, the tackles lackadaisical, but by the end of the month there had been a noticeable attrition of players until the games stopped altogether. Ali tried to avoid the nude women on TV for the duration of the fast, instead focusing on his studies, but hunger pains often meant his attention wavered, and increasingly he found himself lured onto Facebook to link with his cousins and share videos of Arab men rolling their cars on dusty Middle-Eastern highways.

And then Ali received a friend request from Gavin. Accept or Decline? The screen might as well have been flashing at him.

F 12

Having poked his head out between the curtains of F12, Brayden surveyed the courtyard. A seagull taking off. Pastel Nelson blocks. Blue sky. A Polynesian kid – Year 10, maybe – running somewhere. 'Brayden!' Blasco shouted. 'Pull your face back in!' Brayden let the curtains fall back and returned to the dim of the classroom.

'That's nice of you, sir, showing concern for my safety like that.'

'It's not that. It looks bad if the senior management are wandering around. I'd have to explain things.'

'So you don't care about my safety?'

'Honestly, not so much.'

Jun laughed; Akaash – who was still lingering by the door and contemplating an exit – suggested Brayden was expendable.

'How come, sir?' Brayden asked.

'It's a joke, Brayden. I care about you as much as a

teacher can care about a student without it becoming strange. Sit down and let me do what I'm doing.'

What he was doing was trying to figure out whether or not the lockdown bell was a planned drill, however his digital ineptitude and refusal to correspond via email meant searching his inbox was like wading through mud. So much unopened correspondence: House meetings, teacher tips, recommendations about certain students that he probably should've taken, sports announcements that were made, then retracted, then made again; notices about injections, violin lessons, school field trips, school meetings; professional development sessions that he hadn't attended. An announcement about the culinary club and their first place award at a hospitality festival; a month-old message to say that First XV training had been cancelled. 'Sir, so is this a drill or what?'

'I'm checking, Wendy. Keep texting.'

The junior mathematics team came in second place: Hurray! The science club will be operating after school Monday through Wednesday. A message about report writing, a message about a short school day due to heavy rain. Manager needed for girls' waterpolo; Dear all staff, here's a neat game to help introduce your lessons; Dear all English teachers, the junior reading unit starts next week. Manager needed for boys' softball.

'Well?'

While Blasco continued to hunt, Brayden kicked Jun in the shin. Akaash put his hand on the door to leave but took it off again when he noticed Penelope was staring at him. Sean had pulled a dictionary off the shelf and was trying to read, but the bell's difficult rhythm meant he found it hard to focus his energies. The rest of the students were talking. Smiling. Some cupped their hands over their ears so they could hear the music of their headphones. Others played games on their portables or flicked paper at the bin. Jun rubbed his leg and told Brayden to stop it – retaliation would only create escalation. 'You see Danny's new video?' Brayden asked.

'No,' Jun said. 'What's he done this time?'

'Holy fuck it's funny.'

'Yeah?'

'Like, really fuckin' funny.'

'What does he do?'

'I kinda shouldn't explain it. You just have to see it.'

'Was it worth kicking me in the leg?'

'Sir!' Penelope shouted. 'I think Akaash is trying to leave.'

'Move away from the exit, Akaash,' Blasco said without raising his head. Professional Development Monday – How to be Better with Boys; Staff meeting, Tuesday: agenda listed below.

'Sir?'

'I'm getting there, Wendy.' Peer-sexuality group meeting; work experience trip to Argentina; new supervising teacher required for the Amnesty Group.

'Just tell me what it is,' Jun said.

'No. you have to see it.'

'Come on.'

'Ask Sir if you can use his computer.'

'You do it.'

'Sir!'

'Yes, Brayden.'

'Can we use your computer for a sec?'

'No, Brayden.' Dear all teachers, there been a concerning lack off attendance at—; Senior girls' hockey needs a coach; Weekly riddle: What goes up a chimney down but not down a chimney up?

'Come on, sir.'

'I'm busy, Brayden. That should be obvious.'

Dejected, Brayden returned to the curtains and toyed with the idea of prising them open again.

'Uxorial!' Sean said suddenly. 'Of or relating to one's wife. That really doesn't sound like it means what it means.

Akaash was inching back to the door. He could sense the outside world. Wide open spaces. Room to move.

'Sir?'

'An umbrella, Wendy. It's an umbrella.'

'What?'

Brayden poked his head through again. Blue sky. Pastel Nelson blocks. White smoke drifting from somewhere indeterminate. And Henry. Henry walking around, looking left and right. Henry moving his head sharply and suddenly. Brayden knocked on the window and tried to get his attention, but when Henry looked over, there seemed to be something wrong with his face.

STELLA

Stella was groggy but it was hard to tell why. Maybe the light in the guidance counsellor's office. Maybe the dust. Maybe the pot she'd smoked the day before – stone-over. Either way, she didn't appear to feel like talking – this may just have been an escape from the classroom – but Mrs Gershwitz (call me Verna) didn't expect much. She was, however, beginning to get the feeling that she was too nice for her own good, and that in terms of Stella, she was slowly backing herself into a corner.

Lies.

Truth.

Stella's M.O. seemed to be to mix them together and let Verna sort it out.

A special student – a difficult history. A strange relationship with her dad. Maybe. Really struggled with the divorce. Maybe. Has dabbled in hard drugs – like, serious ones that involve needles and require a working knowledge of older men with tattoos in order to obtain. Hard to say.

Stella squirmed and wriggled on Verna's couch and scratched at her arm, then seemed to settle into a stare between the cracks in the venetians. Her hair had been freshly dyed into an almost neon red. 'You don't ever get sick looking at that? Stella asked.

'Looking at what?'

'The blinds. They make me dizzy.'

'Dizzy?'

'My focus keeps jumping backwards and forwards between the inside and the outside. It's making me feel sick.'

'Do you want me to open them?'

'Close them.'

So Verna did, and suddenly the room was all artificial light, much smaller than it had been only a second ago. Stella shifted herself again, curling down into a ball – a familiar position – and cast her eyes at the floor.

An unhealthy fascination with death and death related subjects? Definitely a fascination, but what constitutes unhealthy? Death is an interesting topic, after all. A deep sense of loneliness – a core loneliness – that goes further than your average teenage alienation? A chemical imbalance? Hard to say. All teenagers are in a state of imbalance – that's not news.

'Have you seen your dad recently?'

'…'

'Stella?'

'I don't want to talk about it.'

A desire to be self-destructive and engage in self-destructive behaviour. Yeah, probably, although it's more important to figure out where that desire comes from, and nobody likes to talk about the bad stuff.

'Did something bad happen?'

'I said I don't want to talk about it.'

'Okay.' But is that because something happened or because nothing happened?

History of compulsive lying. Certainly. Absolutely confirmed. Verna had watched Stella do it to her face. But that didn't mean everything was always a lie.

'I've started a relationship.'

'Oh. Do you want to discuss it?'

'He's pretty good looking. Tall, blonde hair. He's into kite-boarding.'

'Kite-boarding? That doesn't seem like a guy you'd normally pursue.'

'You told me I should be more active, so I'm trying to meet guys with adventurous interests.'

'What's his name?'

'Jeff. His name's Jeff.'

'Jeff.'

'Actually it's Steve.'

'Is this a real guy?'

'Of course.'

Delusional, prone to flights of fantasy. Maybe. Or just exercising a rich imagination and burying her self-awareness for the fun of it…Possible. Psychologically sadomasochistic? Surely it's too early for that level of complexity.

'No, this guy's great. Loves his grandma.'

'How long have you been seeing him?'

'About a week?'

'Does he go to this school?'

'Nope. He's left school. He goes to university.'

'And how did you meet?'

'Internet.'

'The internet? What, through a friend on Facebook?'

'No, a dating website.'

'A dating website.' Verna tried to keep her voice even. 'You know, dating web–'

'Yeah yeah yeah, paedophiles and weirdoes and whatever. I'm careful. I don't show him pictures of my tits or anything.'

'It's just, wouldn't it be better to maybe meet someone your own age?'

'At this school? You know I saw a kid here drink his own piss the other day.'

Truth and lies. Hard to sort. Verna shifted in her chair and felt the urge to straighten the calendar above her desk, although it was already straight.

'Besides,' Stella continued, finding, it seemed, some energy for the discussion. 'If he really wants to see my tits I can just show him someone else's.'

'What do you mean?'

'Like just take a photo from another site and copy and paste.'

'Have you actually met this person? In person, I mean.'

'Fuck no. And I don't use my actual photo. I don't even use my real name.'

Intimacy issues? That's probably missing the point. Fear? Doesn't seem like she has any. A need to be loved while giving nothing in return? Trite, but...

'How do you think Jeff will-'

'Steve.'

'How do you think Steve will feel when he finds out he's being lied to?'

'Lying? Like, this isn't lying. Like, it's kind of expected. You just play up to them. I mean, he's probably not the guy he's pretending to be. Fuck, a Biology major, likes walking his dog and playing his guitar. Bullshit. If anything he deserves to be lied to.'

So much fiction. Verna thought back to one of her early sessions with Stella: crying, confessions, the vague indication that she had been (maybe, maybe) sexually assaulted by another student, Stella curled up foetal on the couch. Verna felt she had done well to create a safe space – room for the young and the damaged. It wasn't the same feeling now. This was becoming sharp and nasty and somehow blurry all at once.

'Do you think people are just set up to lie?' she asked. 'Is that the standard we should set for others?'

'Maybe. I dunno. People can be pretty shitty.'

'Well, don't you think you should raise the bar a little and be the better person?'

Stella sat up and swung her legs onto the floor. 'You get taken advantage of like that. People fuck you up. And I don't want that to happen to me again.' The first meeting? The crying? It wasn't even hearsay without details or a narrative shape.

'It's just a hard way to live,' Verna said. 'It takes a lot of energy to put on a mask and set all these traps. If you're honest with people, most of the time they'll be honest with you.'

'Sometimes I fantasise about being a prostitute; that way I'd get to lie for money.'

Shock tactics. Aimed at eliciting a response – any response. Bring it up. 'You're not serious. You're just saying that to see how I'll react. And if you knew what that sort of life was like then you wouldn't be saying it.'

Spoiled obscenely during the divorce and now vying for attention of any kind? Probably. Quite rapidly becoming a bad person.

'I'm thinking about leaving school. Like, I'm old enough now.'

'How would your mother feel about that?'

'I don't think she cares.'

'I'm sure that's not true.'

'You don't know her.'

Subjectivity. Impossible to calculate and quantify.

'You don't want to stay till the end of the year and see if you can get university entrance? It's only a few more months.'

'Do you know who Brenda Spencer is?'

'Is she a student at the school?'

'No… Hey, can I go now?'

MiNA & AHMED

With his pants around his ankles and his girlfriend beneath him in the brush, Ahmed decided the best course of action was to freeze and stay as still as possible until the dog and its owner passed. It was times like these that he yearned for the comfort of a bedroom and the absence of parents. He had been inside Mina's bedroom, of course, but the door always remained resolutely open, Mina's mother pretending to knit or sweep or rearrange furniture from angles that kept her in full view of the goings on. This draconian presence only made Ahmed fantasize more, because Mina's room was Mina's room – a full blown girly affair of pinks and stuffed toys and smiling teen heartthrob posters that made him just a little jealous. If he could have her there, in her room, it would be like sticking it to them as they watched. Conversely, his own room had recently become spartan and sophisticated. In the weeks following his Dad's intervention, he'd tried – somewhat subconsciously – to eradicate any indication that the Ahmed that existed in the present was in any way related to the Ahmed who'd ever cried or spilled things on himself. So down came the posters of soccer players and up went a single painting of a rocky landscape – barren and cool, it hinted at an urbane level of brooding. The duvet cover was next to go (because what self-respecting man still sleeps in the company of cartoon dinosaurs?) replaced with a single block colour, and when his parents found him clearing away old trophies and tidying things, they were proud that he seemed responsible.

Mina was never given a chance to see the bedroom in its original state, since her first visit to Ahmed's home had been after the parental involvement, and when she saw the scarcity of personality and the thoroughly adult state of things, she became a little nervous. 'Where's your stuff?' she said, sitting uncomfortably on the edge of Ahmed's bed.

'In the closet. Under the bed. Why? What's wrong?'

'It's just really clean and empty. Like, I didn't think it was going to look like this. I thought you'd have junk everywhere.'

'You don't like it?'

Mina didn't want to reply; she wanted to skirt the subject and move on. She pressed her hands into the bed and looked around. 'It's just—'

'I'll show you something,' Ahmed said, offering her his hand.

In the laundry he opened the cupboard and reached high up into the darkness – a darkness that he'd hoped was going to be a permanent home – and pulled down the dino duvet. 'This is a stegosaurus,' he said. 'And this is a brachiosaur. Four days ago these were still on my bed. If you look in the box in my wardrobe you'll find posters of Messi and Ronaldo.'

Two minutes after this exchange, Ahmed's mother found the pair in closer proximity than she would've liked, Mina still clutching the colourful prehistoric pastiche.

Mina herself hadn't seen the dog walker. Her only view was of Ahmed's face and the background lining of white cloud. Within that frame she could find herself disappearing into a better context – it wasn't the back of a school in a dead suburb; it wasn't even the same country – and as she slipped into the fantasy her wider senses went with her. So it was a shock when Ahmed forced his hand over her mouth and froze, and at first she felt scared, not of what was around them, but of him, of the fact that she was suddenly being gagged and held by arms stronger than her own. Ahmed's expression didn't make it any better, eyes wide and twitching – the panic of fear being just a little too close to the panic that precedes violence. And so she tried to wriggle free, an instinctual response, and Ahmed was forced to hold her tighter, shushing her until he realised that she lacked the information he had – the legs beneath the branches and the glancing patter of dog paws – and he whispered to her, 'Someone,' and looked in the right direction and conveyed what needed to be conveyed.

This wasn't the first time they'd been this close to being caught. They'd tried the school bathrooms – the girls', which seemed safer – but had been forced to flee when a cleaner had entered to disinfect the toilets and restack the rolls. They'd figured it was for the best, given that the graffiti and the smells were hard to block out, and both had felt sleazier than they really wanted to be. Local parks weren't much better; the variables were too great, and no matter how far into the bush they scrambled, local smokers or – worse – curious kids on bikes, somehow managed to seek them out and force them into quick fumbling and disgraced exits. And now a dog was sniffing in the bramble beside them and its owner was calling for it. 'Chip! Here Chippy boy!' And Chip was marking his territory with a lifted hind leg and small squirts of urine, and before the couple could reach a decision, Chip was sniffing them – a German short-haired pointer, dark brown – and licking Ahmed's ear. It was the kind of moment that would've been funny if it were their dog instead of someone else's, someone who was now making their way around the bush and calling out: 'Chip! Chippy!' A young voice – a voice from school. A voice from next to them in classes and around them in assemblies. A voice that would see them and spread word about the things it had witnessed, and then Chip marked his territory again, this time on Ahmed's shoes, before turning and hustling back through the bramble, and the voice began to recede.

The two of them lay there for quite a while, libidos dissolved, Ahmed with his eyes closed and his forehead in the dirt. Mina could feel the thumping of his heart, the only real signal that he was still alive. She felt a twig poking into the skin of her back and she could smell the dog piss. This was unmistakably a pile of dirt at the back of the school.

MS BAKER

The ringing of the lockdown bell was only a fleeting reprieve. For no more than a moment, both Corban and Joseph found themselves looking around and wondering what was going on, but when Corban looked back and found his opponent distracted, he took the chance to hit Joseph in the face. It wasn't a good punch – high school punches usually aren't. Instead of connecting hard and forward, it slipped sideways across Joseph's nose, and any observer could've seen that it was thrown with ambivalence, that even as it was being delivered, Corban wasn't sure it was a good idea. And it wasn't. Because Joseph was bigger than him, and Joseph – unlike Corban – had gotten pretty used to taking beatings from his dad. So when Joseph grabbed Corban by the neck (the second time his neck had been roughly handled in the space of twenty minutes) he felt absolutely no guilt about putting all his energy and anger into Corban's eye socket, and then his cheek bone, and then his teeth. And there was nothing Ms Stephanie Baker could do.

This was not why she got into teaching. Corban, a Year 10 who seemed underdeveloped for his age and still very much a child, was bleeding from the mouth and half-sitting and pretty obviously crying, and Joseph was calling him a cunt. And the bell was ringing, a bell that, because it was her first year, Ms Baker had never heard – a bell that sounded like a sick or faulty fire alarm. And Corban was noticeably dripping blood on the linoleum in front of her. And Joseph was still standing over him… She didn't remember grabbing Joseph by the arm, but it had happened, and she had a firm hold, one that involved her nails and white knuckles and had managed to get his attention, and he was turning now. And the bell was going. Three seconds on, one off, and the noise of the class was swelling around her, and Joseph was saying something – 'Assault, Miss! You're assaulting me!' He was trying to break free, but she wasn't letting go; there was no way she was letting go; but she'd gone blank now, because what was she supposed to do next?

The feeling of having lost control had hit her hard at the end of her degree. Three years of Biology was enough for an academic credential and a graduating gown, but that seemed to be about all, and around her the world was moving forward. Her friends were pushing on with things, either leaving the country in defiance of student debt or buckling down and accepting jobs. Former law students were becoming clerks and taking up internships; ex-arts students were resigning themselves to more study, lining up Masters courses in what seemed to her to be fruitless or irrelevant areas of history or literature. Her partner, a year ahead, had already put his computer science degree into action and found work as a programmer, and it was on his salary that she spent a year sleeping in and scanning for jobs, keeping up only a token Sunday and Monday at a plant nursery while she tried to figure things out. She cooked and cleaned as a kind of domestic compensation, but the more she did it and the longer she took, the more she got the feeling that she was voluntarily chaining herself to domestic servitude. Yet, the further she got from matriculation, the less appealing the jobs in her field began to look. Who wanted to spend weeks at a time living in a shipping container on the West Coast filling in study sheets about bird colonies, a generator for power and a long drop for a toilet? 'I'd be down there for a month at a time,' she'd told her partner. 'I'd go crazy. And I'd miss you.'

'I don't know. It might be good for you,' he'd said. 'You could get some thinking done.'

And maybe she would've gone, had he not been so keen on the idea. Because his new job was bringing in money, and now he was buying new clothes and going to the gym.

Lab jobs often required more education – an Honours at least – and even then she wasn't sure she wanted one. Lab coats, tests; sterile rooms and microscopes. Her experience with lab people had led her to believe they either had a high tolerance for boredom or rich inner lives they could escape into, and the extra loan debt aside, she was worried she had neither. The alternative was working as a pharmaceutical rep – a reasonable entry-level salary and the chance to drive from client to client and peddle company drugs – but just as she didn't have the hermit-like nature of the lab scientist, nor did she have the extroverted energy required to hawk products and make continuous small-talk. She'd discussed the issue with her partner, and her parents, and her friends, but as with any real decision about life direction, it had to be made alone. Outside advice is inevitably partisan or superficial, and quite often both.

The decision to go into teaching came suddenly as she vacuumed. It was the middle of the day and a TV talk show was doing a special on weight loss, the follow up to an exposé about the obesity epidemic, and Stephanie had been watching all week with an interest that disgusted her. As she vacuumed away crumbs and grit that probably wasn't there and got angrier and angrier about weight gain that was entirely in her head, she looked up and out the window – searching, maybe, for a better place, anywhere but the carpet – and saw two girls in school uniform ambling down the street, backpacks dragged idly behind them. She switched the vacuum cleaner off and watched them walk in lazy patterns and stop and pick flowers from someone's garden and laugh, and the overwhelming innocence of the whole thing, the insouciance, helped her make the decision.

The more she thought about it, the more it took hold. Teaching science would let her use what she'd learned. She could interface each day with people that shared her passion and were doing something positive. She envisaged field trips and coaching netball; eager kids asking questions and addressing her by her last name. Cups of coffee in the staffroom and discussions about the curriculum. Her partner was all for it. 'I think that's a great idea. You'd be perfect for teaching.' And she ignored what he said next about there not being any real money in it, and she ignored the connection between the girls she'd seen walking and the time of day it had been, because if they were out on the street during Dr Phil, then they were wagging, and the park up the road from her house was just a fantastic spot to get stoned.

'Shit, man, fuck!' The voice was a student's, though she couldn't tell whose, because she still had Joseph by the arm, fingernails dug right in as he struggled, and the words had floated out of the shouting around the class, and it's possible they were referring to the blood pooling between Corban's legs, or maybe the fact he was crying, or even just the whole scene of devastation – three seconds on, one second off – 'Stop assaulting me! Let go you bitch!' – and then she did, her fingers coming free, her nails catching and pulling at the wool of Joseph's jumper. The look on his face was somehow both feral and stoic, and for a moment she thought that he might hit her too. Behind her in the class students were moving out of their chairs, a semi-circle forming as their attention drew towards the action. Those who couldn't see were clambering up onto the lab tables to gain a better view. Only Emily remained in her seat, reluctant to break protocol without being told, and the only one in the class, it seemed, to be wondering about the bell. Ms Baker turned, not so much to correct the class, but to escape Joseph's face (surely he wouldn't hit her in the back) and the desire to control the situation made a surging return, her voice coming out with as much authority as she could muster: 'Sit down, all of you, now! Get off the damn tables!' It hurt her vocal cords. Some of them started to climb back, others continued to watch, because behind Ms Baker, Joseph was making his final statement, spitting at Corban – a loose spit, flecked – before threatening her as he headed for the door – 'Gonna kill you, bitch!' The words made her wince.

The post-graduate prospectus for teachers' college had been overstuffed with images of good looking, well-to-do young people who lacked the capacity for sarcasm. It made the course seem as if it was all going to be note-sharing across shade-latticed picnic tables. But while marketing rarely matches reality – people are always uglier and the picnic tables are covered in bird shit – most of her cohort really was as earnest and clean as the advertising suggested. While engaged in her training, Stephanie made new friends, went for coffees, and made a point of opening herself up. She discussed modern pedagogical method over beer and happily spent time helping her fellow students with their assignments. Unlike the atomised isolation of her undergraduate course, teachers' college was big on community, and this helped bolster the feeling that she'd made the right choice. Her school placements were interesting and diverse, and during her first time in front of a class – at a mid-decile all-girls school – the students were responsive to her and forgave her nervousness. They even respected her, because she was young and not deformed in any way, and for Stephanie this was not something she'd predicted or even considered. For teenagers of the right ilk, it seemed, all she had to do to be successful was be there, just stand in front of them and speak clearly and provide an alternative to the ageing men and women they were so used to. It was on her second school placement, however, that she made a decision. The school was in an upper-band suburb, co-ed, and as she drove her car into the grounds – an old Toyota creeping ever nearer to the boneyard – she quickly became aware of how economically out of place it was next to BMWs and Audis and, shit, even a Saab. The problem, she would soon discover, was not that these cars existed, but that they belonged to students.

This was her first real experience in the link between parental ideology and the effect it can have on the behaviour and outlook of kids. Here the students she encountered seemed despondent and arrogantly lazy in ways only easy living and guarantees of future nepotism can produce. There was a mood of entitlement that seemed to linger in the air of the classroom, and when called on to answer a question or provide evidence of their efforts, students often reacted as if the request had been made by a servant. In the teachers' lounge, Stephanie found the atmosphere almost palpably sticky. There was something uncomfortable in the way staff members talked about the overseas holidays students had taken and the companies the parents owned, as if it were all somehow theirs too, as if proximity to wealth and prestige alone meant it had rubbed off. And they didn't seem to notice that they were being treated like butlers (a wilful ignorance?) or that their students had been taught by the economic success their teachers envied that to be a high school teacher was to be at the bottom of the food chain.

Although Stephanie had never been a class warrior, she now found herself rejecting schools in wealthy areas in favour of 'aspirational' zones – suburbs defined by immigrant communities and cultural diversity. She read the *Pedagogy of the Oppressed*, and for a short period following she developed the habit of using terms like 'praxis' and 'oppressor' in casual conversation, words that ruffled her partner in ways he wasn't totally equipped to deal with. Her final placement went well. She acquired a 'student focus' rather than a 'teacher focus,' and she mastered the art of the teaching voice, a clear and commanding tone that cut above chatter without constituting a shout. Her lecturers were pleased with her glowing associate teacher reports, and at the end of the year, with a job already assured and a new sense of purpose neatly folded and ready to go, she went out to celebrate with her teachers' college friends and ended up getting much drunker than she should've.

And now her hands were in her hair and she was making circles, the lost loops and turns of someone utterly overwhelmed. When, between sobs, Corban spat on the floor, it might have been his tooth that bounded and clicked. And with the bell still ringing – three on, one off – it was time to move. She turned and focused on the class and spoke hard: 'Emily. You and Gary take Corban up to the nurse. Corban, can you hear me?' A nod through sobbing. 'Emily and Gary are going to take you to the nurse. Are you okay to walk?' More nods. Focus on the bell. Acknowledge its existence. 'Alright, everyone else, you can hear that. Fire alarm. Leave your bags where they are and follow me.'

'It's not the fire alarm, Miss.'

'It is for us. Let's go.'

The students began to lift themselves from their seats and shuffle toward the door, most watching Corban as he stood and cupped his mouth in a futile attempt to hold in the blood. Bravely, Emily leaned down and collected Corban's tooth for him, and Gary stood dumbly and licked his braces and looked out the window. But things were falling into order again. Clarity was coming back. As the last of the students left the room and filed out through the hall and into the sunlight, Stephanie locked the door behind her.

DANNY

'It appears there are certain ingredients for success,' he said into the camera, having now learned to look directly into the lens and brave the emptiness of its gaze. 'First off, you need to show some skin, which is why, as you can clearly see, I am topless. However, I'm aware many of you will be put off by my pale pimple-ridden chest, and for that reason, behind me, I have placed a poster of a hot girl sponging herself down at a car wash. She'll get dirty before that car gets clean.' Danny recorded the lines twelve times before he had a version without stutters and with the appropriate comedic rhythm. He'd noticed this as a typical vlogger move, a convention of the genre: cut out the mistakes, edit the reality to make it sing. 'It also needs to be funny,' he said in the next recording block, 'Which is why I made the joke about the slut at the car wash.' Cut. Next block. 'It's also vital that I appeal to some wider trends and issues that affect my target audience – you guys – so here come some opinions loaded with swearing.' Cut. 'Girls don't like you because you're weak and boring and sad and frightened.' Cut. 'And your standards are too high.' Cut. 'And internet porn is rapidly turning you into the kind of guy that expects girls to enjoy it when you cum on their face.' Cut. 'That's not the memory they want to have when they think back on how they lost their virginity.' Cut. 'So fuck you!' Cut. 'And fuck me!' Cut. 'And always remember that Jesus loves you.' Cut. 'Even if you don't love him back.'

The final section of this sixty second whirlwind took some preparation and planning – icepack, needle, tissue paper, mirror – because he only really had one shot at it. He cooled the side of his face with the icepack and rested his head against his hand. From the quiet of his room he could hear his parents laugh at something on TV, and in the moments before hitting the record button, he was overcome with an inexplicable wave of love and gratitude for them. He opened his eyes and set himself up, took three swollen breaths and pushed the button. 'But the real factor – the big one – is the mixture of facial jewellery and pain, so here goes.' He dropped the icepack and picked up the needle and forced it through from the inside out (the wrong way, he later discovered). In the end he didn't need the mirror, because he had his eyes closed throughout the entire thrust, squeezing them tight against the sting and pressure as it went in, and then the pop as it broke the skin and shot through the other side. With the needle's end protruding noticeably from his nostril, he stared back into the camera. 'How's it look? I guess I better pull it out now.' The extraction was slower, and with his eyes open he watched his nostril suck back against the friction of the needle before thopping out again as the point went sub-dermal, and then the bleeding began (bleeding not stemming from the intended hole, but from the needle scraping against an area of membrane that had been weakened by his habit of picking). The pain wasn't so bad. Breaking his arm had been worse, catching his finger in a car door had been worse; campylobacter-related diarrhoea had definitely been worse. Comparatively, this was just a dull sting and ache. But the blood meant a theatrical finish, and as it started streaming down onto his chest he felt it was a good time to shout and look wild and hold up his hands in the faux paralysis of someone too shocked to do anything else. Cut. He could hear his dad asking if everything was okay.

Titled *Sluts, Opinions and Self-Mutilation*, the video went up a week after Danny returned to school, but not before he took the chance to bask in the success of his holiday's endeavours. Thanks in large part to Facebook connections with peers he didn't talk to in real life, a good chunk of the student population (regardless of year-level or demographic) had already seen his first two videos. As he lurked from group to group over lunchtime and thought about what his parents had said regarding Year 12 being an important juncture concerning his choices for the future, he could hear his name being spoken and he could tell people were talking about him. The cocktail party effect: although engaged in other thinking or conversation, when the soft syllables of his moniker were whispered, his brain subconsciously registered it. And this was good, because each mention was a number, a viewer, somebody to boost his count and corresponding sense of self.

Although it seemed people were much less reluctant to abuse him or make fun of him face-to-face, occasionally it happened: someone larger than him and dumber than him got up the requisite sack to tell him he was a homo or a queer (always with the gay jokes), usually while he was walking past and they had a wall of their friends to laugh with. Not that it would have mattered if they didn't, because abuse just meant viewership, it meant that he'd managed to steal a small segment of their lives that they could never have back, and so he'd already won by the time they clicked the dislike or wrote the offensive comment or took the time out of their day to mock him, which is why he always responded with a polite bow and a 'Thank you for watching, I love a critical audience,' before walking away. There was no need for anything more.

Anything undertaken outside the recording field of a camera was now extra work; while he still enjoyed the live audience, it always felt as if he were advertising for his channel. But he also felt that it was vital to mature his material. Because Year 12, after all, was a crucial stepping stone to higher education. Instead of copying mind maps about racism off the whiteboard, it was about engaging in critical analysis with themes of servitude and oppression; instead of the simplistic utility of Pythagoras, it was standard deviation and something called a surd. So standing on the desk just to be a dickhead wasn't going to cut it anymore. Where he had simply wet toilet paper and tossed it at the ceiling and got laughs in Year 10 – an audience of easy idiotic pubescence with little to no grasp of the present, the future, or even themselves – Year 12 saw his peers displaying imitations of adult restraint and sophistication that aimed to mask a heightened social terror of the world around them. They demanded subtlety. So Danny responded to this with props – quirky adaptations to his character that would allow him to perform in gentler and more refined ways, and, for the most part, without the presence of bodily fluids or shouting. His small remote control helicopter was a hit. At only thirty dollars, the SG105 was light weight, easy to operate and USB rechargeable, and the flashing yellow light next to the tail rotor-blade helped to give it the feel of a large humming bee as it drifted into classrooms through open windows and attacked the unsuspecting. With its esoteric nature and idiosyncratic bonus points, Danny felt it gave him the air of distinction that blowing bubbles from a pipe might have given a younger version of himself. In the end it was worth the confiscation and trip to the Dean.

'How was your summer, Danny? Did you manage to get a film project off the ground?' The Dean was lifting the SG105 up and down in his hand, as if trying to link the device into an attempt at a pun.

'Yeah, it was good. I made a few things.'

'Like what?'

'I recorded a music video. And a short documentary about the stress potential of clothes pegs.'

'Good. Great. Can I see them?'

'I'd rather you didn't at this stage. You know, it's early on, so I'm still coming to terms with the equipment and cutting things together.'

'Conflict is the key,' the Dean said. 'Conflict and characters.' He put the helicopter down on the desk between them. 'Look, we're not going to have another year of this are we?'

'Of what?'

'The clowning. Because it's not just about you this year. Year 12 is important.'

'I keep hearing that.'

'Universities pick students based on Year 12 grades, not Year 13 – the marks come in too late at Year 13 to make them useful. And you're a quick kid, so I expect your parents will want you entering into tertiary study, yes?'

'They've indicated that a few times.' Danny had his hands folded into his lap, a posture of studious attention that he was trying to master. Done well enough and with a genuine dedication to remaining still, it had the tendency to make people laugh.

'But like I said, it's not just about you. You've got to consider the other students.'

'I do consider them. I consider them a lot.'

'Because they need to do well. It needs to be a serious academic atmosphere in the classroom, and every time you break that atmosphere you're damaging their ability to do well, to get into the courses they want to get into. You're hurting their futures.'

'I understand,' Danny said.

'Good. I'm keeping this for the time being though. It looks fun to play with.'

Danny left the office as the Dean attempted to get the SG105 airborne, the turbulence of its rotor blades causing a pile of freshly printed timetables to flap off the edge of his desk.

And Danny did understand. He understood that for a large proportion of the students in the classes around him, there was no real future to hurt. The butterfly effect of his landing a helicopter on the desk in front of Brayden was not going to prevent Brayden from reaching his goal of becoming a pot dealer that lived out of a caravan; nor would it stop Andrea from becoming the hairdresser she yearned to be. And he always took special care not to impact on the paradigms of the young and studious – the kids who buried themselves in books and went to study groups without being forced: these guys weren't his audience. Nonetheless, he tried to adapt to the Dean's request, and by way of apologising for the intrusion of the helicopter, he bought a guinea pig.

Kept in a transparent plastic container for most of its life (with air-holes, of course) Danny decided not to name it. Given the stress of its conditions, early death was inevitable, so it was better not to get attached, just as it was important not to let to his parents or teachers know that he was carrying it with him. Piebald and fluffy, it was a hit with girls in all his classes, and he was happy to release it into their company for the duration of maths or history, provided, of course, that they kept it under wraps. For Danny, the undercover aspect was what helped to foster the feeling of conspiracy. And girls, he was discovering, were taste makers – leading indicators in the war for attention. Each female viewer was worth twice a male, because males went where females were heading simply to garner the feeling of being involved. And when girls loved the guinea pig, they loved Danny by proxy. They figured he was a sweet guy for having it; a sensitive type, with a soul and everything. Each girl had her own name for it: Melissa called it Skippy; Ivy called it Fuzzball; Mina called it Mr Snugglesworth. And Danny started to notice all the little patterns of mood as they fought over who got to have it next, whose turn it was to put it in their bag and feed it bits of their sandwiches and love it and stroke it. If Sharon didn't get it, she seemed huffy and distracted; if Karishma got it instead of Stacy and Anna, then Stacy and Anna would be rude to Karishma in subtle and awful ways as soon as they were out of class. But while Danny noticed this sort of behaviour, it was more important just to get it back at the end. It was a mascot, after all. A twelve-dollar advertising machine. And when the expected end arrived and it rolled over and put its little feet up in the air for good, he could just get another one and tell the girls that he wanted to keep Mr Snugglesworth (or whatever) at home, but here, play with this little guy. He considered writing the name of his YouTube channel in the guinea pig's fur; only the fear that this might be interpreted as a step into cruelty stopped him from doing it.

The big stuff he kept for his channel, and in the days following his upload of *Sluts, Opinions and Self-Mutilation* he found himself too preoccupied with responding to comments to bother with anything school-related. For the most part, his target audience of males and females in the thirteen to seventeen bracket were pleased with what they'd seen, and with a well networked system of referral though Facebook the video quickly went microcosmically viral, watched by most of his school, as well as being passed on to friends of friends at other schools. The meta-levels to the content worked nicely as a duel hook; half the audience thought it was serious and clicked the like button because it fairly represented them, and the other half got the joke and so hit the like button as well. Brevity also helped. At sixty seconds, he wasn't even asking them for the length of a commercial break, and a minute was the change in their pockets they weren't going to use anyway. Combined with the marketability of the title, and as the infection began to set in to the wound in his nostril, the video slowly began to collect a global audience – teenage viewers from the States drawn in by the promise of tits and blood and maybe even emotion; viewers from Russia pulled by the idea of someone cutting themselves and a thumbnail image of Danny covered in his own gore. 'Fck kid – you an idiot.' – USSR4eva

'Whaddaya doin? Doesn't your mother love u?' – Darren786

She loves me plenty, Danny thought. That's why she took me to the doctor's office.

Because he'd had to lie about how it had happened. He wasn't ready to show them his performance art or even try to explain things regarding audience numbers and the importance of authenticity when it came to increasing his share of global attention. So he told them he'd been using a needle to clear something in his nose when his elbow slipped from the table and caused him to skewer himself in this awkward but – if they really stopped to think about it – lucky place, because it could have been his eye, so let's all be thankful here and just deal with this as a secret blessing. His mother agreed; his dad called him an idiot (a rebuke which Danny felt was fair under the circumstances and so it didn't damage his self-esteem) and they patched him up with tissues, then antiseptic cream, then a small circular Band-Aid that neatly covered his nostril but made his nose itch. But it was good advertising – proof that it wasn't all smoke and mirrors – and in the brief window between the upload and widespread viewership, the Band-Aid led to questions by his peers, all of which could be answered by directing them to his channel. However, his habit of taking it off to show people the hole meant the intrusion of dirt into the wound, and within a couple of days it had become an inflamed carmine pustule seeping fluids back into his nasal cavity. Hence the trip to the doctor's and a pass for a whole week of sitting in his room and responding to comments as they came in. 'Funny shit brotha' – MonkyDog7

'Thank you. It's nice to be appreciated.'

He watched his view counts climb. He loved the world.

TOM & DAVE

Bam! Dave fired an empty beer bottle at the wall and watched it smash. Tom took a drag on his cigarette.

Just like that, Dave said. Nice and fast and you'd get away with heaps.

I dunno. Shit gets shut down pretty quickly. There are probably more factors at play than you realise.

Counterfactuals?

There's no way in hell you know what that word means.

Counter – against. Factuals – facts. Things that are against the facts. Things that you don't know because they're running against the state of play. Bam!

Outside the Midway House the rows of bamboo rustled in a sudden breeze and then fell quiet. On a road beyond the building a truck moved into a lower gear as it struggled uphill.

Alright, Tom said. What about the dumbbell thing?

What?

At school, the black kid with the dumbbell, remember – fuck, what's his name? – He got shut down really quick. Like it was over before it even started.

Yeah, but he's an idiot. And that was pretty clearly like an anger thing. He didn't plan it. He let his emotions get the better of him. You have to be cool about it. Study your area, pick your targets, identify where you're going to go first and second and stuff, think about how witnesses are going to react.

Counterfactuals?

Yeah, sure – see, it works.

You have to be a psychopath to plan like that, Tom said.

That dumbbell thing was pretty weird though.

Howdya mean?

Not like the act itself, but the fact he picked a dumbbell.

That would actually really hurt.

Hurt? Think about it. What if he'd got someone on the ground and tanked them in the head? It could've killed them. Ten kilos coming down hard on a human skull buffered by concrete. Fuck.

That's a lot of newtons.

The skull would just crack open. Your brain would squash. You'd be dead like straight away. Even if you didn't die and the doctors managed to save you, you'd be a vegetable.

Shit, what was that guy's name?

Don't know. You know about Jeffery Dahmer?

The Indian dude in Chemistry?

Nah, that's Jeff Garmah. Jeffery Dahmer D-A-H. Serial killer. Did weird shit.

Is this what you look up in your spare time?

Like, he tried to reanimate his victims. Drilled holes in their heads and filled them with acid.

This is seriously what you look up?

Get this; he'd masturbate with their guts.

You can't research a one-page history paper but you can memorise this.

It's interesting shit.

I'm not helping you with your essays anymore.

Apparently he was just like a really lonely guy, and he'd kill people because they threatened to leave him. They'd be walking out the door and he'd kill them just so he could keep them around, like prop them up in the lounge and talk to them and stuff.

I don't know what your point is.

The dumbbell thing.

Don't follow, Tom said, picking some plaster out of the wall.

Okay, so think about this. Dahmer's first victim was a hitchhiker – a guy – and he picked him up and drove him back to his place, and when the hitchhiker wanted to leave Dahmer got all upset and ended up bashing him to death with a dumbbell. Then he ground up the body and scattered it in the woods.

And you think there's some kind of psychotic connection between a serial killer and the thing at school, like it's the same haunted dumbbell just travelling the globe looking for victims?

That's not what I'm saying. But get this, when he was finally convicted and sentenced to like sixty million years in prison, he was in the weights room when another inmate started a fight with him.

I see where this is going.

And so this big-arse inmate grabs a dumbbell and beats his skull in with it, and apparently the whole time Dahmer just like takes it, like sits back and accepts it as this dumbbell comes crashing down on his face. So it's got this crazy insane cycle. His first kill, his own death. The dumbbell.

It still sounds like you're trying to make a connection that isn't there.

I'm not making it, Dave said. I'm just saying things. You're making the connections.

You're fucking retarded. And I'm serious about your essays – I'm not helping you with them anymore.

ALi

Eid al-Fitr fell on a Friday, and Ali's parents gave him the day off school to celebrate. He was breaking the fast, after all, and it was a chance to gorge himself to an unreasonable degree and play soccer with all the luxury that food and water provided. His mother had made xalwo for the first time since leaving Somalia, and when they arrived at Nasir's home she placed it neatly among the banquet that had been prepared and arranged. His father spent the whole day smiling and chatting – a double celebration, because he'd found a job stacking shelves at a paper warehouse. So the mood was good, and for a full twenty-four hours Ali didn't have to think about school or homework or confusing friend requests from people who did not actually appear to want to be friends.

There were other things on Ali's mind as well. His cousins had frequently been skipping out on large portions of each school day, and this left Ali in a difficult position, because if they weren't there, then he was alone – and being alone was hard. He remembered what Nasir had said about family. If they were there to protect each other, then surely they should stay in school to help him. But it seemed weak to ask; childish. For a while he thought about telling his parents, but somehow that also felt cowardly – sneaky and underhanded even – because Ali's mother would talk to other mothers who would talk to their kids, and then they would know he'd snitched. 'Doesn't the school call your house if you're not in class?' Ali asked Nasir with a mouthful of xalwo, hoping this was something Nasir hadn't considered.

'Yeah, of course they do. But my dad's like your dad; he can barely even read English – you should hear him trying to speak it on the phone. He just says thank you to everything and hopes whoever is calling will go away. One day the police will call and tell him I'm dead and he'll go "thank you, thank you" and hang up and go back to watching TV.'

'It's just, you know…'

'What is it, my cousin?'

'School is not as fun without you and Tarabi in ESOL. And Odawaa is nice, but…'

'I know, he's very dumb.' On the lawn in front of them, and maybe not completely out of earshot, Odawaa was trying to swat a wasp with a stick. 'Okay cousin,' Nasir said. 'I will come to ESOL for you.'

But Nasir's promise lasted for all of a week. While Ali had accepted the conditions of the classroom as something he just had to put up with, an obstacle on the road to success, Nasir was quickly giving up. The desks and chairs and whiteboard were signifiers of prison conditions, and the teacher was a guard, there to torment and punish rather than serve. His worksheets were frequently incomplete and his homework was never done, and when Ali tried to help him by speaking in English, Nasir became frustrated and reverted to Somali. Instead of focusing on the given task, he'd turn to Tarabi and Odawaa and start telling dirty jokes, and they would laugh and return fire, and soon none of them were doing anything. For Nasir, writing anything down seemed painful, as if the action physically hurt him, and as a result his handwriting always looked like a confession extracted after torture, bent and shaky and ugly, a kind of injured awfulness that made Ali's spaced out block letters seem like smooth calligraphy.

It was maybe out of shame that Nasir didn't tell Ali that he wasn't coming, or that he was taking Tarabi and Odawaa with him, but the result was that Ali was suddenly completely alone, and ESOL was no longer the escape it had been. Yes, he could get his work done without the distraction of jokes about midgets and postmen, but he could also hear the others in the class, and having a group of Chinese international students make fun of him in skidding English was somehow worse than when it came with the clarity and speed of a native speaker. 'You lonely, hah hah! You lose your friends.' There were no metaphors to couch the blow, no idioms to render the meaning unintelligible.

But the real pain was inflicted during lunchtime.

Where class provided structure and the distraction of work, lunchtimes brought with them a terrible, terrible freedom, and after eating the apple and sandwich his mother had given him – a task he tried to savour for as long as possible – he was left to walk the grounds and block out the boredom. He tried sitting it out in the library, but against the chatter of other students and the fact he was stuck at the children's books – complete with pictures of dogs and cartoon monsters – the experience was somehow personally embarrassing. For a while he sat on a bench and looked at girls as they passed: girls of all ethnicities texting on phones and sharing music and hugging and laughing, but these girls were not like the naked women dancing on TV. They never smiled at him or even looked at him, and the one time a girl did (he'd been staring for some time, it must be said, at a Middle-Eastern girl with cool dark hair and deep olive skin) it was after a friend had alerted her to the leery gaze of an immigrant loner. The look she'd returned was one of repulsion and disgust. Then her extremely large boyfriend gave Ali the finger and told him to fuck off, and Ali was left with the feeling that TV was providing a disingenuous reality.

It was on his third lunchtime alone that he finally found the grass bank above the basketball courts. The night before he had chatted with Nasir online and Nasir had come close to what seemed like an apology for the abandonment, and Ali knew that Nasir hadn't informed his parents that he'd given up on education and was, instead, riding his bike aimlessly around the suburbs and hanging out in parks. 'Just try to make some friends,' Nasir's message said. 'You're a smart guy, people will like you.' And Ali got the feeling of being pawned off, although maybe Nasir wanted for him what he couldn't get for himself – to run around with people he wasn't related to, to actually socially interact, just like the students on the courts below him. For the time being, Ali felt he'd found a workable equilibrium. From up on the bank in the shade of the trees he could watch other students play pick-up games of rugby and soccer and cricket without being so close as to make his spectatorship uncomfortable. The wire fence gave him protection, and from a distance the whole thing was safer and more balletic. He followed a ball hit by an Indian kid as it skittered though the field of a rugby game, and he watched Gavin tackle Xiao, probably harder than was necessary, and it was like watching TV, passive but without fear. And then Mr Gleeson was standing above him and eating a sandwich, making his rounds on lunchtime duty. 'Hello, Ali.' From the ground Mr Gleeson looked like a giant, mingling with the canopy above him.

'Hello, sir.'

'Good view from up here.'

'Yes. Good view.'

'Why aren't you down playing with the others?' Stupid question, you idiot. They don't like me. Don't ask me that.

'I don't play.'

'You don't play? Seems a waste. It looks like fun. Take it easy, Ali.' And then he was off, chewing his sandwich and heading for the field.

Ali was back on the bank again the following day, but closer to the action this time, Mr Gleeson's annoying intervention having highlighted Ali's social deficiencies. He was close enough to see the expressions on their faces, and when a basketball shot over the fence, he took the active step to chase after it and hurl it back to the player with a throw that felt uncomfortably inept, but with this action he'd been seen. Gavin had spotted him – the game of rugby having paused while someone chased the unpredictable bounce of the ball onto the makeshift pitch of a cricket game. 'Ali!' he shouted, and for a moment Ali was going to pretend he hadn't heard it, but then it came again a second time with a lot more force: 'Ali!' The small bits of eraser were still coming during maths, tiny bounces off his page and the laughter that signified they'd managed to land one clean in the tight curls of his hair – 'It's like a fucking carpet!' – and the friend request was still left unanswered, since Ali had hoped that a lack of response might be the best response, because what good could possibly come from either of the other options? 'Ali you little bitch; wanna play?' And now he had to respond, because he was too far down the bank, and when he turned back up to look where he'd been sitting in the safety of the trees, it seemed distant and unreachable, an old friend leaving on a train forever. 'Oi, you wanna play?'

'Oh, no, I don't know.' His whole mouth to form the vowels, his palms growing moist.

'Come on, it's easy. Suck it up.' Idioms.

'Easy?'

'Yeah, it's fuckin' easy. New Zealand game, man.'

'Okay. I play.'

He made his way through the gate in the fence and stood in the courts. At ground level he'd lost his bearings, and now there seemed to be a lot more going on. People were running in every direction as different games overlapped in the crowded space; balls flew at the corners of his vision, and without proper perspective he found himself wincing and ducking as if he were under attack. The game was already back in full swing: students with red faces and dirty uniforms, shirts un-tucked, pants rolled up: Ali in a vortex. Ali spinning. People bobbing and weaving and grabbing around him. 'You're on their team,' Gavin said, and Ali watched him wave a hand in a general direction, indicating what could have been any number of other guys whose names he didn't know and who gave him no signal that they were on the same side, and he hadn't played this before, this game with a deformed ball and full contact options, where the goal seemed to be to run and throw and hit. 'You know the rules?' someone asked, and Ali shook his head but it appeared that whoever asked the question wasn't all that concerned with the response, and then someone threw him the ball and he caught it. He looked around: a basketball was being bounced on the other side of the courts; a flock of seagulls was flying overhead; someone was laughing – female, loud – but he couldn't see them or fix its position, and he wondered what it was they were laughing about, whether it was at someone or something. ESOL worksheet number six: Adverbs with two forms: She laughed hard? Or she laughed hardly? 'Fuckin' run you dopey cunt!' So Ali ran, and he made it a full two steps across the court before something hard and fast crashed into the side of his body and knocked against his head, and even before he hit the ground he could hear the others make that sound people make – the same in every language – when they've witnessed something painful, that emission of one elongated syllable that expresses everything about how agonizing and brutal it must have been for the party involved. He felt his vision arc and lose focus, the ball leaving his grip with it, and then the inevitable thud as he settled into a sick and breathless ringing against the warm grit of the pavement.

He wasn't angry that it had happened. Yes, it seemed unfair to blindly hit someone who barely knew what they were doing, but he'd agreed to play, so he had to respect their decision to do it. Nor was he angry that no one helped him up, because the game had to continue. And he wasn't angry about the fact that he couldn't breathe (he'd been winded before – his lungs would open up again soon) or about the blood that was coming from somewhere around his ear. But as he stood up and tried to dust himself off and recalibrate to the swirling of the world around him, he found that his shirt had been torn in the fall – shredded against the hard ground – and this was what hurt more than the ache and graze of his side or the throbbing of his head. 'You look like you're on your way.' His dad's voice. 'Now tell me, what is the boy on the left saying to the boy on the right?' That he wants to inflict pain on something. That this is no way to live. Blood on teeth in dirt and sunlight. And now the seagull was flying back the way it had come (the same seagull?) and the basketball was bouncing again, and the laugher had returned, this time louder, swelling, waxing: ESOL worksheet number seven: Adjectives – Order: I bought a knife sharp? Or I bought a sharp knife? And then the ball was in front of Ali, lolling against its shape, and he was staring at it, and then picking it up, and he could hear himself being addressed – 'Oi, Ali, retard, you're offside. You can't pick it up' – but it made no difference, because the ball was already heading skyward and long, a big clean punt that sent it over the cricket game and over the fence and into a neighbouring property, a pure catharsis, and Ali was so impressed with its flight – a ball that would've sent Odawaa hard down the left wing and toward the opposition goal – that he didn't hear Gavin charging up behind him, and for the second time in as many minutes something hard stuck him in the side of the head.

That afternoon Ali found himself in the deans' corridor awaiting a meeting with the boy who'd punched him. In the light of the admin block his shirt looked even worse. Streaks of his blood and grit had adhered to the fabric, and against his dark skin it looked more like a burn than a graze. His whole left side ached from the fall, and he could feel fluids pulsing in his skull, as if his brain had its own heartbeat. Someone had seen the punch and reported it to a teacher, however they hadn't been specific – a fight, they'd said – so both boys had been called up to explain their side of the story and go through the process of conflict resolution.

Gavin was already in their Dean's office when Ali arrived, so he was asked to wait in the seat outside the door until it was his turn. As he sat and studied the abrasions on the palms of his hands, other deans and senior teachers passed him without looking, eyes fixed straight ahead. 'No, of course. Yes, Mrs Chambers.' The door had opened and Gavin was coming out, flanked by the Dean. 'Hey, buddy!' he said to Ali, and Ali found himself reacting to Gavin's mood with a rote response to friendliness, an automatic grin and a 'Hello, yes' that he wasn't sure why he was giving.

'You two look like you're on the way to mending.' Mending? Definition, please. 'Come in, Ali.'

He took the seat in front of the Dean's desk as his pupils darted about and gathered information: pictures of Mrs Chambers in a sundress and holding a baby; pictures of a man in shorts holding a big fish above his head; a reddish painting that looked like crayon of a ghost holding its mouth open. 'How are you, Ali?' Mrs Chambers spoke slowly and had smile creases forming at the edges of her eyes. This was the first time Ali had ever spoken to her, and he found the immediate assumption of familiarity a little off-putting.

'Okay, yes.'

'Gavin tells me that you kicked his ball away. Is that

true?'

'Yes. I kick his ball. But he hit me.'

'Did he hit you before or after you kicked away the ball?'

'After. But I tear my shirt. See?' Ali pulled up the torn and bloody area of his shirt to emphasize the damage.

'That looks sore, Ali. I think we should get you to the nurse after this. Did that happen before Gavin hit you, or after?'

'Sorry?'

'What happened first, the tear in your shirt, or Gavin hitting you?'

'Oh, de tear.'

'And how did that happen?'

'On de ground.'

'You fell on the ground?'

'Yes, I fell on de ground.'

At this point Mrs Chambers felt she had pieced it all together. 'Okay. I see. Now I want you to listen carefully, Ali.'

'Yes, yes.'

'If things aren't going your way, it's important to behave like an adult. If you fall and hurt yourself, you can't take it out on other people, because they have every right to their space as well.'

'Yes.' Ali didn't understand.

'So now I'm going to have you boys apologise to each other, and then we're going to get you off to the nurse. Okay?'

Gavin stood up when the door opened and Ali and the Dean emerged into the corridor. 'Alright,' she said, 'Gavin, you first.'

'Sorry, Ali,' he said, putting out his hand. 'It won't

happen again.'

'And now, Ali, it's your turn.'

'Yes. Sorry.' He found himself shaking Gavin's hand and looking back into his smile and feeling something had gone wrong.

'Good,' Mrs Chambers said. 'And we'll leave it at that shall we.'

Outside the admin block the sun was hot and in the distance Ali could hear someone shouting or laughing. A breeze was starting to blow and it made his mouth feel dry. Gavin had walked with him as they left the building, but now he was looking around himself, off at other things. 'Do you know where is nurse?' Ali asked.

Gavin stopped and looked directly into Ali's face. 'Fuck off, cunt.'

The breeze blew again. Gavin walked away. ESOL worksheet number four: Adjectives and Adverbs with the same form: In the phrase 'Everything went wrong,' is 'wrong' an adjective or an adverb?

When Ali returned home that day he said nothing to his mother or sister and went immediately to his computer. Later that evening he would lie to them, concocting a story about how he'd tripped and fallen during physical education. But first things first. He logged into Facebook and accepted Gavin as a friend.

HENRY

Henry saw Brayden at the window but didn't really see him, just a face in the curtains that he passed over before pressing his own against the sky and listening for the scream between the urgent syncopation of the ringing bell. He moved without being sure where he was moving or why he was moving there, his feet plodding beneath him, head arched up, his body guided by his ears. White smoke, wispy, dispersing. Footage he had seen of the Boxing Day Tsunami: barefoot and wearing shorts, a man walks forward and into the path of the destruction, because he can tell something is coming and maybe he wants a better view, like a front row seat of the raw power surging toward him, although it's possible that he doesn't quite understand what's happening and can't see the boats being flipped and rolled in the surf beyond the palms, or the jetty that's being torn apart; it's possible that he doesn't know he's walking blindly into Armageddon. In the footage, the sea towers above him, and as Henry sat on the floor and looked up at the TV to see it – a kid at this point – the images loomed above his perspective, and he felt the end of things, mortality, the crushing possibilities of the world around him...but the footage would always end with a cut, and then the screen was all news presenters again. 'What happened to the man, Dad?'

'I imagine he was killed, son.'

But how did he know? Surely anything could've happened. At the last minute the guy could've turned and run. Or he could've scaled a palm tree super quick. He looked like a native; he was probably more than adept at climbing with speed and knocking down coconuts; when the crucial moment came he'd simply flown right up one, the tide's violent force sliding harmlessly underneath... And up there he had a better view. He could wait it out in safety, clinging to the trunk with his arms and legs while he looked out over frothy wreckage. Because the reality is we didn't see what happened; when the camera stopped, facts and objectivity went with it.

If only he could block out the ringing, then the world would be calm. Some earmuffs would work nicely. Sunshine, blue sky. In the early summer the school looked much better, like the winter had cleaned the pastel paintwork and polished the handrails and wiped down the benches. Spring had blown away the garbage and washed plastic pie wrappers into the drains and out to sea. Everything was brighter now – crisp even in the afternoon's heat. Everything was tidal. Henry looked up at the stark straight lines of flat roofs; shadows and light, almost chiaroscuro with a squint, much like all his work in photography class. He held up his hands to create a picture frame and studied the image. He liked the simplicity when just about everything else was complex. 'The problem of Palestinian intransigence is a sticking point in Israel.'

'What's intransigence mean, Dad?'

'And frankly I don't see a solution that doesn't involve the creation of two separate states.'

Leila Grey's legs. She crosses them, left over right, while she's waiting at the bus stop. She has to know that her skirt is too short for that. She has to know what it does to him. He imagines a world in which they are married and she stays home and he catches the subway to work and holds on to the roof-straps of the carriage because there aren't any seats left, and in one hand he holds a briefcase and in the other a newspaper, and he tries to read it but the words are unsettled, and this world is black and white. After work he gets a drink at a bar and tips back his hat before he's on the subway again, briefcase in hand and speeding home to his wife. 'How'd you do today, honey?'

'Wonderful, sweetheart, but even better now.'

'Have you been drinking again? I thought we talked about this.'

'Just a quick one to ease the pain. You know I love you.'

Together they stand on the beach in the warm light and the wave is coming. The colours are richer in Indonesia – the blues are truly blue and the greens are really green - and they can see the wave beyond the palms as it tips boats and destroys the jetty, and he looks at her and she smiles and takes the hand he's offered. A warm hand to match the warm light. It's simple.

MiNA & AHMED

During a science lesson in Year 11, Mina's teacher delivered the story about frogs in boiling water, how if you threw one straight into a hundred-degree broth it would jump right out again and hop away to a better world, but if you started it at room temperature and left it to get hot, then the frog would just sit there until it died and became a soup. At fifteen years old and having never heard it before, for Mina it was powerful and new and seemed to have wider implications, and she enthusiastically relayed it to Ahmed as they sat and ate their lunch. 'Don't you think it's fascinating?'

'How? Frogs are dumb.'

'No, like, it's a metaphor for the way people behave and how they react to things.'

'I don't know,' Ahmed said, chewing his apple. He'd learned to be careful about what he disagreed with when talking to Mina. Fights, even small ones, often left him with the feeling that a vital organ had been abruptly removed. 'I just don't see how it relates. Like, if you put me in a pot of boiling water, sure, I'd jump out. But if you slowly warmed the water, I'd be like, ouch, this is getting hot. You know what, I'm going to get out.'

'You don't get it.' Mina felt frustrated.

'I think I do.' Ahmed felt right.

'It's a metaphor, so like, think of the pot of water as the environment or something. If you were thrown into an environment that was totally polluted and gross and full of smog, you'd want to get out of it straight away. But if you started off somewhere nice and clean and then it slowly got worse around you, then you wouldn't really notice it happening.' She used her hands to make her point, illustrating smog with her fingers.

'No I get that. It's just that we're not frogs. We have brains and we notice things. If the world was getting like that, we'd do something about it.'

Mina let her argument fall.

Sexual inconveniences aside, as the year wore on they became more and more like a regular couple, the relationship growing into a developed entity. While the intensity of lust and yearning still regularly made an appearance, they had settled in, and now, during the times they were separated by timetabling or obligation, they weren't so completely incapacitated by the absence of the other. Both had started to make regular friends again, members of the same sex who could help fill in some of the social gaps created by the all-consuming nature of their early courting, like playing Xbox and calling each other names (Ahmed) and going to the mall to shop in stores where the most expensive product was a twelve-dollar hairbrush (Mina) because without a job that's all she could afford. And Mina had started to really enjoy that stuff:

trying on dresses and sampling lipstick at the testing counter and giggling about things that would make Ahmed want to shoot himself. And Ahmed needed the time to release male energy and bond in simulated war environments and exist in a place where it was acceptable to stab someone in the back with a military-grade bowie knife. Their arguments were regular but not frequent, a residual side-effect in the war between co-dependence and personal space. Why, for example, did he have to play games with his friends tonight? It was a Friday and they should go to the movies with people and eat popcorn and do all that other dumb shit like watch her try on dresses that she wasn't going to buy and then have to make a comment that wasn't going to come out right, and why did she have to go to the mall with Veronica when she could meet him after soccer practice and they could try to find a place in the park to be alone for an hour. Why with the parks all the time? You know how I feel about that stuff; can't you come up with a better idea? I've tried, I really have. Well maybe you should get your licence and then we could drive places together. What, Jason's going to the mall with you guys? So as soon as someone has a car they're useful to you. You know that makes you seem like a prostitute. Fuck you! How dare you! I'm sorry – I just don't like the way he looks at you. Like, you don't understand what guys are like – he's definitely into you in *that* way – and it seems like you're flirting with him. Don't worry. Please don't worry.

I love you.

And I love you too.

And they did love each other, and they trusted each other completely – a trust that can only exist in the antebellum of one's emotional life, a time before being scammed or rejected or cheated, before love becomes a philtre to be eyed with cynicism and caution. Ahmed was her cute boy, the one who wrote her poems and kept his dinosaur duvet in the cupboard, and Mina was the girl who scribbled metaphors about their love and hugged him when he needed it and told him he could do it.

But life can play quite elaborate jokes on people, the sort that can even take years to get to the punch line, and while it might be funny for an outsider, to live the joke is another thing entirely. Because what good joke that doesn't involve a pun isn't about pain or disgust or the fundamental problems with being human. Hey lady, the man said to the woman in front of him on the bus, you have semen on your bag. Semen? She replied. No, it's probably yoghurt. I don't think so, said the man: I don't ejaculate yoghurt. And Ahmed laughed when Jun told him this one, but the joke being played on him and his girlfriend was already in its second act, and there was nothing they could do about it.

At age fourteen Ahmed was a good looking kid. His hair was dark and his eyes were well set in his face, and compared to the other students in the class he was above average height. Even without overlooking the traces of acne, which could be put down to the period of hormonal shifting, he cut a pleasant figure – a little gangly, if you wanted to be picky, but he would grow into it. With this in his favour, onlookers were surprised when he developed an infatuation with a girl that bordered on pudgy and who had hair that seemed to stick at odd angles and shiny pimples that dotted her chin. But that was his choice and they appeared happy, and good on her for scoring someone that was aesthetically a division higher. Then the holidays happened, six long summer weeks for trips away to beaches and family Christmases and a general amnesia concerning school and the people in it, and when everyone returned there was the routine assessment of bodily changes, because teenagers of the right age mutate and morph at the rate of bamboo: hey check it out, Darren's got the beginnings of a moustache and Suzie's dyed her hair black, and Mina, it seems, has shed her fat in all the right areas. But it wasn't just the bodily shift, it was also attitudinal. She wasn't a kid anymore; why should she continue to look like she owned and operated a junior science kit? So she found a way to manage her hair, cutting it shorter and employing a brush to leave it smooth and unkinked. It changed the way people talked to her; it made them listen when they hadn't before.

Throughout the year that followed she grew increasingly impressive; the pimples on her chin vanished, and with the light application of a powder her skin began to glow with an olive Persian iridescence that made her classmates jealous. By the time of the winter holidays she was garnering the easy attention of a beautiful person, as well as the craning leers of older single males who seemed disinterested in issues like the age of consent. Each day her face seemed to mature, her cheekbones rising, her smile widening. With the help of her friends she picked out dresses that would match her eyes and pigmentation, and on mufti-day in late spring she wore one that made Ahmed hurt in ways he found very hard to describe. Yes, this was the same clumsy girl he'd fallen in love with, but his duties regarding her had changed. Now he was swatting away competition, catching Mina in conversations with guys who had the pretext of needing notes or help with something – at which point he would sidle up behind her and touch her hip, and she would turn and kiss him, and he had proved that he'd won. Mine, the touches said. Not yours. Now fuck off.

But this was only one half of the joke, because although Ahmed knew that his girlfriend had grown quickly into beauty, and to a large extent he understood why guys might want to linger and try their luck, their frequency and persistence was becoming unnerving. Like they knew something he didn't, like they were outside the heating pot of water.

Ahmed's change was more gradual than Mina's, but it was happening, and the fact was that she'd met him at the high point of his physical attractiveness. While he was taller than most at fourteen, he was freakishly so by sixteen – the kind of tall that elicits questions about basketball and that Ahmed had quickly come to hate, because he had neither rhythm nor flow nor coordination. It was as if his balance and hand-eye dexterity had been squeezed out of him inch by inch, and around the house he frequently bumped into tables and caught his head on edges that should've been out of reach, and his mother had been furious when his right foot destroyed an heirloom while making the protracted journey to his left knee. With height alone Ahmed would have looked fine, but the ravages of growth were stretching him in other unexpected ways. His face became elongated and his nose flattened, and in the process his eyes retreated further back into his head and gave him the look of a reaper or the recently dead, and then to really rub it in, his teeth, over the course of a year, began to jut out ever so slightly, so that even when at rest his mouth never fully closed. And *this* was the guy that was dating *that* girl. *This* lanky cadaver was with *that* vision from a dreamscape. To those new to the situation, it just wasn't feasible. It was an affront to the rules and to natural justice. How could she be with someone like that? Doesn't she realise? What's he got that I fucking don't? And although Ahmed didn't know why it was happening, as Year 11 bled its way into Year 12, other guys were becoming increasingly rude to him, aggressive and competitive without ever explaining things. Because despite all contrary evidence provided by mirrors and digital photography, he wasn't aware it had happened. He had no clue. When he saw himself, it was with Mina, and he found little in the world that was more gratifying or fulfilling or good at bolstering his sense of self than knowing she loved him – which she did, utterly and blindly. She loved him so closely and intensely, in fact, that she herself lost all perspective of his face: terms like 'good looking' or 'ugly' were unsuited to what she felt about him. He was Ahmed. The boy with the poems. So the two of them went out in public together, the giant figure of death and the Arab beauty, and people made jokes from the safety of their cars, or even just flicked their eyes in the food court and stored it away as evidence of the abnormal. 'Shit, man, check it out. Totally an arranged marriage.' But what they didn't know couldn't hurt them.

The fight started the same way others had. He wanted to play games; she wanted the world of people and movies and talk. They had been waiting together at the bus stop after school. The sky had the flat grey oppression of an afternoon that was already sick of itself. 'You always want to stay in and do nothing; you're like an old man.'

'I just don't want to go out with a group of people,' he said.

'That's an old man thing to say.'

'It's fine for you. People are nice to you. People are

scared of me, and I always get the feeling they want to stab me and steal you.'

'You're being jealous again.'

'No, I'm not – and it's not just guys. Everyone wants to steal you.'

Mina tried to change the conversation. In order to get around a blockage with Ahmed, she'd previously found it was useful to digress before coming again at a different angle. 'Danny brought a guinea pig in to class today.'

'Is this another metaphor?'

'No, it's a real guinea pig. And he let me name it.'

'Oh yeah.'

'I've called it Mr Snugglesworth. It's really cute.'

'I think it's a metaphor. I don't like Danny.'

'What? Why?'

'The metaphor is that the guinea pig is his penis.'

'Stop it, Ahmed!'

'And I bet he was happy that you were touching it and stroking it.'

The digression hadn't gone as planned, and Mina was immediately annoyed that as stubborn and jealous as Ahmed was, he was right – Danny had been unreasonably happy that she was handling and playing with it, and now she wouldn't be able to feed Mr Snugglesworth without it seeming sordid and pornographic. The shouting began. Couldn't he be normal? Couldn't she wake the fuck up already? With a complete disregard for the traffic that slowed to watch them, they argued and waved their arms, and eventually Mina banged her fist on his chest, because he was stubborn and stupid, and Ahmed told her where she could go and turned and walked off – to hell with the bus, and to hell with other people – because she wasn't worth the stress.

For the duration of the ride to the mall, Mina's hands were shaking, and when she found herself in the food court with Veronica and Jason, the remnants of anger and adrenaline all but compelled her to talk about it, to do what she never did, and discuss what was personal and problematic. And Veronica and Jason, who weren't so much friends as lackeys of convenience, acquaintances by accident of geography and timetables, listened the way people listen when beautiful people are talking, with a reverent desire to agree and say yes and feel included in something that seemed better than themselves, and with no little level of sadism did they answer her question when she asked what she shouldn't have asked: 'Why should Ahmed be jealous of other guys?' and she was given the answer no good looking teenage girl who doesn't know how good looking she is should ever be given. She was stunning. She was amazing. In every single respect she was better than him – and hadn't she noticed what a possessive freak he was, because frankly, sometimes, we're a little scared of him: you know that look he gets when he fixes you with that stare. The Ahmed Stare. You're in the right with this one; you have every reason to be angry and upset. We can't believe it's taken you this long to see that. You know, it's like you've been with him for so long you couldn't even see it happening. Everybody's behind you on this one. Everybody will understand. Because you're so beautiful, and so smart, and you could do so much better.

And it went on.

And on.

And by the time her phone started to ring with Ahmed's flashing name, she had been totally rewired, a harried convert to the religion of herself. Her palms were wet and what seemed like electrical surges were sparking in her chest; the universe was peeling open. Do it, she told herself. A snap decision, sure, but that's how real decisions get made. And in the fantasies of her future his limb-heavy figure was abruptly evaporating. 'Don't answer it,' Veronica said. 'Let him suffer.' But she had to. She owed him that now. She would go to see him and she would explain it all and he would have to understand. They were young, and people change, and he'd get over it; really, she was doing it for him… a lie to make it easier to digest. His name continued to flash.

She moved into the noise of the food court and away from the ears of the others. She answered. 'Don't bother apologising,' she said. A long silence followed. '…Ahmed? Are you there? This is childish.'

'My dad,' he said. 'He's had a heart attack.'

STELLA

For a long time Stella pretended she liked abortion clinics. When the opportunity arose, she fictionalised detailed narratives about her personal experiences with them, how she'd drop in and say hi to the nurses and doctors and how they all knew her name, and then she'd ask for the usual. She would've stopped doing it had her audience not been so ridiculously credulous, but even in Year 11 her classmates just sat there and swallowed it. Unable to complete their worksheets, they asked her follow-up questions, and she was more than willing to provide answers. 'Yeah, they let you keep the foetus. They put it in a jar for you.'

'So you've still got them?!'

'I keep them lined up on the mantel at home. My mum likes them. She says she's proud of me.'

'Really?'

'Yeah, she says she wants me to be a slut just like her.'

The actual abortion clinic was nothing like she'd

imagined. For some reason, she'd always envisioned it being small and a little dirty in a way that was almost quaintly rustic, with one room for the procedure and another for the reception desk and a tiny car park at the front designed for no more than four vehicles at a time. She'd expected a fan blowing – small bits of paper taped and billowing off its steel exterior – a radio playing talkback and waiting room chairs with stained wooden arms and nervous fingernail markings. Instead the seats had no arms at all and the waiting room was cavernously large and hospital-clean and there was no fan and no radio; in fact, there was very little noise at all, save the squeak of a wheelchair and the whine of an automatic door.

It started with a period that wouldn't. In the en-suite bathroom that adjoined her bedroom she sat on the toilet looking at boxes of pads and tampons that weren't being used. According to the small print, the pads were manufactured in Hungary, the tampons in Thailand. She'd hoped this information might distract her from thinking what she was thinking. It didn't.

It wasn't like it was a decision, because decisions necessitate a choice. In this case there wasn't one: it had to go and it had to go fast and no one would know, and then she could forget about it. Like really forget about it; shove it deep and hard into repression until even the repression was repressed, and then maybe, at forty – if she lived that long – she might remember it one night in a cold-sweated nightmare, but by then it wouldn't matter.

Unlike anything involving structured learning, when it came to matters of deceit she was capable of sustained periods of concentration and extremely high levels of analytical complexity. So she did her research by the glowing light of the computer in her bedroom, and when her mother came in to say goodnight, she admitted she wasn't feeling well, that her cramps were really bad this month and the headaches worse than usual, and because her mother was conscientious and caring and wanted the best for her daughter and loved the way she expressed her fiery individuality with neon red hair, she advised that maybe she stay home – 'See how you feel in the morning, of course, but use your judgement' – and would she like a hot water bottle to ease the pains…?

'I love you, mum.'

'I love you too, Stelly-Welly.'

'Love is for cunts,' Jeff said. Stella looked up at him in the night, the orange warmth of his cigarette turning the lower part of his face into a momentary hearth. 'Love is a fucking cheeseburger that arseholes use to feel better about themselves.'

She called the doctor's as soon as it was open, then two hours later she told her G.P. in the relative comfort of confidentiality. 'Are you sure about this?' they asked.

'Absolutely,' she replied.

'There will be a mandatory session with a counsellor before the procedure…'

'I just need the referral' (such an adult thing to say).

Something about surgical suction curettage. Curettage – the removal of a growth or tissue. Curette – a surgical implement designed for said removal and scraping. A growth – pretend it's a cancer, because it might as well be.

There's no such thing as fast tracking. School became white noise, a shiftless blur of light and sound with no definable edges. At home in the garden, caterpillars were chewing on swan plants.

'Love is a corporate product: there's nothing personal

or unique about it. It's fucking mass-produced.' She could see the light of the moon glinting off his eyebrow ring; black hair that dragged in the matter of the universe and destroyed it. 'It's soma. It makes people stupid and pliable. Fuckin' shoot me if I fall into their kind of love.'

The lies were easy: it's a school trip, we're staying overnight at a camp and studying the bush – here, sign the permission slip I drew up and printed out in like two minutes. It costs sixty dollars. They'd prefer it in cash…The cramps are back; I can't go in today… We're staying overnight in the school hall to raise money for Mali. I'm not allowed to eat. Feel free to sponsor me, it's a good cause…

The first referral. A bus ride in sunlight – a four stage fare, $6.40 – a walk through a huge car park where windshields and bright paintwork attacked her retinas, and by the parking barrier she threw up a little and when she stood again it felt like she had boot prints on her innards. The waiting room – a hall, really, an airport terminal – and then a room with big windows and more light and a few chairs and fucking venetians. And here's a joke: a social worker, a nurse, and a medical practitioner all walk into a room and ask Stella questions about her mental health. The social worker asks pretty direct questions about the situation surrounding the pregnancy, the nurse plays the good cop role, and the medical practitioner reiterates what she's already been told about suction curettage. And then Stella doesn't say 'I'll have the usual, please.'

'In some cases, women want to keep the products of the pregnancy. But in your case I don't imagine-'

'What?'

'The products, they like to keep–'

'Like the dead bits that are...?'

'Yes.'

No. Fuck no. Throw it in a fire.

Caterpillars chewing swan plants.

Jeff staring back down at her. Jeff pushing into her.

School desks into which she carved his name with a compass and could etch the word love without him ever having to know; tiny rebellions.

White noise.

The day of the procedure.

'Your pupils are huge,' Jeff said. 'I could probably climb in and hide in there.'

By nine a.m. she was swallowing the misoprostal and sitting in a room by herself and watching traffic from the window. Uterine contractions and a much less euphoric kind of dilation. And then the bleeding. And the cramps – real this time – a fact that should've signalled relief but instead messed with her chemistry and made her cry.

'Should I say I hate you then?' she asked him. 'If love is for cunts.'

'Hate's just a different product.'

She found herself groggy and beneath paper sheets. It had all been explained, and she knew the steps by heart: antiseptic solution and bimanual examination; local anaesthetic and a pinching feeling and metal dilators. Cramping. Breathing. Cramping. The good cop nurse now Gaussian soft, holding her hand and squeezing it and telling her she was brave, it'll all be over – breathe slowly now – soon. The cannula reaches the uterus and the suction begins and instead of thinking about a foetus or placenta or bits of broken tissue she drifts into other places and blocks out the sound and the ceiling is filled with small back holes, like a thousand open pupils, and when she lives inside them and climbs in and hides she hears nothing about the forceps required to remove what can't be sucked free. Jeff's face is glowing in the dark and she's holding his chest. 'Words have been co-opted,' he says. 'So let's just not use any.'

The bus ride home was four stages with a transfer after three – $6.40 – but before she could get on she had to sit down on a curb between parked cars, and after she vomited for the second time on that same stretch of concrete she stared at a tyre, at an empty pack of cigarettes, at what might have been a shard of broken glass.

'How have you been, Stella?' Verna asked, swivelling in her office chair and smiling her counsellor smile. 'How are things with Steve?'

'Jeff,' Stella said. 'His name is Jeff. And he's a cunt.'

F 12

'Try using the search function,' said Wendy.

Library closed on Wednesday; Testimonial sheets due. 'The what?' said Blasco. Marking schedules for external moderation.

'The search bar.'

Blasco raised his hands in defeat. 'I give up. I'm a Luddite. Here, you do it.' He rolled his office chair away from his desk and stood, giving Wendy the space to hunt through his emails. The lockdown bell continued to sound, three on, one off, but the majority of the class had settled into its presence. This wasn't an alarm so much as an escape. It meant lesson plan disruption of the kind that was impossible to fix, and even if the bell stopped now there would be no more Willy Loman. At best there would be a game of hangman where Blasco picked words that none of them knew, but more than likely he would just let them sit and talk.

Penelope was scratching her head. 'What's a Ludd–'

'One who is broadly opposed to technological changes,' Sean said, leafing through Merriam-Webster.

'The etymological root,' Blasco added, 'comes from nineteenth century workers who had a tendency to smash the machinery that was making them redundant.'

Wendy sat down at Blasco's desk and began tapping at the keys and fiddling with the mouse. 'See, sir? The search function. Type in a word and it'll find it in your emails.'

'Type in *cock*,' Akaash said.

'Akaash!' The teacher technique: say their name and nothing else and they should infer their transgression. 'Type in drill.'

She did, and up came a list of fire drills over the last year, but nothing indicating a lockdown practice.

While all this went on, Brayden had his head poked through the curtains and was trying to piece together what he was seeing, because Henry had looked at him but not seen him, and this was unusual. And white smoke was coming from somewhere. And maybe Brayden would've spent more time meditating on this, thinking about Henry's strange gaze – the distended lines across his face and his dreamlike movement, the expression that suggested something bigger than a dumb look and a generic cry for attention – had Jun not taken the opportunity to kick him in the back of the leg and hobble him: a clean kick, right in the tendon behind the knee, that caused Brayden to collapse backwards onto the floor. 'Eat it!' Jun declared.

'Shame!' shouted Akaash.

And there were no more thoughts about Henry as Blasco was forced to move into the fray and prevent it getting worse. 'Jun, sit down; Akaash – that's called sadism; Brayden, up you get. Serves you right for looking out the window.'

'Sir!' Brayden rubbed his leg and got up into a seat.

'I've tried practice, lockdown, and intruder,' Wendy said, 'but nothing's coming up.'

'Okay, then. I guess we have to assume this is a real thing.'

DANNY

It's all subjective, and of course it's relative. In the darkness of his bedroom Danny watched the numbers continue to climb. He stroked the guinea pig like a villain; he let the colours of the screen wash over his face. This was a full-time gig now, and with the monetisation of his videos it was about more than just viewership. There was capital to consider, actual coin that he could watch collect – albeit slowly – in a bank account, before reinvesting it back into equipment to make his work even better. There was a manic perfection about a cycle where the goal was the cycle itself.

On his first day back at school following the infection to his nose, someone threw an apple at his head. It hit him in the ear and exploded and left a long buzz and ring, but when he turned to find out where it had come from, all hands were down and all backs turned. A critic, no doubt – a viewer jealous of talent. But he could show them. And he did show them, because it was later that same day that a collection of Year 11 kids dared him to down his own urine – 'chug some piss' – and as soon as they offered up the money, Danny was more than willing. He was destroying detractors with sheer weirdness and showing them how it was done. This is how you swallow an ego, you wash it down with your own hot fluids, and when it trickles from the side of your mouth you just wipe it away with your sleeve and howl.

Although he'd rinsed the filmy remnants from the back of his tongue immediately following the act, there was an aftertaste that lingered all the way home and somehow got worse, until he wasn't sure whether it was real or imagined. And this worried Danny, because by all rights he should have felt good about things. It was sunny and he was making money.

After ditching his uniform and counting his cash, he gargled and settled down at his computer. A new video was already pulsing along the threads of his Facebook feed. Filmed on a pixelated cell phone, the most noticeable part of the video was the sound, the decibels pushed into static red as a blurry audience whooped and cheered and Danny drained the frothy yellow beverage into his own throat.

There were different ways to respond to this, of course. He hadn't wanted the act filmed, but here it was, done with minimal skill, posted on someone else's channel, and clearly designed to make fun of him. The title *Piss Drinker* didn't help. The rational course of action would be to contact the site and have them take it down. Students had reacted over less, however most of them had been swiftly ostracized – reaction led to reaction. Danny remembered what had happened to Jasper Slukins. Cursed with a stupid name to begin with, Jasper also had to overcome the terrors of red hair and a speech impediment, but when Vincent had periscoped his cell-phone camera over the top of the toilet door and come away with pretty damning footage of Jasper deep in the throes of self-pleasure, the burdens of everyday living became too much. He'd been moved to another school after that, but the video – stateless and digital – had followed him, and whenever he felt he was free from its ability to destroy his already fragile reputation, up it surfaced like a rotting corpse. The details of the story varied after that. In the gentlest versions, Jasper was placed in counselling and home-schooled to avoid contact with the real world and given strong tranquillisers on a daily basis to help keep him fogged. In other versions he'd killed himself, each student tagging on their own favourite gory method of suicide, depending on who was telling it or who it was being told to – an easy urban legend passed from year to year as a cautionary tale. But where teachers and peer-support counsellors saw this as a story about the perils of bullying and the importance of empathy, the students knew better. The message couldn't have been clearer: Don't Masturbate At School: *Everyone Is Watching*. And now Danny felt stupid for having ignored this nugget, for having let his guard down. Telling the school administration was certainly out, because what could that do but aggravate the scenario: soon he would have remixed versions of himself repeatedly wiping the urine from his lips to the thump of dub-step. The Dean would end up seeing it; his parents would see it; and he would look, as warped as these things might seem, like a snitch – which is exactly what you are when you complain about defamation or abuse within the walls of a high school.

He toyed with having the video flagged in order to put up an R18 wall around the content, but it was only a momentary idea. Most of the accounts had fake ages on them anyway, and to flag a video meant drawing attention to it. It was the lure of a late-night porn shop; contraband made consumption sweeter. In the end, he did what any good politician or marketing guru would've done. When market monopoly is attacked, when the policies of an opposition party are more popular than one's own, the only acceptable course of action is to steal, to co-opt. Copy the product. Mimic the policy. So he downloaded the video and threw it into his editing program, and within an hour he had his own version, set, as it had to be, to the rank digital migraine of dub-step: he drank, it rewound, he drank, it rewound – a looped video of the moment of ingestion that forced the audience to flap their hands and get involved – and then a howl that worked nicely as a climax. And up it went: *Piss-Drinker Remix* on his own channel. It was the same with everything. Own the humiliation and render it flaccid.

And this strategy would have worked perfectly had it not been for the unrestrained behaviour of the Year 11 kid who'd filmed it in the first place, because rather than letting the video take its course and find an audience through the accepted avenues of social networking, he'd been eager to be a direct messenger – to grab some kudos – and having downloaded Danny's version onto his phone he was apprehended during maths while trying to show it to friends, and the device was confiscated and the video watched, and passed on, and passed on, and suddenly Danny found himself with the Dean anyway, this time answering questions he had never really wanted asked, and the Dean was looking flustered and concerned in entirely new ways. 'Jesus, Danny! This is worrying.'

'Why?'

'You know why. Or you should know why. Do you know why?'

The SG105 was sitting on the filing cabinet behind the Dean. 'Have you played with that much?' Danny asked.

'I can't let you deviate here, Danny.'

'Look, I really don't see what the problem is. I haven't broken any rules.'

'It's not about that,' the Dean said, although he wasn't entirely sure whether or not Danny was right regarding rules. If he'd wanted to, he might have been able to say something about appropriate comportment in a school setting, but he chose not to. 'This sort of behaviour is not healthy—'

'The piss was fresh.'

'You know that's not what I'm talking about.'

'And it was mine.'

The Dean sat back in his chair and looked out the window and then turned back to Danny. 'Do your parents know about this?'

'Yes,' Danny said. 'They encourage it.'

'I find that hard to believe, buddy. How about I give them a call and we discuss it?'

But this Danny didn't want, and for the first time sitting in the Dean's office, his ears began to get hot, and the Dean was already making the requisite movement to the phone, as if he already had the number memorised, as if Danny's parents were waiting nervously on the other end, chewing their cuticles and expecting the worst.

'Yeah, I just don't think that's a great idea.'

The Dean settled back into his seat. 'The guidance counsellor it is then, because that's the only other option

I'm going to give you with one this one. I mean, think about it, Danny. The senior management haven't seen this yet – and hopefully they won't – but how do you think they'll react? You're in school uniform. What sort of image do you think that gives off to prospective students?'

'So Mrs Gershwitz then?'

'I'll set it up for you.'

'Can I have that back yet?' Danny pointed to his helicopter.

'No.'

TOM & DAVE

Ah fuck! Dave jumped around and waved his hands and blew cool air on the patch of forearm skin he'd just burned with the hot steel tip of the lighter.

What was the point in that? Tom asked.

Sexual thrill.

I think you're supposed to mix it with something else before it can count as sexual, like having a girl play with your nuts.

And you're an expert? Dave continued to blow on the patch of red skin. In the corner of the room, where the walls and ceiling met, a spider was in the process of spinning a web; in the harbour beyond the window the tide was beginning to change.

I know what I know, Tom said.

You know what you know?

Yup.

He knows what he knows!

Tom took a drag on a fresh cigarette. So I don't see the point in what you just did. What, are you depressed?

Do I look depressed?

When you're intentionally burning yourself you kind of give it off. Like, it emits from your general direction.

It's not like I'm a cutter. Like, I'm not doing it to get over the death of my dog or so I don't have to remember my mum beating me. This is strength training. This is about wearing myself in.

Yeah? Tom said.

Yeah, Dave replied. Like kick-boxers. They smack their shins against wooden poles so they can deaden the nerves and make themselves more effective weapons.

I don't see how burning your forearm helps that.

I'm just increasing my tolerance; lifting my threshold. When the time comes I'll be able to take a ton of punishment.

You want me to hit you in the face then? I mean, like, for training purposes.

I dunno. You might enjoy it too much.

No, serious. You ever been punched before? Like, really smacked in the face?

Fuck, again, you're spouting this shit like you're an authority on it – like you've got this secret history of beating up pimps and being tortured in brothels.

So you haven't been punched before? It's okay to admit it. It's nothing to be ashamed of. Lots of guys are punch-virgins. Tom ashed his cigarette in a way that seemed to represent experience and expertise.

Punch-virgin? That's how you're going to play this? You're a punch-pussy. Fuck.

Wow! Really? You were on a winning streak with counterfactual, but man, *punch-pussy*.

Fuck off. I know you haven't been punched.

Oh yeah?

I fuckin' *know* it.

Okay. If I convince you I've been punched in the face, then I get to punch you. How's that?

It's bullshit, Dave said. Because you won't.

I will.

Fine. Fuck it. Convince me. Prove it.

You sure? Because if I do, then I get a free one in your face, and I mean a good one that you can't resent me for afterwards.

Yeah, I get it.

Okay. Alright. So you remember Rachel?

What, she punched you in the face? Doesn't count.

No, just listen – you need some backstory on this. So I went through that brief patch of seeing her at the beginning of last year. We went to the movies a few times and went to the mall together and stuff like that.

You ever get anywhere with her?

Just listen. So we'd been sort of together for about two weeks and I'd gone to this movie in the middle of the day with her and one of her friends and her friend's boyfriend.

You should've just got drunk with her.

Maybe, yeah. But anyway we're in this movie and it's the first time we've actually made out and so I'm not really watching the film, but half-way through it someone behind us starts throwing stuff at us, like bits of popcorn and shit like that. At first it's small enough to ignore, but it just keeps happening until it's like two or three pieces a minute bouncing off our heads. So eventually I turn around and say something.

Were you like, fuck you cunts, I'll fucking kill you!

No, of course not. I was polite and stuff. I was like, hey guys, do you mind? That's really annoying. And as I said this I noticed it was a big group of fat girls doing it –

like trash-fat, you know, with tits half out and sticky eye-liner that you could see even in the dark.

Wait, so they hit you?

Just listen. So, you know, I have to say something, because I'm with my date and it's required that I don't act like a pussy, but after I turn back around and some time passes and we start making out again, here come the bits of popcorn. And so for the second time, a little more pissed off now, I turn around and tell them to fuck off – like, I've paid for the movie and everything, so leave me the fuck alone. But this time instead of like smirking back at me and saying nothing, they've crunched their faces into this I'll-fucking-kill-you look.

The fat girls…?

Yeah. And so I turn back around and Rachel tells me to ignore them, but you know that she doesn't mean it, but what am I supposed to do, like wander up and start stabbing them?

Maybe. That's why it's important to carry a switchblade – who knows when you might wanna casually stab some fat chicks in a cinema.

So things get kind of tense and we stop making out and I can't enjoy the movie because it keeps happening, and Rachel's friends don't want to leave the place because it's not happening to them – they're a few seats over and so they don't really feel the situation. Eventually Rachel stops holding my hand, and the popcorn's still flying into us, and I'm pretty pissed off but essentially useless, like there's nothing I can do now. And then the movie ends and when I turn around the gaggle of fat chicks are already making their way up the aisle toward the exit. And in the light now I can see that Rachel's face has got all tense, like her lips are shut tight and she's not looking at me, and I know she's thinking like to hell with this guy, he's a pussy, and so that makes me kind of angry. Like angry at her as well as the fat chicks, but I don't say anything and we get up and leave.

Is this like a symbolic punch? Because that doesn't count.

So we walk through the front of the cinema and Rachel's friend and her boyfriend are holding hands, and I remember thinking, there's no way I'm holding Rachel's, and then we get outside into the full light – it's still mid-afternoon – and we're standing in the car park and I see the group of fat girls, four of them, standing next to a car smoking, and I know I have to do it. I have to go over and say something otherwise the anger is going to stick to me, and it's the kind of thing that could really easily blow a new relationship, you know. So I have to.

Switchblade, brother.

So I break off from my group and walk straight over, and Rachel doesn't say anything – there's no like, oh, no, don't, just leave it alone – she just watches me go. And when I get there and I'm standing in front of these girls it's pretty clear they don't recognise me, like they have no clue who I am or why I'm looking pissed off, and because they're so blank about it I wonder for a moment if I've even got the right group, like maybe I'm about to make a huge mistake, and it's during this delay that one of them recognises me and puts it together, and before I've even said anything she's like, hey, it's the faggot from in front of us. And when she says this it kind of hits me in the face, like who are these bitches, and so I start to let loose on them.

Good.

Nah but here's the thing. When I start to swear at

them, I get the feeling that I sound like my parents; I say things like how dare you be so fucking inconsiderate. I mean, that's shit from my mum's mouth. And even as they start to swear back at me, saying like obscene shit, that's all I'm thinking, like, how sheltered I am; like, there's no way I can compete with them. So I try to actively ramp it up and pick on the easy thing and call them fat fucking whores, and at that point one of them like steps forward and pushes me, like a hard push in the chest with her painted nails, and because I can't push her back—

I would've.

I spit at her, like a pretty clean glob of phlegm, and it lands on her tits and then everything turns to shit. Suddenly one of them is saying Michael, Michael, and the car door opens and out comes this big guy – like the kind of guy that makes fat chicks look petite, the only possible type of guy that could ever be a boyfriend to one of these things – and he looks really calm, and at first I sort of think, okay, yeah, a male, he'll understand, and as he's walking into the action I start to explain things. You know, hey, these girls pretty much ruined my date and now they're calling me a faggot, you need to help me out here and keep them under control, and Michael just wanders in and takes the girl that pushed me by the shoulders and moves her aside and then kind of smiles a bit, and then that's that…

That's what? What happened?

I hit the ground. He punched me in the face – a couple of times, actually. Up came his fist and then smack into the side of my head. And you don't actually feel the pain when it happens. You just feel like a really hard compression, like pressure popping something really fast. And then I think I might have said something in between punches, but

I don't remember what, and then he hit me again. With the same hand, I think. I think he was holding my collar with the other one. And after that I don't remember anything until I was on the bus home.

What happened to Rachel?

You know what happened to Rachel. Who gives a fuck? You know…think of the early stages of a relationship as a baby. What happens if you shake the baby really hard and then throw it on the concrete?

Dark.

But this brings us full circle. Where do you want it?

Shit, I don't know. Where do you suggest?

I'd recommend the side of the head.

The side of the head… Alright. Let's do this.

ALi

When the bell rang for lunchtime and ESOL was over for the day and Nasir and Odawaa and Tarabi packed up their things and said they were leaving for lunchtime and maybe even for the whole afternoon, Ali asked if he could go with them. Nasir stopped and paused in the courtyard and scratched at his chest and considered the blue sky and any number of abstractions before answering. 'Are you sure?' he asked. 'I don't want to be the bad influence that that you blame if you get into trouble. And I would feel bad if you missed your classes.'

'Just let him come,' Tarabi said, bouncing his soccer ball. 'Then we can play two-a-side.'

Nasir looked at his younger cousin and measured the issue. 'Come with us for lunchtime, and before the bell we will drop you back for the afternoon, yes?'

The solution lifted the weight from Ali's chest.

As the four of them made their way to the exit, Ali felt protected by the height of his relatives and by the volume of Nasir's voice. Nasir talked like he wanted other people to hear, as if the jokes he told in Somali and that were laughed at by his friends needed no translation for the passing groups of students. The volume was a weapon of confidence. It was a power Ali wished he had.

At the back of the school the four of them veered onto the field and toward the fence to avoid the duty teacher, and one after another they made the quick leap to freedom. As soon as he was on the footpath, Ali understood why Nasir liked to leave. The world opened up. The roads were deserted and long, and he could hear birds and the hum of distant traffic. There was a lingering redolence of freshly cut grass and hot tyres recently passed – if liberation had a smell, this was it.

They played soccer alone in the park. They practised slide tackles and set up game situations, like finding the head from an in-swinging corner. Odawaa and Tarabi competed to see who could stand on their head longer; Nasir tried to perfect the rainbow flick, looping the ball back up over his shoulder mid-run. And before returning to school they stopped at the dairy and bought cold Cokes – Nasir paid for Ali's – and they drank them in the pleasant heat as they walked. And Ali was happy, because for the first time in days he wasn't thinking about the messages that were being sent to his Facebook, or the looks he was getting from Gavin and the rest, or the curdling mixture of rage and fear that indicated there was nothing he could do. Because typing answers back only seemed to make things worse, and what had started as a desire to gain some clarity and maybe a proper apology was now a relentless barrage of hatred that oppressed him and confused him in equal measure: 'U know how bad you smell cunt'; 'Guess who's a faggot? You.'; 'Somalis are fucken rapists'; 'How do you get a Somalian chick pregnant? Just jerk off into the gutter and let the flies do the rest.' And Ali received this all in isolation, alone at the computer – unable to tell his mother or father, unwilling to tell Nasir. He was well aware that he'd become a sport – the fox in the fox hunt, overmatched by hounds and horses and a sense of the inevitable. Waiting for the maths teacher to arrive for class, he was ill-equipped to deal with the casual attacks that pretended to be normal conversation: 'So I hear you guys are pirates.'

'Pirates? What is this?'

'You steal shit and hold people hostage.'

Or:

'My dad says Somalian taxi drivers are fucking it up for everyone else. He says you overcharge and steal customers.'

'I don't drive taxi.'

And it might have been manageable if there had been just one clear antagonist, but although Gavin had been the catalyst, he was no longer the sole source. It had been picked up like a catchy beat, and now they were all dancing to it, regardless of race or gender. It was squashing Ali.

Maybe things would have been different if he hadn't lied about how his shirt had been torn. Maybe his dad would have tried to sort things out. Instead, Ali had fended off questions and taken the shame. 'Why were you wearing your regular uniform for P.E.?' his father had asked, fresh home from work and well aware of the value of a dollar. 'Don't you have a P.E. uniform? I thought we bought you one.'

'I left my P.E. uniform at home. I'm sorry.'

'That was thoughtless, Ali. Thoughtless. Now you

only have one good school shirt.'

'I can fix it,' his mother said. 'I will sew it back together.'

And she did, but the result left a long line – a clear stich mark that might as well have been a scar – and whenever Ali fingered the crenulations in the fabric as he tucked the shirt in, it was like revisiting the guilt of the lie, the love and concern of his parents colliding with the bile of the playground. And so each time he touched it he became angry, because the tear signalled the point where it had leaked into his family, where the dirt of the world crossed over and affected the sanctity of his home. Watching his mother stitch it had almost made him cry.

Yet as he walked with his cousins in the sun of the afternoon and drank his bubbly Coke and watched Odawaa accidently stand in dog shit, everything was okay. ESOL worksheet number 19: Conjunctions: Despite, Though and However: A) Despite it was wrong, he was having fun. Or B) Though it was wrong, he was having fun. And it wasn't so much that Odawaa had stood in it, it was that his reaction had made it funny – his arms raised as if this was somehow God's fault, his removal of the shoe as he hopped around looking for something to wipe it on, eventually deciding that Tarabi's shoulder might provide an ideal surface. 'Okay, cousin,' Nasir said. 'It's time for you to go.' They were down the road from the back exit of the school and as close as they wanted to get before retreating. 'We'll see you tomorrow. Go and learn something.' Ali watched Odawaa hop after his brother and throw his shoe like a grenade, and then he turned and ran up the hill to the gate. This system would work. He could manage things this way. It was the freedom he needed to maintain his effort. And as he turned the corner into the school – a smile on his face for the first time in weeks – he ran directly into a cluster of duty teachers. Three teachers, all white, all male, all young, all towering over six foot. Three teachers in the early stages of their profession: one a P.E. teacher who knew Ali by name and class but when he'd come to write a report had nothing to say, so copied and pasted the report of another kid and simply changed the name; one a maths teacher who liked to use sarcasm and favoured the kids who managed to get it; the last a social studies teacher, a bullish devotee of the church who enjoyed the power and responsibility of his new role – because kids need discipline, and it's important to treat them all the same, and sometimes it's important to scare them, shout at them, really get into their bones, because it's the only way they'll learn – and does it matter if he takes pleasure in it? 'Ali!' The P.E. teacher said. 'What are you doing out of school?'

'Answer him!' The social studies teacher. 'Come on!'

'I…?'

'That's not any kind of answer. Show some respect. And stand up straight.'

'Um…?'

'You're in big trouble.'

'After school detention at least.'

'And maybe a caning…'

'Almost certainly a caning.'

'And we'll be contacting your parents and putting you on an official warning.'

'Will we need to get the police involved?'

'That might well be the case.'

'Oh, this is a big problem. A very big problem.'

'What makes you think you're special? What makes you think you can just leave like that?'

It went on this way until the bell went, Ali unable to explain things, his hands shaking, the men standing above him and around him and laughing with each other in a way that was totally exclusionary, Ali the in-joke in the middle as they tried to trump each other with threats, the social studies teacher propelling the torture as if his DNA had stalled in The Crusades. 'If you've got his name, I'll do the rest. Get the hell out of here!' And although Ali had struggled to follow the meaning of the words, he understood their cadence and volume.

That evening Ali spent much longer than usual watching the naked women dance on TV, although his focus went beyond the screen and into his problems, and when his father arrived home and asked why he wasn't on the computer doing his homework, he said he didn't have any. He said he was feeling sick. He said he wanted to stay home tomorrow. He felt besieged; he felt hatred, and although it didn't show up as a measurable fever, it was a real kind of sickness. It clouded his thinking and stymied his appetite. It made it hard to laugh at jokes, and when his dad wanted the TV translated, it made focus and accuracy that much more difficult. 'What did he say was his motivation for killing the shopkeeper?'

'He was angry. He needed to take it out on someone.'

'Are you sure? I thought it would be more complex than that.'

But a day off sick is only a day off sick, and while his father was at work and his sister was at school, Ali was back on the computer and staring at the disease. And then he was back and waiting outside maths class, and around him his peers were listening to songs on their headphones and playing games on their portables – technology Ali had never touched – and when someone asked what music he liked, a question that he knew was a trap, he chose not to answer, opening his bag instead and looking for something that wasn't there. 'Ali! Ali! What do you listen to?' The inside of his bag was black and deep and he wished he could fall into it and zip it shut. 'Ali? Is it sax music? I bet you like sax music? I bet you listen to it in the bath and rub your nipples to it.' Look into the bag and find the darkness. 'Bullshit, dude; Somalians don't have baths. They don't wash.' But the longer you look, the more your eyes adjust. 'Nah, they wash. They just do it without water and use shit for soap.' And then you can see that it's not a hiding place, that it's shallow and finite. 'Ali! I bet Somalian music is all just like clicks and whistles and shit. I bet you go to like Somalian raves where everybody's just clicking and whistling and jumping up and down and rubbing each other with shit.' The bag is nothing at all – just threads and material and an apple and books. 'And then they all get together and have this big black shit orgy, and the only thing you can see is their teeth.'

And at interval Ali told Nasir everything. Holding the stitch of his shirt while he did it, he told him about the bits of eraser and the rugby game and the messages on Facebook. He told him about the teachers that stood over him and the jokes about their culture and poverty, and he made sure that Nasir understood every detail – jerk off into a gutter and let the flies do the rest – and Nasir sat quietly and listened to it all. 'I'm glad you have told me,' he said. 'It is very good you've told me.'

'It's why I need you to come to ESOL,' Ali said, and Nasir nodded with benevolent understanding, and before the day was over Nasir had absconded with a dumbbell from the weights room and used it to brutally beat a kid named Gavin.

MS BAKER

For her first day on the job Ms Stephanie Baker bought a new dress. Educational cream and with a conservative neckline, she offset it with brown leather boots and a navy cardigan and glasses rather than contacts. It was meant to whisper its effortlessness and exist in the space that indicated she'd made a choice to look good but hadn't overdone it, and in the staffroom it gave her the confidence to feel like she belonged. Her partner liked it. It was a step into the professional, and on image alone it was, to him, a vast improvement on the torn jeans and domestic scruffiness that had defined her year of unemployment. 'We look like we belong together again,' he'd said, clumsily indicating that for a long time he'd felt that they hadn't.

On her first day wearing it, as she waved a board marker in front of herself and pondered what she would write up next, the inky tip somehow traced itself across the material above her knee and left a blue line that would later refuse to come out. She resigned herself to it – it was a mark of the job, a battle scar. But the next time she wore the dress, it happened again, this time with a red marker, down in the same spot where her right hand unconsciously hung during periods of thought. And then it happened again.

And now she was standing in the corridor as her students filed into the light and she was looking down at the asymmetrical collection of lines that had formed above her right knee, the streaks in the material, her boots beneath her hemline, scuffed at the toes after banging against lab tables and dragging against stairs – evidence of maladroit steps made while carrying boxes of photocopying and hurrying from room to room. The bell continued to ring, much louder now that she stood in the corridor and close to its source, and the release of the students as they filtered away from her, and the movement of the marks on her dress, and the stress of a tooth that had been dislodged, and the shouting that had strained her vocal cords, and next period was supposed to be an assessment for senior biology and she wondered where all the test papers were and someone was calling to her against the ring – three on – where is it coming from? – one off, and she could hear their voices, and she felt dizzy. Truly dizzy. She followed the kids out into the courtyard and looked up. Blue sky; white smoke. This was herding cats: they were already fanning out into the school, kicking bins and hiding around corners and pulling the leaves off plants. Darting silhouettes against the light. She felt for her nose, a sharp left-handed movement beneath her nostrils to check if blood was beginning to run.

MiNA AND AHMED

In the space between the first heart attack, which sent him to hospital and psychologically crippled his wife, and the second the following week which ended his existence, Ahmed's father had the time to tell his son – through breathing tubes and from the weakness of a hospital bed – that he had given up on God, that the universe owed him nothing, and that if Ahmed wanted to live a worthwhile life, then it was entirely up to him to make that happen. Ahmed had been there day and night listening to his father's stories, his dad dredging up anecdotes from his past that he felt were important to impart, and in four days Ahmed learned all the information that should've been drip-fed to him throughout his twenties and thirties, pieces of advice that were meant not for sixteen-year-olds but for expectant fathers or men approaching mid-life. He made reference to books he wanted Ahmed to read, to philosophy he thought he should look in to – 'Try the existentialists,' he said, and Ahmed nodded – and he told him to hang on to his girl, to make the most of youth and beauty while it lasted, because both were fleeting, and you never knew when you might break your neck on stairs or suddenly be overcome by the feeling of a car driving over your chest.

While his mother broke down completely at the funeral and had to be supported by relatives, Ahmed remained stoic. He hadn't cried in front of his father, and he wouldn't cry now. He towered above the other mourners and looked into a space that wasn't there. He wore a black suit. From any kind of distance, he looked like the spectre of death lurking over the proceedings, his long fingers dangling awkwardly at his sides. If someone had cared to look, they might have noticed that he had ceased to blink. Relatives and friends conveyed their sympathies, shook his hand and moved on, intimidated by his stature and a face that didn't seem to move, and puzzled by the girl that shadowed him – an Arab beauty in a black dress and black hat who didn't seem to know where she was or why she was there.

Following the wake – after all the guests had left and his mother had been put to bed with the help of prescription drugs – Ahmed and Mina walked together in the twilight. In the week following the initial heart attack, the two had barely spoken. When the news had come through, Mina's mother had driven her to the hospital to be with her boyfriend. She'd hugged him and sat with him, but there seemed to be little else she could do, and as he closed down almost entirely, she felt that her role was simply to be there. To be a presence. She took time off school to be with him. She held his hand in the hospital waiting room. She tried to block out what she'd been thinking. She tried not to think of the future. But now they were walking together. His dad was dead. The sun was going down and cars were passing them on the street. She wanted desperately to be in one of them, to be somewhere that wasn't this street with these problems. Ahmed held out his hand; she took it because she had to. It felt huge and clammy.

When he led her into a park without saying anything, she thought it was going to be for sex. She thought they would head into the bushes and that he would kiss her and lay her down, and for the first time in their relationship she was truly frightened of him, because she feared he wouldn't say anything, that he would lean over her and into her and use her as if she wasn't there. But instead of the bushes, he pulled her to a bench and sat her down and stared again at nothing, his shirt un-tucked now, his hands resting on his knees, and in its own way this was scarier. In the distance cars continued to pass. The light became purple. She didn't know what to say. 'We need to leave,' he said.

'What? You want to go home?'

'No. We need to leave the country.'

'What? When?'

'As soon as we can, like we've always said. We can work hard for the rest of the year and get university entrance, and then we can go. We won't have to do Year 13. We can live in Algeria, open a store.'

'Algeria?'

'And we need to start having children.'

'Children? Ahmed…'

'Because we don't have much time, and no one is going to help us unless we help ourselves.'

This was too much for Mina to process. 'But, what

about your mother?'

'She'll be fine. She has her relatives and she has God.'

'But…'

'We can have lots of children and we can run a book store and we'll never have to think about this place ever again.'

'Ahmed.' She looked up at him: his flattened nose, the eyes that receded back into his face and in the falling night resembled dark lagoons, his hair combed in a way that was so far out-of-step and anachronistic that it was absurd. She loved him, this odd monster, but it was now in a way that was built only out of shared memory; it had a past and present tense, but no future… 'But…' And then he started to cry, and he put his head in her lap and wept, and his big chest convulsed as everything came out, and Mina didn't know what to do. She wasn't equipped for this. She wasn't ready for the weight of adult responsibility, and as Ahmed's tears poured into her dress she began to cry too, not because of the sympathy she felt for him and not because of his father, but because she desperately wanted to be back at the mall and talking and giggling and trying on lipstick, and she hated herself for wanting it – but there it was. Ahmed was a burden, and his size and his veneer of maturity were all tricks of perception: he was a baby, a mewling infant that needed to be fed and cared for, and she was far too young to be a mother. This was the truth. Except now she was trapped. Now there was no way out. She was crying. The water was boiling.

The following weekend, while Ahmed was at home with his mother, Mina slept with the first guy she could find at the party.

DANNY

'I've been thinking about the meaning of it all,' he said. He'd decided to tell Mrs Gershwitz everything; there didn't seem to be a reason not to. 'And I feel a lot of it is coded in our genes. It's part of the human search for significance, you know?'

'I think so, yes,' Verna said. The Dean had filled her in on Danny. A quirky psychological make-up; wildly precocious – gifted and talented in a way he wasn't quite able to control… Let's wait and see.

'And I really like attention. I know that. It's not a secret. The Dean thinks this is the bad thing; he tells me there's a difference between the right and the wrong kind, and there is, I'll admit that, but it's nowhere near as big a gap as he thinks it is. I mean, I'm not making porn in my bedroom or anything, and I'm smart enough to know that most of the messages in the media are retarded. Like, I don't want to be a reality TV star. I want to have levels, you know. I want to be smart and connect with people that way. And what's so wrong about feeling good when you get noticed? Like I said, it's encoded in our genes. It's part of being human, right?'

'Right,' Verna said, although she had little idea what Danny was talking about because he'd simply jumped right in and prefaced nothing.

'Yeah,' Danny said. 'You know, I feel we're on the same page, you and me. That we're reading from the same book.'

'What makes you think that?'

'You understand the creative spirit. You seem like you know that we all need an outlet. How about you?' Danny leaned in to Verna with his hands together. The question seemed genuine. 'Have you got anything you like doing creatively? I bet you're a closet novelist.'

'As a matter of fact, I like to write short stories.'

'Wow, can I read one? What are they about? What are your themes?'

'I don't know if I'm ready to share them with you yet, Danny. We've only just met.'

'Adult content, huh? I understand. I won't pressure you. But it's important you give it to someone. You could publish under a pen name. There are plenty of blogs dedicated to literotica that would love to have your work. I'm sure it's good too. You seem like the—'

'Danny.'

'Yes?

'I'm not comfortable discussing this with you.'

'All I'm saying is it's not an outlet until it's *let out*, you know. If you keep it in your drawer it might as well not exist, and then you don't get the catharsis – the feeling that it's gone somewhere and that it's meant something.'

154

Verna shifted in her chair and shuffled some papers that didn't need shuffling.

'Is something wrong?' Danny asked.

She took a moment to collect herself and order her thoughts. 'Danny.'

'Yes, Mrs Gershwitz? It is Mrs, right? What does Mr Gershwitz do?'

'Why are your grades so low?'

'I bet he's an intellectual. I bet he lectures at university in history or something.'

'Danny.'

'I don't know. The usual reasons. Video game violence, I think.'

'Are you not stimulated enough in class? Do things move too slowly for you?'

'No, they move at the proper speed. I mean, I don't really see the point in rote learning essay answers, and I'm never going to be a chemist or a biologist or a physicist, and they don't let me into the school plays anymore.'

'Really?'

'I know. I'm as angry as you are.' Danny didn't seem angry. 'Have you ever thought about swapping the venetians for curtains? Those things dick with your perspective.'

'Why aren't you allowed in the show?'

'Politics. Nepotism. And I have a tendency to make it all about me.'

'Oh.'

'Yeah,' Danny said. He moved his hands into the shape of a tepee and pressed the tips of his index fingers against his chin.

'Maybe you should join a club? Are you interested in social justice?'

'As much as the next man.'

'You could join the Amnesty group. Or the computer club.'

'I feel we're hitting a wall here, Mrs Gershwitz.'

'Well…'

'Yeah, I know.'

'…Do you have many friends, Danny?'

'Not in the traditional sense. I mean, I don't have people I cling to for acceptance or safety. And frankly it seems kind of bigoted to have friends – choosing one person over another to share your feelings and secrets with. That seems arrogant. I love everybody equally.'

'How about the boy who posted the video of—'

'The piss-drinking video? He saw something funny and wanted to share it. Why hold it against him? It's nice that he was paying attention to my life at all. Human community and stuff. Even the guy that threw the apple at my head the other day. He's just struggling through it all like the rest of us. Maybe his dad hits him or something.'

'Would you call him a friend?'

'Sure. Why not? Look, shouldn't you be encouraging me to make friends rather manufacture enemies?'

Verna felt her cheeks flush and her throat go dry. There was a fine line between the remarkably well adjusted and the totally unhinged; in this case maybe they were interchangeable. 'What do you want to do when you leave school, Danny?'

'I'd count my guinea pig as a friend.'

'Guinea pig?'

'Check him out.' Danny reached over to his bag and produced a murky plastic box containing something noticeably furry and almost certainly alive.

'I don't think you should have that at school.'

'He provides the emotional stability I need to make it through my day.' The animal lurched about in the box. 'He has a nice simple outlook, he puts up with the rough conditions of his life, and he lacks the ability for critical thought. He's a model for what I admire.'

'Does the Dean know you have this at school?'

'And he's an easy audience, you know.' He poked a finger through the top of the container and let the guinea pig nibble at its end. 'I don't have to impress him, and that's hard to come by in a world where everybody wants something bigger and better. But I don't know. What did you want to do when you finished school? Surely you didn't want to step into counselling straight away.'

'I wanted to travel.'

'Why?'

'To broaden my horizons. To see what else was out there.'

'I know it's not the same, and I'm all for experience and everything, but I can get all the horizon-broadening I need from a fast internet connection and a decent screen resolution. I'd prefer to focus on the here and now rather than fantasize about a future that's inevitable anyway…' Danny held the box up to the light. The guinea pig was trying to turn around but was having trouble in the confined space. 'Unless I kill myself, of course.'

The backs of Verna's hands began to itch. 'I wouldn't throw words like that around so carelessly, Danny. Life is a gift. You shouldn't treat—'

'Yeah, I hear people say that.' He put the container down beside him and opened the lid and picked up the guinea pig. 'You know what a white elephant is?'

'The idiom?'

'The kings of Siam would give a white elephant as a

gift to people they didn't like. That's the etymology of the phrase. Basically the recipient couldn't kill the thing – because that would be an insult to the kings and the elephant was really valuable – but the cost of keeping it alive ended up crippling them financially.'

'And you think life is like that?'

'It's just a thought. So what does Mr Gershwitz do?'

'He lectures in sociology. I think we should probably leave it there for today, Danny.'

'Brilliant. Keep up the writing, Mrs G. And work on that pen name.'

He left the room with his guinea pig in one hand and his bag in the other.

F 12

While Mr Blasco was leaning back in his chair and thinking about the world beyond teaching and Penelope was reviewing homework she didn't understand and Jun was stretching his arms out across his desk and Sean was leafing through Merriam-Webster – hubris equals an overbearing pride or arrogance – and Akaash was still standing by the door yearning for an escape that seemed less and less likely and Wendy was married to her phone, Brayden was back at the window, his head through the curtains as he continued to survey what he didn't understand, couldn't compute, struggled to piece together: yes, that was Henry – it looked like Henry – although it was hard to see because of the angle, and Brayden had to press his face hard up against the glass, but even then it was tough to tell, because Henry was lying down, arms akimbo, face to the sky; and yes Henry was weird and all, but who lies down in the middle of the school and just takes a break while the lockdown bell is chiming? – a bold move for anyone given that he was just across from the admin block and in full view of the deans and the deputies: surely they would see him and no doubt that would result in a raft of detentions and school service duties...

But there was more.

From his left, emerging from the bowels of the school, was a whole class of juniors (Year 10s maybe), one of whom was bleeding quite badly from the mouth and had taken off his uniform shirt to mop up the blood, the shirt itself soaked almost to saturation, and behind him the other students were beginning to fan out and stand on benches and chase each other with sticks – behaviours that seemed out of place considering the mood that was beginning to settle over the scene (is that smoke or fog?) – and finally Ms Baker, who had poured all her energy into teaching Brayden biological concepts but had only really succeeded in turning Brayden on through proximity and attention and a pair of leather boots that seemed disciplinarian, and silhouetted as she was against the light, Brayden found himself caught in an uncomfortably erotic daydream that he refused to deconstruct (the maternal aspects of the whole thing, you see) and then Ms Baker moved up toward her class and shouted something – a movement into full view – but, because the bell was drowning her out, Brayden couldn't tell what she was saying, although he could see that something was wrong: more blood, Ms Baker holding her face, red droplets staining her cream dress, and in that moment Brayden felt the need to save her – to run to her rescue and carry her away, to be there for her – and yet he also felt the urge to hide, to go foetal beneath a desk and close his eyes and suck his thumb. So he did neither. The contradictory impulses had drained his ability for action or cogence or clarity. He found himself watching. He didn't understand.

STELLA

At the time, she was thinking about the heliocentric universe and sex crimes and the stains on this guy's ceiling. She was thinking about the trip to the mall she took with her mother last Tuesday and simultaneously about how little she revealed of herself to anybody, including this guy with arm tattoos whom she didn't really know and who owned two dogs that he kept attached to the fence at the front of his house, presumably for the purpose of intimidation. She definitely wasn't thinking about Jeff, because Jeff was a cunt who hadn't called her or texted her, and when it came down to it he was just a pussy with dyed black hair and an eyebrow ring and a whole load of faggoty words he used for self-defence – words that couldn't hide the fact he was actually well-to-do and white collar, and even though she couldn't know for sure, she was pretty certain his mum worked in a kindergarten and his dad was an environmentalist, that he grew up in a nice house with a dishwasher and a dog and a whole set of model trains and books featuring anthropomorphised animals. She was certain that he loved them and was loved and that he was a total cunt. Not like this guy. This guy was beaten and wretched and smelled like neglect. This guy didn't spend time thinking about colour coordination or the right thing to say. He just was. 'If you really want to hold your shit together in a fight, you can't let anger get in the way.'

Cool, I'm listening.

'You have to channel the adrenaline and let it focus you. You gotta have control.'

Wicked, yeah.

'Guys that get their heads stomped are always the ones that get drunk first and fuck out. That's why I don't drink much until I get home. I mean, this one time…'

This one time was like a lot of other times now. An easy lie and Stella is free for two whole days and absolved of any obligation outside a short text to her mum on Saturday afternoon (because she doesn't want to intrude – she doesn't like to seem overbearing. Daughters need autonomy, space to grow and develop, or so say all the latest texts on parenting) and the city is where it all happens, you know, it's where she has the room and the opportunity to explore and be real, and with make-up and red hair the bars are easy to get into, and you don't want to bring friends because they'll only get in the way. Friends are makeshift. Friends are to be met rather than kept. Neon lights and bass lines. A small dress and a small bag with everything you need: a change of underwear, make-up, tampons (manufactured in Thailand) and a sweater if it looks cold. Money is for other people. Fifty dollars is all she needs as a start-up cost: $4.60 for the bus ride; $19.99 on a bottle of vodka that will last more than a night and can be tucked away or left in shadows to be collected later; the rest is safety money that she won't need and can always return to her mother to garner good will, because once she's in she's in, and guys will buy her drinks and pay for taxis and flick her freebies. In the end it's just about attitude: listen to their shit and nod, and after a drink or two maybe rub their leg… Because in spite of everything, like their history of control and dominance and advantages in pay rate and their overrepresentation as CEOs and politicians and their ability to inflict violence, *men are the weaker sex*. They crumble easily; they can be manipulated, and deep down they all have mothers whom they hug and love: even this guy, with his wretched smell and the scar along his cheek. 'The key is to stay sharp and focused. I practise meditation to control myself.'

Really? Fascinating. Do go on.

'So when it happens I can focus on the target areas, like the knees and the eyes. Or the neck. If you punch someone in the neck just right, they usually don't come back from that.'

At dusk on Friday Stella drank alone in a city park and watched the sun go down over apartment buildings. She imagined she lived in one of them and that she worked downtown and had just stopped off after work to ease out and stare at the dog walkers and students. She imagined she had a job in an office and that she did office things. She fictionalised an affair with her boss, her eventual marriage to a co-worker, a kid of her own, and a divorce. It seemed to be the natural cycle of things.

She went to a bar and talked to a guy with a beard.

She went to another bar and talked to a man in a suit.

At the third bar she was refused entry due to a lack of I.D. and spat at the bouncer and moved on, her small heels clicking on the pavement as she left. Given that the Earth revolved around the sun and that she was made primarily of water and meat, legally defined age restrictions on alcohol didn't make a lot of sense.

'I thought I killed a guy once – like a quick punch to the neck and down he went. He must've hit his head on the pavement and cracked his skull.'

What did he do to deserve such radical treatment?

'He was harassing this woman, so I felt I had to step in.'

That's very gallant of you.

'No one should get away with harassing women. It should be in our instinct to protect them, you know.'

Another bar and another guy and for some reason Stella's in a mood to tell all, because the guy's got black hair that reminds her of someone and he says he's a computer programmer and why not? So she tells him the truth: she's a legal secretary, though she's not sure she likes the industry because a lot of the lawyers are sleazebags, and once you have an inter-office affair, you know, it makes the working environment kind of uncomfortable. And she's pretty sure that the guy – who was married, you know, and so should've had a bit more discretion – went and told everybody else at work, so now everyone looks at her like she's some kind of easy-access slut-card they can use for a free ride. And the cunt never found out about the abortion… And for some reason Stella is thrown out of the bar. And this is a shame, because she was enjoying the atmosphere, and on TV women throw their drinks on guys all the time, so what's the big deal? It's like a convention. You sound like you're a little messed up, he said. How dare you: reaction… It's the adult thing to do.

And now outside in her dress and with her bag she stops to sit on a bench and have a little cry, because she's a touch drunk and maudlin, and because after the bus ride home from the clinic she had to keep up the lie and be sick and her mother brought her a hot water bottle and let her stay home from school.

'Women are for babies, right? They need to be respected and cared for. And I'll gladly kill any fuck-face that disrespects that.' Outside the dogs are barking at something. Inside the paint on the ceiling is peeling away.

Your ideas are Neolithic. Did you know, did you know, that the Earth revolves around the…

Weak guys always stop for the crying girl. They break off from their group and check if she's all right. They sit and feign nurture. They speak with soft voices and ask if there's anything they can do. What's the deal? You need to wait until a girl is broken before you make your move? You don't have the social nous to handle a fully functioning female? Sex crimes. Creep. Fuck you. If that's the way it's going to be then watch this: Stella accepts the help of a guy who might only be nineteen and who sports a poor impersonation of a goatee. His pants are too long for him and his arms are vegan thin. She goes with him to a bar where he joins his friends and she wipes her eyes and reapplies her make-up and pretty soon she's all smiles and anecdotes, like the one about the teacher she used to have who had an erection during class whenever he talked to the boys, and the one about the kid who drank his own urine for money, and then she takes this guy and his facial hair aside and leads him out the back of the bar and into an alleyway, and it's here that she makes the offer: forty dollars is all it'll cost him. It's a good price, and she swears she's not normally like this. She wouldn't be saying it if she didn't need the money. And then he gives her the money and wants nothing in return. He says she just better take it and go – he doesn't want to see her denigrate herself for any amount of money. He's a vegan, after all. Thank you, she says. She's rapidly becoming someone she doesn't want to be. She swears to him that she'll change – this is just a phase, you know.

Stella leaves.

Stella has forty extra dollars.

'There's a lot of fucks out there.' The dogs continue to bark.

And cunts. Don't forget cunts.

'It's human nature, you know. There's a lot of bad people who'll kill you just to get ahead.'

And you meet the best people after midnight in the shittiest bars. The guys look like they'll stab you for the fun of it and the girls look like they know the names of the charge nurses in the emergency room. Karaoke is playing and the felt on the pool table has a tear in it, and no one cares to ask what a girl like Stella is doing in a wasteland like this, all by herself and in that dress. Because *she's* the danger here. *She's* the issue. In class they talked about the problem of racial profiling: you're a taxi driver in the bad part of town and two different people are hailing you for a ride. The first is dressed ghetto and has his hood up and looks like the stereotype; the second is wearing a shirt and tie and looks like an accountant. Which one do you pick up? Easy, Stella says. The first one, because what the fuck is the second guy doing in that part of town? And she senses the men around her now feel this instinctively; they avoid eye contact and make no advances and punch the white ball across the tear in the baize like it's not even there, and so she's forced to buy her own drinks from a bartender with maxed-out pupils and sweat lines casting a deep V on his tee shirt, and she does rancid tequila shots by herself and gets up to sing bad karaoke to a popular song – one about a girl wanting a boy, notes that are impossible to reach, whole sections where she trills and grinds and dances and still gets little attention: 'You're brilliant, Stella,' says her mother. 'You can do anything you want and don't let people stand in your way.'

And there are sections of blur. She's only seventeen. She's standing in a cramped alleyway that doubles as a smoking section. Some guy with shadow on his face is laughing from right down in his gut and some woman in a singlet is trying to tell a story about a guy named Mason, and Stella is trying to catch expelled cigarette smoke as it drifts into yellow shards of light, standing up on her toes and breathing in deep, and maybe she thinks the action is quirky and quaint and might get her noticed, but in the end all the extra breathing just makes her feel sick, and her little chest begins to heave and her brain feels like it's swelling, and there it is, she's vomiting a mix of tequila and vodka and beer into a little puddle in a darkened corner, and for just a second – the fleeting moment when the alcohol washes against the back of her teeth – she nearly wants out and away. She's not thinking. 'Take a hit of this,' says the voice – 'It'll clear you up,' it says – and she doesn't think about where it's come from or who's offering, and the yellow shards are really hurting her eyes now, so she just sucks against the burn of a blue and orange flame and sees her own nose lit up and glowing. 'Just give it a minute and you'll be okay.'

'Just wait a second and you'll be fine.'

'Just hold on for a moment and it'll be sweet.'

'Just let it hang for a bit and see what happens.'

'Just focus on something else
and we'll see you in July
or maybe August.'

'Just chill for a while and
wait for
the asteroid to hit
the atmosphere.'

→ 'I knew this guy once, and he like…
He like what?
'Nah, you don't wanna hear that story.'
Believe me, I do. I'm all ears. Tell me everything. Tell me the origin of your tattoos and the history of the scar. Tell me why your forearms look like weapons and why you think it's okay to wear a shirt with noticeable stains and holes out to a bar, even if it is a dump like this. And if you know what other people's blood tastes like, tell me that too… But first tell me about this guy.

'He was into heroin pretty bad, but he was also holding down a job, and he was a dad and all – but there was a divorce, so he only saw the kid on the weekends. Anyway, so he has to hide the needle marks, right. So he's started injecting in really weird places, like…'

On Monday, Stella will sit in English class and be force-fed a short story about the perils of discrimination, and the story will finish with a lesson about how it's important not to judge people based on something as superficial as race, because when you get to know each other personally, you might realise that we're all the same underneath. That we breathe the same air and digest food with comparable intestines. That our wounds scab up in remarkably similar ways.

'…Eventually the area gets really infected and they have to amputate the thing. Basically he castrates himself, you know.'

Did he get to keep it, like in a jar or something?

Stella watches the lights of the city from the window of the car. Arab men pull on hookahs; guys in polo shirts look sweaty and heavy and fucked, leaning on walls until the walls don't lean back. Something hard is playing on the stereo and a guy like this shouldn't own a car this clean and this fast. And the bars recede; the darkness of the suburbs swells up. Houses. Thousands of them. Houses where people actually fucking live their lives, eating microwavable food and incubating tumours and preparing to die and have you ever actually sat there and watched the frost develop on the grass, like just sat down in a field before dawn and watched it freeze up around you?

'Anybody ever tell you that you're all over the place?'

No I'm not. How can I be all over the place when it's all the same thing?

Yeah, sure, there are categories. There's discrete data and words that help us sort shit out – but it's all fundamentally the same. A foetus is the frost on the grass which is the vacuum of space. The vacuum of space is two dogs tied to a fence and an overgrown front lawn and an incongruously expensive car and the paint peeling away from an asbestos-heavy ceiling and the sweat and the smell of a guy with a deep ugly scar on his cheek. It's the fact he doesn't have a name and the weight of his body and the Earth revolving around a sun that appears to be coming up now – through the lime curtains – just like Stella's coming up again and will be until her brain gives way quite a few hours down the road at the bus stop she'll have to wait at in order to get home.

ALi

If students were only sorta kinda whatever about the issue of the small Somali boy in their class before the beating, afterwards they all had an opinion. And maybe the senior management and the deans might have done something about Ali's class placement and shifted him to somewhere less hostile, but they didn't know. Nor could they know, because the whole thing seemed utterly random. A one off. A freak. And like all good inmates inured to the system, no one was talking. There were the facts: Nasir had used a dumbbell as a weapon, and in the space of about thirty seconds, the period of time between the first strike on Gavin's back and the moment when Nasir had been pulled away by a mixture of Year 13 rugby players and a quick-thinking Phys-Ed teacher, Gavin had been left with a hematoma, a broken arm and a broken collarbone. Thank god they stopped it when they did, because a murder on school grounds has a tendency to damage future roll numbers. They also knew that the two didn't know each other, that Gavin was very much the victim, and that Nasir would not be returning to school and would almost certainly be hearing from the police. But that was that. Even on his return from the hospital, Gavin was reticent. He didn't know why it had happened; he'd never met the kid, and his parents were suitably shocked and had considered taking the issue to the media. But they'd been quelled; in times of crisis schools can move very quickly into damage control. The principal had visited Gavin in the hospital and conferenced with his parents, and Nasir's family had been contacted and told that their son would not be coming back, that the wheels of the justice system would soon begin to turn. Not that they understood any of it. Throughout it all Nasir said nothing. When the community constable spoke to him in cool clear tones, Nasir simply stared back, and when his parents asked what was going on, he translated for them in a measured voice: 'The school is full of racists. They don't want me there. The policeman is for my protection.'

But it had worked, at least in the short term, because even if the adults knew nothing and couldn't see the incident as anything other than a random act of madness, maybe culture clash, maybe (and let's keep this one quiet) the actions of a violent and dangerous ethnicity, the students knew the truth, and for a time the world around Ali became quiet. It was clear what had happened: he'd called in a hit. And the rumours began to swirl. He was part of a gang; he had connections to some aggressive and pretty hard-core guys; he was Somali royalty that had escaped the conflict of his homeland and had a whole network of underlings to protect him. 'Gavin's fucking lucky he's not dead.'

'I've heard about that Somalian shit; guys are ruthless

– skin you just for fun, then salt your body so they can feed off it for weeks.'

'What, like cannibals?'

'You eat the body you eat the soul. Fuckin' dark stuff.'

'Shit.'

So once again Ali found himself sitting alone in his classes – at least a desk between him and the next student – but now there were no bits of eraser, no antagonisms, no finger gestures or jokes, just carefully selected visual pathways that aimed to dodge eye-contact or any other form of non-verbal communication.

Ali conveyed the situation to Nasir after Gavin had returned to school and Nasir had already spent a week riding his bike around the suburbs with nowhere to go and nothing to do, a plastic bag filled with solvent hanging from the left handlebar in case he stumbled across a park that looked nice – a place for him to sit down and enjoy midday quiet and scramble some of his brain's pathways for an hour or so. And of course he wasn't going to tell anyone about this – it was his business and his alone – but it was the reason his head throbbed and he felt groggy; and it was the reason he seemed slower than usual to his cousin, who sat with him on the steps of his house in the afternoon sunshine and tried to communicate the less than subtle shift in social interaction: Ali, who wore his uniform, the sewn-up tear tucked away in the waistline of his trousers. 'They are scared of me,' he said.

'Good.' Nasir was smoking a cigarette, rolled rather badly from his father's pack of tobacco. It was an affectation he'd decided to acquire following the expulsion.

'But now no one talks to me.'

'So? You are not there to make friends, Ali. You are

173

there to get an education.'

'But…' Ali wanted to tell him he was stupid. He wanted to say that he didn't need the pressure and he didn't want the guilt. Because now he owed Nasir something, and he didn't want the responsibility of paying it back.

'Look, Ali, I don't want to talk about this.'

Ali shuffled his feet and looked at the grass – too green; always green. 'What are you going to do now?'

'I'm going to go to bed and not think.'

'I mean, are you going to go to another school?'

Nasir's cigarette had gone out. He spent some time trying to relight it. His hands were shaking. 'You don't know much about the world, do you, Ali?' The cigarette failed to ignite and he threw it on the step. 'Ali, my young cousin. Ali, Ali. You know what your name means?'

'You could get a job.'

'Ali means you're supposed to be the Leader of Islam.'

'You could work with my dad.'

'But you know how many people are called Ali? – Millions. Millions of them. There are millions of people who decided their son would be the leader.'

'Get your dad to talk to my dad.'

'So you see the problem there. That's the way the world works, my cousin. That's how it is.'

TOM & DAVE

It's hard not to resent you after that. Fuck. Dave rubbed the side of his head, nursing the area above his ear where Tom had managed to connect.

At least you popped your cherry.

Do I get to hit you now?

That wasn't part of the agreement.

Because I really feel like hitting you.

That's only natural. It takes a big man not to be emotionally affected by a punch to the head. But if you really wanna hit me, then sure, I understand, go for it. Tom leaned forward and stuck his head out and closed his eyes. Remember, he said. I understand completely.

A container ship had begun to cross the harbour; smoke from a factory on the far side of the city was smearing into the horizon line.

HENRY

He looked up from his book. He'd never really noticed how messy his handwriting was, like backwards calligraphy; it must have been hell to mark. He suddenly felt extremely sorry for Mrs Vanderbilt and all the other teachers who'd been forced to pick their way through his obtuse symbols to find meaning.

'Henry?'

'I'm sorry about this, Mrs Vanderbilt.'

'You're sorry about what?'

'My handwriting. It's a nightmare.'

'It's not a problem, Henry. Just answer the question.'

He looked around the class. Everyone was staring at him: Ben, Jason, Veronica. Leila, to his right, looked anxious and expectant. He tried to think about what the question was, but it seemed to have escaped him. 'I'm sorry,' he said. 'I don't know what the question is.'

'Sure you do,' Ben said, pulling off his glasses and cleaning the lenses on his shirt.

'No, I don't. I have no idea.'

'What, you haven't been listening?' said Veronica. 'Mrs Vanderbilt. Henry hasn't been listening. He doesn't know what's going on.'

'Don't worry, he knows,' the teacher said. Her tone suggested that she believed that Henry *did* know, that he just wasn't focusing enough. 'Come on, Henry. It's there. You just have to access it. Tap into that part of your brain.'

He looked over at Leila. She was waiting. Her eyes wanted him to answer, believed in him. 'Did the question have to do with society?' He glanced about, examining the faces for any sense of affirmation.

'In a way, yes,' said Vanderbilt. 'But it's also a lot more personal than that. It's an individual issue, but one that affects us all to some extent.'

'Is it a question to do with history?'

'Everything's a question about history,' Ben said. 'Everything.'

'What?'

'Do you want us to spell it out for you?' Jason said.

'Honestly, yeah, that would probably help.'

'G. A. P. P. A. L. 4. 7. E. 9. F. Z. 6.'

'What?'

'I'm spelling it out for you. Come on, man. You're a smart guy. Keep up.'

'He's right, Henry,' Vanderbilt said. 'You're an intelligent kid. You should know this.'

'You should know this,' Leila said, anxiety bleeding out of her. 'Please know this, Henry.' They were all still staring, waiting.

'Look, Mrs Vanderbilt, I'm going to be honest. I tuned out for a bit there. I'm sorry. I'm going to need the question again.'

Vanderbilt flattened her dress with her hands and looked for a moment at the world outside the classroom, light washing over her maternal face. 'Okay, Henry. But you need to listen carefully. This is the last time I'm going to repeat it. Are you ready?'

'Yes.'

'Because it's not an easy question to repeat.'

'I understand that. I'm sorry.' Henry suddenly had the urge to cry.

'Given what we already know about dialectical materialism in both theory and practice, and given the current geopolitical and geological situation in North Africa, when we think about the rapid advances and regressions caused by a savage and aggressive form of globalization, to what extent can we measure our sense of self with reference to a rapidly mutating cultural and technological zeitgeist?'

Henry paused for a moment and tried to really consider this.

'He doesn't get it,' Jason said.

Vanderbilt made no move to quiet him. The words jumped and squirmed and tangled in Henry's mind; he saw them as lines on a page, still for only a second before they warped themselves into incoherent knots. 'Could you write the question up on the board, please?'

Vanderbilt made no reply; she continued to stare at him. Henry took this as a no.

'Can I answer?' Ben asked.

'Fuck, Ben. Wait your turn!' Henry was becoming flustered.

'He can't do it.' Ben sat back in his chair and folded his arms.

'Okay…' He took a breath and tried to focus, but the

extra oxygen seemed only to make him dizzy. 'The insurgent situation in North Africa means that our sense of self... when we think about technology... and current cultural trends...'

'He's talking shit.'

Again, Vanderbilt made no effort to intervene. Henry persevered. 'It means that it's changing, like... When you really consider the thing, it's sort of loose and... It could be that we're being influenced by the notion that...'

'You don't get it at all,' Jason said. 'You're out of your depth, man.' And now something was caught in Henry's throat and he was struggling to speak, and Leila was still staring, and Ben had launched into an answer that Henry was finding it difficult to listen to, the words dropping in and out or doubling up on themselves. He desperately wanted to be outside.

'It's a pretty straight up and down question,' Ben was saying. 'I mean, without drifting into a conversation about Hegel and method acting and the nature of team sports, when you look at the problem from the starboard side it becomes opaque enough to answer, because in the end its really about human nature and nurture and the fluctuations in the abortion rates that we see on a minute to minute basis.'

'Very good, Ben.' Vanderbilt moved to him as he spoke and patted him on the head in the way one might pat a dog, slowly and with care and affection, her fingers running though his hair.

'But it's also important to note down that shifts in the economic landscape can lead to a sort of verisimilitude.' It was Jason's turn now. He spoke directly at Henry, into him. 'And that has a doubling up effect when it comes to policy decisions in the Congo.'

Henry had it. He understood, and for a moment his throat cleared and he found a space – a breath – to answer. 'I get it. The answer is nonsense. The answer is meaningless because the question is meaningless.'

They stared at him.

'Like, our sense of self is defined largely by a mixture of stock market rape and historical injustice, and if we add to that a finite degree of porridge then it always rains on Tuesdays, even when it doesn't.'

They stared at him.

He looked at Leila. She was crying. He looked back at Vanderbilt. She was now rubbing her hands through Jason's hair. 'He doesn't get it,' Jason said.

'He doesn't fucking get it,' Ben added.

Henry looked down at his book again, then out the window. He could see the wave coming. 'I don't like this.'

'Yeah,' Mrs Vanderbilt said, kneading Jason's scalp with her fingers. 'Well there's nothing you can do about it.'

The wave hit the jetty and tore away the palm trees and raced up through the school. Any second now it would hit the windows of the classroom.

'Yeah,' Veronica said. 'There's nothing you can do about it.'

DANNY

It was an English exam and he was meant to be writing an essay; the pen was supposed to be on the paper making marks and making sense, but neither seemed possible at this stage. Making sense would require sorting information, but the information refused to be sortable. Danny looked up from the paper. Someone coughed at the other end of the hall. As its echo receded he could hear the fragile gnaw of approximately three hundred ballpoints scratching at their pages, a subtlety broken by the occasional flipping of a question sheet. Someone shifted in their chair, steel legs grinding abruptly on the wooden floor. The clock at the front read two forty-five. He'd been sitting for over half an hour. The paper provided for his answer remained blank. The clock read three.

That morning he'd uploaded a video of his guinea pig against a green-screen backdrop of Tokyo. Shot with close-ups and careful lighting from his desk lamp, the guinea pig was an invader, an homage to Godzilla, and with small twitches of its nose and a slight turning of its body, it destroyed a whole legion of plastic soldiers. Above a Beethoven piano sonata, Danny narrated in a soft, loving voice: 'All he wanted was love and acceptance, but he was not made for this world, and as they fired hatred into his soft flesh, he wondered whether he would find love in the next.'

The clock read three-fifteen. The invigilator was looking at him, staring. He stared back. Afternoon light was pouring into the hall through the side windows. He looked back down at his page and found it empty once again. What was the question? He picked up his pen and drew a face at the top of the sheet; he made the eyes into crosses; he gave the face a tie that looked a lot like a cock and balls.

On the way to school that day his dad had asked him if he was prepared. 'Yes,' he replied. 'I have my gun; I have my vest; the monster will be dead before the day is through.'

'Good. A metaphor. You'll need those, right?'

'Yes, father. Yes I will.'

His YouTube channel now had over one hundred thousand hits. The *Piss-Drinker Remix* was doing particularly well. Top comment: 'Fcukin weird.' The day before going on study leave, someone had thrown a hot mince pie at Danny's head. He didn't know who it was. He didn't care all that much.

Three twenty-five. He'd folded the page with the drawing of a face into his top pocket. Best to start fresh with a blank sheet. Still, he needed sense and nothing was coming. Nothing wanted to come. He looked at the invigilator – a teacher from the Technology Department with a white beard and a bulbous nose. He didn't know his name. He stared. The invigilator stared back, then pointed down, signalling that Danny should return to the task at hand. He collected his pen and slumped into his chair, looked left, right: rows of students, hunched and concentrating. He visualised their deaths. The hall caught fire and the doors jammed closed: they ran in screaming circles until their uniforms were engulfed in flames and their skin started to melt; inside the heat and pressure he saw eyeballs exploding, tongues boiling. He walked through the aftermath of charred and blackened bodies. He struggled to empathize. The clock read three thirty.

Before his morning maths exam he'd sat next to an African kid with big teeth and skin so dark it seemed to absorb the sunlight. He sat with him because the kid wasn't sitting with anyone else, so why not. He showed him his guinea pig, let him hold it; the kid seemed happy with this.

Three forty-five and the paper in front of him was somehow even emptier. It had become a hole he could put his hand into – a void. He wanted to put his face on it, let it slip inside and enter the blank space, enter the nothingness. A lack of things would make more sense; lack of form would mean there'd be nothing to sort. It would be easier. Questions would cease to exist.

At three fifty-four he saw men in black balaclavas smash the windows and run screaming into the hall. To make a statement one of them grabbed Veronica from her seat and slit her throat and used the blood spraying from her neck like a hose to soak nearby students. Then they opened fire, muzzles flashing as bullets rattled the bodies of the captive audience. Danny watched the kid next to him take one in the face, his cheek bursting open, the loose skin like a meat flap, and then one in the skull, his body slumping to the floor. Danny pressed himself into the white emptiness of his page and closed his eyes.

Four o'clock. The invigilator crossed the time off the whiteboard at the front of the hall. An hour and fifteen minutes to go. Nothing written. The girl to Danny's right put her hand up to signal for extra paper. Danny used the opportunity to ask for a toilet break.

Before his morning exam that day, Danny had sat in the sunlight and fed his guinea pig bits of lettuce from his sandwich. He stroked its fur and tried to consider what he'd studied. He knew there would be something to do with asymptotes. After giving the animal to the African kid – his wide smile reflecting the morning – Danny tried to explain things. 'It's a maths problem, right. Like it's an expression. And the formula is pretty simple. But it's not really a maths problem. I mean, its applications are bigger than that. You know what I mean?'

The African kid looked up at him and nodded. He was cupping the guinea pig in both hands. 'Very soft!'

'Because an asymptote is basically a line that gets closer and closer to zero, but it never actually gets there. It's jammed on this march to infinity.'

'Infinity?'

'Like, *forever*. Like it'll never reach zero. But the thing is, it keeps getting closer and closer, so there's this illusion of progress, right. You always think you're getting somewhere, but then you don't. You can't. It's a trap.'

'Can I give food?'

Danny gave the kid another chunk of lettuce from his sandwich and watched him feed the animal from his hand. 'So I think this is an expression for all kinds of human trouble. Like the search for objective truth. Like god and love and meaning. We get the feeling of getting closer to something, but it's only an illusion really, because we're trapped on the journey to infinity.'

'Forever?'

'Forever. Exactly.'

'What is name?' The kid was holding up the guinea pig.

'Whatever you like, buddy.'

'Buddy?'

'Sure.'

'Goodbye, Buddy.' He handed the animal back to Danny who slipped it back into its container and into his bag. It would spend the morning in the dark, waiting in the hallway while its owner sat his maths exam.

At six minutes past four Danny stared into the bathroom mirror. One of the toilets had been blocked with rolls of toilet paper and was overflowing. A lone slug lurked at the edge of a pool of waste water. On the wall someone had carved a swastika. The ceiling bulb had blown and the atmosphere of urine was thick enough to taste. He looked at his reflection. There was nothing wrong with the kid gazing back at him. He wasn't abnormal. He wasn't deformed. In most respects he was smart, even likeable. He punched the mirror with his left hand, cracking the image and cutting his flesh. Blood began running into the basin. His fist throbbed and pulsed, the pain surging through his whole arm and blocking out thought. He ran it under the cold tap and wrapped the wound in a full roll of toilet paper, dragging the cheap single ply over and over until his hand was mummified. He returned to the hall.

Four fifteen and still *carte blanche*. The throb mixed with a sting; the first traces of blood began to seep through his bandage. He watched the invigilator's eyes go red as sweat began to collect on his forehead. He watched the man vomit suddenly and violently, a mix of bile and oesophagus clinging to his beard. He watched the student next to him put down his pen and vomit onto the page and reel out of his chair and begin to feast on the throat of the girl next to him, skin and tendons caught in teeth. When you cut open a slug, you expect it to be gelatinous all the way through, a single gloppy muscle. Instead you find organs, a whole system of tubes and sacks.

Four thirty and blood was dripping onto the floor. No one seemed to notice. He lifted the dripping hand up to his answer sheet and let it mark up the first page until it resembled a Rorschach test. He repeated the process for the next ten available pages. This was an answer. Fuck the question. Four forty-seven.

The maths exam had gone well. He'd stayed the full three hours. Used his calculator. Refrained from writing jokes as opposed to answers. At twelve thirty time had been called and Danny had closed his answer booklet. Other students started talking. Rather than join in, he chose to sit quietly with his eyes closed, attempting as best he could to zen away the sea of fractions. He was the last to leave the room. He collected his bag from the hallway and sat alone on the field to pass the time before the English exam.

Five o'clock. Blood on most of the pages. He was beginning to feel dizzy. Around him the room began to shake. A ceiling beam broke free and crushed a row of students, their bodies pinned and limp and lifeless. At the rear of the hall a crevasse opened up in the floor, swallowing desks and chairs and all their occupants. He listened to the screams as a wall came crashing in, dust and debris rising, a severed head knocking against his feet. When the windows imploded, flying glass cut soft faces and the wind of a cyclone blew in hard, then sucked back, dragging out the corpses as if into the vacuum of space. Danny sat back and dripped the blood from his hand onto the white of his school shirt. Five fifteen. Pens down. Stay in your seats until all papers have been collected… It was then that they noticed. 'Dude, what the fuck?'

'Sir, I think something's wrong.'

'What? What's going on?'

'Just look, sir.'

Alone on the field between exams Danny looked across the grass. He could see houses in the distance. He could see clouds. If he looked hard enough, he could see infinity. He could tell there was no answer, no reaching zero, no certainty or objectivity. There was no divinity or supreme sense to it all. He saw it in the grass beneath him and in his own quivering hands; he saw it in his dopey leather school shoes and in the dead eyes of his pet. Someone had opened his bag and opened the box and broken its neck, and where was the truth and love and meaning in that?

MiNA & AHMED

His big hands were around her throat. He could feel her pulse, the skin of her neck stretching against his fingers. He needed both hands to lift her up and press her against the wall, so he didn't have a free one to muffle her screaming, and when she screamed it made her ugly again; it distorted her features, distended her jaw and loosened her eyes in their sockets; it crinkled her forehead and flared her nostrils. It was with her pinned like this, two feet off the ground, her legs trapped by his hips, her arms free to lash and claw at the side of his face, her hair popping free like wire, tears smearing her makeup and casting channels in the powder she had applied to her cheeks that morning; it was with her teeth bared like an animal, wet and afraid, and her body a primal sack of meat and instincts and howling – a violent sub-human cacophony of fear (fear that he could smell, fear that he could wash himself with): it was with her jammed like this against the brick backing of the school's hospitality block that Ahmed saw what he needed to see.

...Because Mina had gone ahead and done the decent thing, the adult thing. She'd waited a full two weeks to give him space, to let him adjust after the funeral. She'd made sure it was a Friday so that he had the weekend to piece himself back together. She'd even gone to his house to have the conversation so he wouldn't have to go anywhere afterward.

They'd sat out on the front lawn in the green plastic chairs next to the washing line and she'd started to cry, because there was no other way to begin. 'What's wrong? What is it?' he asked. She sobbed and looked at the flax plants in the garden. She covered her face with her hands. 'What? Tell me.' He reached over and tried to hug her, but she shifted her body, a quick instinctual jerk. The movement opened the conversation. 'What have I done?' Ahmed waited. Looked at her. Looked at the road beyond the front gate.

'I can't.'

'What?'

'Algeria!?'

'Oh, shit, look, I just said that because I was upset. We don't have to go right away...and we don't have to go there, we can go somewhere else.'

She looked up at him. She knew she wasn't being clear. She took a breath and prepared herself. 'No, I can't go anywhere.'

Ahmed felt blood run from the back of his skull; his neck strained and tightened. 'What? Why?' His voice felt high and whiney. His hands suddenly seemed in the way.

'It's time, Ahmed. Just, you know...' She never used

his name in direct conversation with him. It was a marker for other people denoting who he was. Saying it to him, saying it as he sat in front of her, it sounded like a pointed shape.

'Like, so, what?'

'We're really young. And…'

'You don't love me anymore?' Ahmed had heard people ask this on TV, but it was the first time for him. It sounded forced and useless. Infantile. And even before she answered, the conversation tracked out ahead of him, clichés leapfrogging to the conclusion of a breakup that had played out a billion times already: of course I still love you, that's not the reason. Then what is it? It's that this is too much for me right now; we have our whole lives, you know; can we still be friends? Of course we can – I'd like that.

'Of course I still love you,' she said.

He was silent. A car passed on the road. Somewhere inside the house his mother was watching a soap opera.

'Ahmed?'

'It's fine. It's the right thing to do. You're right. I'd still like to be friends—'

'Of course we can still—'

'But I think you should go now. I don't think we should see each other for a while.'

'But I'll see you at school… How are we—'

'I won't be there next week.'

The crying, which had dried up as she launched into things, now returned. It seemed more genuine this time, mucus and shudders, and it appeared to Ahmed that she was only just realising what it was that she'd decided to do. He knew he could help her with a hug, that this time she wouldn't move away, but he restrained himself. He wanted her to feel alone. He needed her to feel the bitter scrape. 'You should go,' he said again. Her face was puffy and pathetic. His hate for it was sudden and total.

And then, that night, after she had left sobbing and confused, he loved it again. He sat alone in his room with books he couldn't focus on. He loved her because she was right and there was nothing he could do and because he'd known her for too long. But he had to hate something, so he hated everything else. He took a walk through darkened streets. He smashed the window of a parked car with a broken piece of cinderblock. In the irritatingly optimistic wattage of the supermarket he stole a bottle of wine and drank it in a park. He let down someone's tyres. He went home and wrote her a poem about bees and fire and death that didn't make sense. When he woke up the next morning it was to the sound of his mother crying. Women were always crying. He couldn't eat. He felt dizzy. And that's the way it stayed.

All weekend he wanted to text her, or call her. He didn't. He had real trouble operating the buttons on his phone; his brain wasn't connecting with his fingers – his synapses were preoccupied. He sat in the lounge with his mother while they watched TV in silence. He hadn't told her. He wouldn't. On the screen, characters of the soap operas looked neat and washed; he looked past their faces and into the pixels until the shows became nothing, refocusing only when a guy on a beach at sunset spoke directly to him: 'So you don't love me anymore?'

'Of course I still love you,' the girl replied, a tanned body in a tight bikini. 'It's just…'

And then on Sunday night he was at it again, his fingers fumbling with the keypad of his phone, trying to work out drafts with emotional significance, trying to contrive the language to convey an abstract he couldn't define within a concrete and limited space. He wanted to say something that would express everything. He needed to communicate that he hated her and loved her and needed her and that she needed him and this was foolish and let's move past it and into a future of… But it wouldn't happen. Everything was jumbled. Nothing was clear. His mother was crying again. He needed to call her.

Pacing his room he pressed the phone hard against the side of his head, as if the volume of the ringtone equated to proximity, and when her voice came up on answerphone he hung up and dialled again, and dialled again, and dialled – and then he was out on the street in the darkness, a lurking *momento mori*, and for the second time that weekend he smashed a car window and stole a bottle of wine, and even though he was as big as he was and clumsy to the point of embarrassment, in the soft dark of the night he moved with a purpose and a direction: he would watch her – that was all. He needed that. *She* wanted that. He knew. Because you're not together for two years without forming some kind of instinctual bond, a preternatural link that transcends words and lets you know their moods and desires, regardless of physical presence. That's the way it was. It always had been.

Mina's period of mourning lasted the whole of Saturday. She told her family. She told her friends. She updated the school via a relationship status adjustment on Facebook. Yes, looking at him was hard: his dark face and looming figure behind her in photos, hanging above her shoulder like an extended shadow – it was *her* shadow, and now it was gone, and she missed it and wanted it back. So she took down whole albums (Ahmed and Mina at Rainbow's End; Ahmed and Mina at the Beach; Ahmed and Mina at the Winter Gardens…) and filed them away. She put his notes and poems and presents into shoes boxes and slid them deep into a cupboard. It was best not to read anything he'd written for her. Words meant meaning and meaning meant emotion, and at this stage – according to a number of different websites that specialised in issues like this – nostalgia was a toxin that she needed to purge from her system. And she didn't want to cry again like she had on the walk home, a tragic blubbering, vision demented by tears, her chest heaving. It had lasted all the way to her street, where, as she turned on the footpath and made the final stumble home, a car of passing guys had honked their horn and whooped from their windows, and she'd felt the mature thing to do was stop crying and fake a smile.

On Saturday night her friends dressed her up and took her out. 'It's the best thing for it,' Veronica said as she helped apply eyeliner. 'You need to feel pretty again.' And by ten o'clock Mina was drinking an R.T.D. in a car park by a beach and talking to a nineteen-year-old guy with strong arms and a symmetrical face. And although he'd seemed ugly to her at first, somehow too squared off, too well defined, after an hour of talking about his car and his apprenticeship and the movies he liked, she started to notice the cool movements of his hands and the clarity of his posture and the gentle slope of muscles in his shoulders that seemed to flex calmly at the fringes of his singlet. She made out with him. He tasted of beer and liberation. She got his number. Veronica agreed that it was the right thing to do. 'But don't you think it's too soon?'

'Don't ever think that, Mina.'

'She's right,' Jason said, both hands on the wheel as he piloted them through the night.

193

'But I don't want to hurt him.' She tried to avoid his name.

'You've already waited. You were going to do this a month ago. And he doesn't have to know. Besides, it's none of his business anymore. Remember that.'

A song about love was playing on the radio. Mina could still taste the beer. 'You're so pretty,' Veronica said. 'I'm so jealous of how pretty you are.'

'She's right,' Jason said. 'You're hot.'

For two full hours that Sunday night, Ahmed sat in the bushes outside Mina's window. He finished his wine and watched her sit at her computer. He watched her leave the room and return with a cup of herbal tea that he knew was infused with peach; he'd tasted it on her lips many times before. He watched her type and move the mouse and laugh and scratch her head. He watched her tie up her hair, her arms pulled up behind her, nipples protruding against her tee-shirt. It wasn't a conscious decision to begin playing with himself – his cold hand in his pants pulling against warm memories – but it was happening, and when he had finished and the loneliness returned, he watched her laugh and type something else, and for a moment he believed that she knew he was there, that she could feel his presence, that the laugher was for him – because she loved him, she would always love him. He wiped his hand on the leaves beside him. He would've blown her a kiss had it not felt ridiculous. He was back there again the following night.

The mood at school was now very different for Mina. Without the dominating figure of her ex, other students talked to her more freely. Girls who had never spoken to her before asked how she was and flattered her and invited her places. Guys flirted. They showed off in her vicinity, messing with teachers for her entertainment alone and punching each other in the shoulders as a way of advertising virility. At lunchtime on Wednesday two guys began a chin-up competition on a support beam at the back of her cooking class; they did it audibly, calling each other names and flicking glances in her direction in the hope that she might cast her eyes back and flick her hair and take feminine note of their existence. This was adolescent freedom. This was the carefree stupidity she had yearned for without knowing it: the right to be dumb and not give a fuck. All week she felt like dancing. And Tim (that was his name – the apprentice) had been texting, the content of his messages getting heavier, libidinous, and she'd been playing along, just a little, just a bit. He'd wanted a photo of her, something dirty, but that would have to wait. For now it should just be words: 'I bet your all coverd in grease,' she sent. 'Id like to rub it all ova u,' he replied. And she showed Veronica, who suggested sending back something much more obscene, and Mina was tempted to tell her (in a way that she'd never told Veronica before and that could only have happened with this breezy new confidence) that she didn't understand the dance – that the eroticism was in the gradual build up, not in a violent escalation.

And with all this going on, Mina didn't even have time to think about the guy she'd slept with at the party (what was his name? – he tasted like cigarettes and smelt of cheap deodorant) and she didn't have the space to mourn or worry or reflect (like the websites said, it was better not to) and by Friday she'd managed to not only stop the bleeding but heal the wound. All she'd had to do was ignore his calls – calls without messages, calls that started on the Sunday night while she was Facebooking with Tim and looking through his photos and laughing at his jokes and loving a whole new world. So when Ahmed's name flashed on her phone, she knew it was important for both of them to ignore it. Healthy. Mature. And then if she could last out the week with no contact, then maybe she would see him, meet him somewhere. Maybe. That would be enough time. After that, who knew? Of course she would love to be friends with him again. Although they couldn't be like they were, they could share coffee every now and then, catch up and talk about things, like adults, like people. This is what she was thinking on the Friday night when he called again, the screen of her beat-up Nokia flashing with meaning. She let it go to answerphone. He left no message. She waited. She texted him back.

When his mother asked him where he was going at night, he told her directly: 'Seeing Mina.' His mother replied with a generalised, 'Oh'. She'd never liked her. Never would. But it meant something to her son, so she'd let it be. And since the weekend Ahmed had been better. He had his clarity back. He was more productive. 'Look, mum, I'm going to clean the house, okay. This place is turning into a dump.' The dishes were unwashed and laundry had piled to unreasonable levels, spilling from the washing basket onto the floor; ashtrays sat in illogical places – next to the toilet, on bookshelves, in the middle of the kitchen floor, overflowing with crushed butts. All day Ahmed cleaned around his mother, vacuuming under her legs while she stared at the TV, until the place regained a semblance of order. The act of cleaning allowed Ahmed to sort through his mind and focus on what was being neglected. Where was the extended family? Where were they when his mother was collapsing? People can only spend so much time and energy on others before they get bored and tired. When the immediate obligation wanes, they return to their own concerns. Ahmed's father, breathing through tubes: 'You can't rely on god or other people; if you want to live a worthwhile life, it's entirely up to you.' As evening began to settle Ahmed set the table and made his mother dinner, then called her in from the living room. 'Can't we eat in front of the TV?' she said. The ashtray beside her was already beginning to restock.

'No. I've set a table. We'll eat together and talk.'

'You're a good boy,' she said. It was a stir of cogence.

Over rice and poppadums that were almost certainly stale, Ahmed laid everything out. He told her he was leaving school and finding a job in order to support the household, and he recommended (albeit delicately) that she find one too. 'It's you and me now,' he said. 'We've got to do this on our own. And we will.' His mother didn't protest his desire to part ways with education, nor did she put up a fight when he suggested that maybe she try to get work at the supermarket. Ahmed was the patriarch now, and this was how it was going to be.

'I don't know what I'd do without you,' she said. He hugged her, told her he loved her, then, as she got up to do the dishes for the first time in weeks, he said he was going out to see his girlfriend.

By the third night it had become a comforting routine. She gave him stability. Her warm room and peach tea invited a sense of psychological calm. Looking in at her while she played with the mouse, half-heartedly attempting to balance her homework with social media, Ahmed clutched the warmth of his own flesh and pretended to live in a better version of the world. The pretence was enough. At times he pushed himself close to the window, dangerously close, where a glance away from her computer would have led to his discovery – a grim face hiding in the darkness just inches from the glass. But it was worth the risk to bring them closer, to imagine that he could feel her. And although he called each night before leaving his own home, he'd come to expect her answering message: the same lilt to the same five words, said just a bit too quickly, a flustered teenage girl caught between moments of makeup and confusion: 'It's Mina leave a message.' No, I won't, he thought. It's enough for you to know I'm there. That's how we remain together. I'm always there.

And then on Friday, after his call and before he left the house, she texted him back, a message that was brief and casual and full of promise: she wanted to meet up. She would be at school on Saturday morning working on a cooking project. They should meet and have coffee and it would be good to see him.

Good to see him.

So on Friday Ahmed stayed in with his mother and cooked her dinner again and watched TV with her, and they prepared a C.V. to drop at the supermarket and talked about what Ahmed might do next – maybe a call centre (they pay well, don't they?) – and Ahmed felt good about all this, like things were moving forward.

And then it was ten a.m. and Ahmed was nicely dressed and standing at the gates of the school. And it felt strange to him already, because he knew he wasn't coming back. His father's dress pants were a little too short, but they were an important addition. They said he was working – or had the potential to – and that things were looking up. He walked around to the hospitality block with wet hands. He felt awkward. His stomach had started to cramp. He hadn't planned what he was going to say, and as he got closer, the whole situation started to seem unnatural and weird.

He found her in the cooking room. She wore a hairnet and a red apron. Other students looked up as he ducked his frame through the door; someone said hello to him, though he couldn't tell who. She came up bouncing and smiling and hugged him, her arms tight around his big body, and suddenly the knot released, his nervous system let go, and the pressure that had tightened his shoulders and clamped his back and that he hadn't realised was even there magically disappeared. He felt like he was melting, cells deliquescing into the room. 'Come outside so we can talk,' she said.

On a bench in the middle of the school she relinquished the hairnet and apron and folded them up. 'I'm sorry I haven't been answering,' she said.

The hug had taken care of everything. Words came out clearly. 'It's fine. I know you can't answer. I kind of don't want you to. I just need to send something in your direction, you know?'

She asked him how he was. He answered. He was fine. His mother was fine. He was getting a job. She thought it was a good idea.

She thought it was a good idea.

'You don't think I should come back to school?'

'I guess it's not really up to me.'

'Well, I value your advice. You're smart.'

'Well, maybe you *should* get a job.'

'Why?' he said.

'You know, to help your mum.'

'It's not because you don't want me here?'

'No, of course not.' She stopped when her phone beeped and answered her message. Ahmed thought it was rude. He didn't say anything. Instead he watched as she attempted to navigate two tasks at once, her pretty face moving in the light, her skin almost polished. 'I would never think that. It's just, you know…' She moved her fingers on her phone.

'Know what?'

She put the phone down beside her and looked up. 'It's just I understand that you need to support your family. I mean, you can still go to university. You just have to do a foundation course or something.'

'Do you still love me?' He couldn't help it. She went quiet. '…What?'

'If we're going to be friends we can't keep asking each other that. You just have to know it.'

'I'm sorry.' He put his head down and shuffled his hands; the movement was childlike and utterly vulnerable and she couldn't prevent herself from hugging him. He put his arms around her, squeezed – maybe too hard – and then felt her pulling away.

'Okay. Come on. Let me go to the bathroom and then we'll go and get some coffee, okay?'

And then she got up and went inside and Ahmed played with his hands again and really noticed, now that he was sitting down, how small his father's pants were on him. Too small to be sensible. Too small for a grown man. And as he sat there wishing he had better looking socks and less ridiculous shoes, he picked up her phone and opened the messages and read everything. He processed the lot – received and sent, received and sent – and felt the world tighten again on his shoulders, wanted very suddenly to vomit.

When she returned she found him standing. He handed over the phone. He tried to hide the quaver of his hands. They walked around the back of the building – a narrow passageway of brick walls that led out of the school – and alone in this adobe corridor, jammed between Hospitality and Science, he blurted the question.

'What?' she said. She was still smiling. He'd said something, mumbled it – too fast to hear.

'I said, who's Tim?'

'Who?

'Who the fuck is Tim?'

And then she too did some processing. She understood what had happened. She stopped. 'You went through my—'

'Have you fucked him yet?'

'Oh, god – I knew it was too early to see you again. Fuck this.' And as she turned to leave, a quick angry turn, a total reversal of direction, she had every intention of saying, 'Goodbye, Ahmed! Go home!' But she didn't, because she couldn't, because his big hands were already on her, jagging her back by the arm, thrusting her hard into the wall, hauling her up by the throat. He lifted her high. He could feel her pulse.

MS BAKER

William Prout wrote a book called *Inquiry into the Nature and Treatment of Gravel, Calculus and other Diseases Connected with a Deranged Operation of the Urinary Organs.* Prout also discovered that the main component of urine is urea, with a chemical formula of $CO(NH_2)_2$.

Stephanie Baker didn't know why she recalled these things. She just did. It was something she'd written down in a lecture but never repeated to anyone. Maybe she'd turned it over in her head afterward while waiting for a bus, like a piece of a poem or a lyric. She may have even mouthed it to herself quietly, but that was all. Now, five years later and with a class fanning out in the courtyard around her, Corban missing a tooth (an incisor?), her own blood spilling onto her dress, and feeling dizzy and febrile – a thick sweat on her temples – here it was again. It was a senseless factoid, but it was the only buffer she had between herself and the concrete. Her logic seemed to go that if she held on to Prout, then maybe she wouldn't fall over. Maybe her legs wouldn't buckle and she wouldn't collect the pavement with all its grit and fossilized gum. Because that would be bad. A self-evident breach of her role as a teacher. And she hadn't even joined the union yet. No: Prout was important. He was keeping her responsible. He was a serious man with serious jowls; the kind of physician she could see wearing a cravat to bed. And what would he say about her dress? It wasn't just marker anymore, it was covered in her nosebleed, speckled and flecked, and if she didn't keep the stains damp, then what were the chances they would ever come out?

It was this thinking that led Stephanie to stumble not forward but sideways, an awkward trip-step to her right, to the drinking fountain. Beyond her a senior student was lying down and appeared to be sky-gazing, and the rest of her class were scattered outlines against light, and Jeremy had tipped over a garbage bin and Nathan was shouting the word cunt. Cunt! 'Stop it!' she heard herself shout. 'This minute!' But she was shouting at her own dress, its hem pulled up against the basin of the water fountain as she tried to pin it down with the thumb of her right hand while reaching the button with the tip of her ring finger, her left hand still cupping her nose, warm and streaked and running, the midsection of her body arched forward uncomfortably, like a small boy craning to pee at an adult urinal. The water started and tinkled forward onto the bloodied hem. Urea. She coughed. Had she told her partner about Prout?

'Yeah, look, you know I don't know about science-y stuff, Steph.'

'But this is interesting.'

'Interesting's pretty subjective.'

She wasn't sure whether the conversation had actually happened or not. She felt like puking. It had all come on so hot and sudden. It wouldn't have been so bad if only someone had done something about that bell. Three on. A digital woman in a digital bikini being sliced open by a digital chainsaw. One off. Three on, one off. Three on. Her hip felt hot. The buffer was disappearing, and then the vomit came for real.

TOM & DAVE

Nah man, I can't.

You sure? I mean, I'm letting you. It's no big deal.

You're a cunt, it's true, but I can't... I kinda feel like I'm on drugs.

Tom stood up from where he'd been hunched over and waiting for Dave's punch. Dave was standing back and deliberately blinking both eyes, like he was clearing his vision. Here, Tom said. Let me check your pupils.

Dave stood in the light and looked up, blinked again.

They seem alright, Tom said. Look left... Now right.... Now follow my finger.

What are you looking for?

I dunno. I've just seen people do this.

Well fuck off then. Dave shook himself free and went to light a smoke.

Are you dizzy?

A bit.

Maybe I concussed you.

Maybe.

Maybe my massive hook knocked your brain against

your skull and now it's swelling and if you go to sleep…

What?

Well, you might die…

Stop it dude.

I'm serious. Tom lit a smoke too. That one punch may well have done far more damage than all the pot you've smoked.

You think?

And even if you don't die, you might slip into a coma, and when you come out, the word confusion will taste like eggs and you won't be able to pronounce 'Q's anymore.

Dude, stop it.

I'm just saying it could happen. I mean, it's pretty rare a head injury's a good thing, and it's true, I did see a doco about a guy who had a concussion and when he came to he could speak fluent Greek and play the harp, but I don't think that's likely with you.

Dave sat down with his back to the wall of the Midway House and rubbed his head and looked pained. He rolled a stray bottle along the exposed floor boards and ashed his cigarette mindlessly. Please, man, he said. Just leave it alone, yeah.

Why? What's up? I didn't hit you that hard.

Remember my brother's mate, Pranav?

Nope.

Remember what happened to him?

I said I don't know him, which means I don't know what happened to him.

Jesus, shut up.

Fine.

He was at this party.

Your brother?

No, Pranav. He's like nineteen. Like first year uni.

And your brother was there?

No, fuck, shut up. Anyway, it was basically like a bunch of guys sitting around drinking and smoking pot and taking pills.

Pills? Like what kind?

Ecstasy. Or like a substitute, like mephedrone or something. My brother says it's almost impossible to get real ecstasy anymore, so dealers hand out this grubby shit that's mixed with meth and makes you all greasy and stupid.

Your brother's a connoisseur of low grade drugs?

They all take heaps of these pills – these guys – like four or five each, and they're sitting around in this kitchen at this guy's house and they start to come up, but like Pranav reacts really bad to it.

Badly.

He starts heaving his chest and sweating heaps, and then he just folds over and hits the floor. But like, everyone else is coming up really hard and they're telling each other how awesome they are and so they don't pay much attention to him while he's lying there on the carpet.

The kitchen has carpet?

Whatever, linoleum, fuck. But he starts foaming there, like on his back, and eventually someone notices and they roll him onto his side and finally someone starts to worry about it, but they're all still really fucking high, and so they don't know what to do.

Call an ambulance? Seems obvious.

Maybe in hindsight, yeah, but like think about it. As soon as they do that it's like an admission that they've been taking drugs, and then their parents find out, and they all start to worry about the police, and then the guy who's holding the drugs is like, fuck, this guy hasn't paid me for those yet – and that's like five pills right, so it's over two hundred dollars.

You're serious?

Yeah, they're expensive.

That's not what I meant.

So they've pulled his tongue out of his mouth an' everything and just let him lie there while they're high and eventually one of them drives Pranav to the hospital.

Finally.

And apparently he just like carries him into the waiting room and leaves him there and gaps it back to the party and that's the end of it – they like continue on with their night.

What happened to Pranav?

I'm still kinda dizzy.

Finish the story and we'll deal with it.

Pranav?

Yeah, the guy in the hospital. What happened?

So it turns out they left him way too long. Like, if they'd taken him to the hospital straight away, then it would've been okay, but because they just left him the oxygen started to cut away from his brain.

Shit.

He's out for like four days and when he comes to, his parents are there. They'd been contacted by the hospital. Like, his friends had just cut him out and said nothing and pretended he was never there. But when he wakes up it's pretty clear something's wrong. He can't form any real words. He just looks up at his parents and goes hnnnn, fuck, hnnnn fuck! Like, it's a huge strain for him to produce anything except fuck, and his eyes are rolling around in his head, and it's clear that they like register his mum and dad, that he knows it's them, but nothing coherent is coming out. The doctors say his brain went without oxygen for too long, and that he's probably going to be like that for the rest of his life, just going hnnnnn fuck! I mean, he was doing computer science. Now he has to have twenty-four hour care just to wipe the shit and spittle off his face.

That's bad, but it's not going to happen to you.

How do you know?

I was lying before. Your pupils are dilating; you're fine.

You sure?

Yes. Stop being a pussy. You were talking about cutting people open before and now you're moaning about a bruise.

The urge to hit you is coming back.

How do you even know that story's real? It's totally likely it's just urban legend bullshit. They spread it to keep you from experimenting.

Because my brother told me. It's as legit as legit. And he says he won't touch that shit anymore.

That's the lesson he took from it? Surely it should be about getting better friends. Get that sorted and you can take all the drugs you want. You need someone responsible enough to know you've had too much heroin.

Remember that time you smoked a whole fifty bag and then you couldn't piss? And then you just sort of fell over and vomited for a while... That was funny.

Marijuana's a fun drug.

I could totally go for some.

You sure? You don't want to go back to class?

We could do both.

What is peer pressure? Tom asked.

It's proof you have peers, Dave said.

STELLA

She was even less communicative than usual, more shut away, although she was sitting upright, which was a good thing. Nothing foetal. No returning to the womb. But the wall was a concern: blank and impenetrable, it swelled between them – between Verna's little swivelling office chair and her couch of compassion. A fly had landed on Stella's arm; it twitched forward a centimetre and rubbed its forelegs, twitched to the left, but Stella's arm didn't move. She barely blinked, her focus somewhere between her pupils and a patch of floor.

Verna had made a special effort to pull the venetians right up and let the light in. It was a sunny day, and in the courtyard outside two junior students were busy trying to construct a sundial out of cardboard, and Verna couldn't help but let her concentration drift in their direction. The juxtaposition with what sat in her office was depressing and inescapable. 'I'm reluctant to suggest this,' she said. Stella made no real sign of understanding. 'But it might be time for us to book a doctor's appointment.' The fly moved again. 'You don't have to think of anti-depressants as a cage. In many cases, they can be quite facilitative. The science is getting better.' Stella looked up, catching Verna's eye. 'They can give you a stronger sense of who you are by allowing you to forget about some of the things that bother you – they'll push them to the back of your mind... They could really help, I think is what I'm saying.' Stella lolled her head back to the space of nothing in her foreground. The fly lifted from her arm and circled the room, and Verna took the chance to lift out of her chair and open the office door and herd it out before settling back. 'Would that be something you're interested in looking at?'

Stella shrugged. At least it was movement.

Verna had already gone through the basics. How was she finding her classes? Was everything alright at home? I'm here to listen, remember. This is a safe place... Stella's attendance reports were somehow getting worse. A good week meant three days. Her Monday had become her Wednesday, and her presence during any first or last period was an exception rather than a norm.

The patch of floor.

'Do I dare ask about Jeff?' Verna tried a smile, just a small one – girl talk, something to draw her out.

Another shrug.

'So he's off the radar then...?' Time for a personal revelation, half an opinion to lighten the mood. 'That's the problem with older men – at least in my experience. They always treat you like a child, even when you're thirty-five and they're forty. It's something to do with the male brain, I think.'

Stella tilted her face and looked up at the light and for a moment Verna believed she was going to say something.

'What do you think?'

Her head wilted again and found the floor, but there was a glimmer – eyes shifting focus. She was thinking.

'Relationships are dangerous, Stella. They can be the best thing in the world – they can make you feel connected and fulfilled. But because of that people become over-reliant on them. And the world can be a pretty difficult place. Uncaring. You know that. People can be uncaring. And just as quickly as it arrives, all that good feeling can be taken away, and you can feel like your supports have been pulled out. It's important that you are complete by yourself. That doesn't mean you have to live a cold and distant life and never get close to anyone, it just means that you have to be emotionally and psychologically self-reliant. You have to believe in yourself first. Do you understand?'

'I do believe in myself. I'm fine.'

First words. Verna weighed things, contemplated stating the obvious, then went for it. 'It doesn't look like it.' Stella looked up at her, her expression blank and inscrutable. 'Sometimes I see you and you're talkative and passionate and very much manic. Other days are like today. Now, I'm not a registered medical practitioner, but I have seen bipolar disorder enough to recognise it. Which is why I think we need to look at the possibility of medication.'

Stella shifted her legs up onto the couch in a more classic Stella position, hugging them into herself. She looked out the window, noticing, for the first time it seemed, that the venetians had been pulled up. 'I've just got a lot on,' she said. To Verna, the remark seemed at once vague and cryptic and fairly reeking of adolescent hyperbole.

'To go back to relationships for just a minute, and I don't want to be condescending here, Stella, but you're still growing. Your brain hasn't fully formed yet. Right now it's in the process of forming a lot of new pathways and trying to develop and to sort of figure itself out. So it's a really dangerous time to attach yourself to people. Because you're changing. And what you need today might be completely different tomorrow.'

'I'm not attaching myself to people.'

'What about Jeff? It seems like he had a fairly big emotional impact on you, and it's important to acknowledge that. To function in a healthy way you need to be aware of how things affect you.'

'Fuck Jeff. He's not important.'

'Fuck Jeff?' She heard herself swearing. The word wafted about the room before coming to rest in the silence.

'I've just got a lot on,' Stella said again. She was looking at the juniors now. One was recording notes in a book – 1B5, ruled – while the other adjusted the cardboard dial.

'Is it the pressure of the exams? I know how hard it can— '

'Nah… My swan plants are starting to die.'

'Swan plants?'

'Some of the caterpillars made it to the chrysalis, you know.' The animation in her voice came suddenly. She was looking directly at Verna. It was like a damaged wall socket had been kicked back into place and the stereo had started blaring half-way through a song. 'But the fuckers destroyed the plants in the process, like ravaged them. Like, by the time they were finished gorging themselves there weren't even branches to hang on, and a bunch of them migrated to other parts of the garden but heaps of them died. I found one on the concrete curled up in the sun, all shrivelled…' She trailed off and returned her attention to the window.

'Okay… Were you upset that it was dead, that it didn't make it?'

'What?' She looked back at Verna vacantly. The socket was out of place again.

'Were you upset that the caterpillars died?'

'They're just insects…'

'Well, what I'm saying is, sometimes people can find greater significance in small—'

'No, I get it and I don't. They're not significant. They're just bugs.'

'Yes, but, you can see the parallels can't you? They start out eating leaves, they go through a big transitional phase – like puberty—'

'I get it. I'm not stupid. But it's not the same.'

'How so?'

Stella took a frustrated breath and scratched at her neck and looked at her feet – her non-regulation shoes, the words 'FUCK YOUR MOTHA' scrawled in black vivid along the white instep of the left. 'I got a tattoo,' she said.

'Okay. Is this recent?'

'It's a tramp-stamp. You know what a tramp-stamp is?'

'I th—'

'It's on my lower back, which is good because I don't have to look at it, you know. I only see it on video. It's a dead pixie – I thought that kinda suited.'

'Does your mother—'

'Tony paid for it. He's got a lot of tattoos. And he smells like shit, but I'm sort of getting used to it.'

'Who's—'

'He's a cunt, but they're all cunts. And he's not that bad. And you're wrong, you know, because he treats me like an adult – like I'm capable of making some choices and stuff – even though he's way older. Fuck, I haven't even asked how old he is. But he's a choice, right.'

'I'm not sure I follow,' Verna said. Her heart was beating faster than she wanted it to.

'Caterpillars don't make choices. They just do shit and they either live or die, and then they die anyway.' She found the floor again, picked her nose. Verna wanted to say something but didn't know where to start. 'But I'll give you that, though. That's a parallel. Most people don't notice *shit* – they don't even realise they're making choices until way after they've made them, and at that point it's not really a choice. It's just leaf munching.'

'But you know when you're choosing?'

'Yes. I want to do something and I do it. I choose it. I want to flush a baby down a toilet, that's on me. I want to spread my…' She stopped. She reined herself in. Her features rippled for a moment, fluxing, apparently unable to decide which way they were going to travel.

'Look, Stella – is there anything you want to tell me?' Verna's couch-surfer looked down at her shoes again and her chemical-red hair fell over her face. She shook her head the way a child does when refusing vegetables. Verna couldn't tell whether what was beginning beneath Stella's fringe was sobbing or laughter. 'If you're in any kind of trouble, I can help.'

'It's all the same.'

'What is?'

'Everything. Everything's all the same.'

F 12

Brayden's face was pressed against the window of the classroom when it shattered, because despite what he'd been told, he was there with his head beneath the curtain and staring. When the glass broke and the curtain behind him jerked up, as if it had been whipped from its ends, his first thought was that *he'd* done it – that it had been *his* presence that caused the window to burst and scatter shards that cut his cheek. The popping crack was sudden and confronting, the pane exploding into his face. It numbed the side of his body and shut down his brain. It sent him spinning sideways in an ungainly rotation. He stumbled backward into the dim of the class, unable to form any recognisable human expression. 'Sorry,' he said. 'I think I broke the…'

'Holy fuck!'

Panic. There was a scream from the exterior courtyard. It cut hard and clear and piercing against the urgency of the bell. As Blasco rose from his seat he felt himself become disembodied, and when he heard himself shout 'Under the desks!' it emerged with an animal tone he didn't feel was his. But the students were already on their way, diving and crawling to the nearest wall. Sean had dropped his dictionary; it landed strewn and bent somewhere in the Ts. Akaash was lying flat on his stomach, his gaze twitching across the top of dirty carpet and scanning other students as they coiled and hunkered. Penelope had begun to cry. They could all smell smoke now, an acrid lick, and they could hear the next blast, something tearing and snapping, and the lockdown bell dragged: three on, blood soaking from Ms Baker's dress, one off.

Screaming outside.

'The fuck is going on?'

'The fuck is happening?'

'Brayden!'

'Be quiet!'

'Brayden! There's blood on his face.'

'Shut up. Shut the fuck up!'

Wendy was whimpering, holding her mouth; she was looking at Brayden as he looked back at her but registered nothing, his own mouth open, eyes distant, the side of his face pimpled with fragments of glass. And then all they could hear was the bell, and it was like silence.

NASiR

When drivers pulled up at the intersection, the act of coming to a stop had a tendency to dissolve their hypnosis. It was a big intersection, four lanes arriving from each direction, and so they had to be conscious of what they were going to do next, of which lane they were going to indicate into, and at almost all times of the day during the working week traffic banked up and sat in its own monoxide haze. As music from radio stations in neighbouring cars conflated, drivers with their windows down were suddenly aware of the existence of other people, and they did their best not to look left or right, avoiding the possibility of momentary eye contact. The phase of the lights was an interval in which to correct lipstick and adjust hair, or to fiddle with the dial and find a song that better suited the mood. Most did all this instinctively, but it was also a way to block out any genuine consideration of the environment, because at this particular intersection there was nothing heartening to look at: state houses with overgrown lawns that somehow expressed an objective aesthetic of depression; run down shops; a bakery with a partially obscured hygiene rating of D in its dirty front window; chipped footpaths next to berms that seemed poisoned and toxic. Better to keep one's mind on the immediate – the reality inside the car itself – and presently the journey would resume and one could slip back into daydreams of better things and prettier destinations.

Sometimes though, this was impossible. The soapy water hit the windscreen and sloshed over the wipers before the driver knew what had happened. 'No!' they said, waving their hands in a way that was identical to the motion one uses to shoo pigeons or pets. But it was too late, because the brush was already on the car, and when it flipped over and the squeegeed lines cleared the view to reveal a smiling black face – oil black – and big teeth glinting and eyes that seemed too red to be human, a deep fear overcame them. They sunk back into their seats, they desperately shuffled though their glove compartments for change that had already been dedicated to parking costs. Their hands shook embarrassingly as they fed it through the window and into the suede-coloured palm of their attacker.

'Yes, tankyou,' Nasir would say, nodding his head. And then the traffic would begin to move again, and he would be left in the middle of it all, blocking the potential for lane changes and feeling it rush around him, like tidal water pulling back into the sea.

In most respects it was a clean operation. Nasir had lifted the buckets and the brushes from service stations, and with the help of Odawaa and Tarabi, it was a moderately profitable enterprise, providing enough to keep them in tobacco and bakery food and the guttery extras their new professional lives seemed to require.

It hadn't been difficult to convince his cousins to stop going to school. They were bottoming out anyway, and without Nasir they were both at a loss. Neither of them had Nasir's sense of humour, and in lieu of this external coping mechanism, classes were a torment they were unwilling to deal with. So the three of them had gone into business, bettering themselves fifty cents at a time.

That's not to say there hadn't been some initial teething problems; when he ran out of the soapy liquid provided by Nasir, Odawaa didn't see anything wrong with refilling his squirt bottle from a puddle; the oleaginous grit he then splashed on windscreens tended to just make them dirtier. When he befouled the glass of a BMW, the owner took offence, got out and shouted, lifting his right arm into the posture of a well-practised punch. Odawaa was saved only by the light changing and cars further back in the traffic honking at the delay. Tarabi, too, needed coaching. He was frequently still washing when red flicked to green, his work left half done and unpaid for. 'You only have time for two per light,' Nasir said. 'You need to leave time for them to find money.' Tarabi listened and nodded. It was sensible advice. But then he did it again, and again, seemingly trying to break some kind of record for how many unpaid jobs he could do per phase.

It might have been the paint. A few times each week – always after the work, because, all else aside, he appeared to have a work ethic – Nasir took his cousins to the back of the park, over the fence from the adjacent Christian Science bookstore, and huffed spray-paint from a plastic bag. He didn't have any real reasons for it other than that it made him giggle, and although the psychological victory was a pyrrhic one (the thumping in his head, the auditory hallucinations, and the sense that his tongue had swollen to twice its size and lay bloated and dead in his mouth were not good things) it momentarily alleviated the feeling that the carriage had derailed. Most times they stayed in the park until sundown, Odawaa lying in the grass, his cousin vomiting, Nasir propped against a tree, and when they collectively regained the world under their feet – when the sea legs and the slurring were gone and only the violent headache remained – they walked home and slept. For Nasir, there was the quality of the anti-drug about it. Actively seeking to damage himself was a way to get well below zero. It made him feel so bad that just getting back to normal was like getting high. To wake red-eyed the following day was a blessing. Yes, his chest felt like it had been squashed and the taste of paint never really left, but he was alive and walking, so when he refilled his squirt bottle and scrubbed bird shit off a window for two silver coins, it didn't feel so much like the end. In fact, it felt good. And the suit was a nice touch. Purchased at an opportunity shop for ten dollars, his cousins saw it as a waste of money. 'You look stupid,' Odawaa said.

'I look stupid, sure,' Nasir replied, examining his pinstripes. 'But you *are* stupid. This is an investment. People will remember this. How many times have you seen a guy washing windows in a suit?'

'None,' Tarabi said. 'Men with suits don't wash windows. They work in offices.'

'Why am I trying to explain myself?'

Nasir moved out into the traffic and offered his brush to a slowing car, and even though the driver shook their head and tried to reject the advance, Nasir proceeded anyway, streaming his water bottle across the glass before the Mazda had even come to a stop and going to work like a consummate pro. When the window came down the woman behind the wheel blurted the inevitable: 'I don't have any money.'

But Nasir was smiling. 'No charge,' he said. 'Tell people about suit.' He pointed at his pants and the lights changed and he walked back to his cousins, weaving smoothly through fleeting gaps between accelerating vehicles.

'You didn't get any money,' Odawaa said.

'I've laid the foundation – that's advertising. She will tell her friends. Then everyone will come.'

Although it's hard to say whether it had anything to do with the suit, Nasir tended to make twice what his cousins did. At the end of the day, however, they would pool the money and split it evenly, and then, if the weather was right, or if Nasir's sense of self needed retooling, it was back to the park to fizz away brain cells and flirt with death. If Nasir had been asked how long it had been, he couldn't have said: days bled into each other, weeks overlapped with weeks, and it wasn't until Ali told him – 'I haven't seen you all term' – that he realised just how disengaged he'd become from his young cousin's life, as well as from his own.

'You're never home,' Ali said. 'And you don't respond on the internet.'

'I'm sorry.' Nasir was smoking on the steps of his house. Somewhere behind him his mother and father watched TV, their English and understanding too limited to truly realise what was happening to their son. 'How is school? Are you working hard?'

Ali had been. Following the incident that had led to Nasir's expulsion and Ali's subsequent fear-based alienation, there had been little else to do. His English was improving. ESOL without his cousins meant there was nothing to do but focus, and with any luck, Ali would be getting a certificate at the end of the year to recognise his hard work. There was even a suggestion he might be able to cope with mainstream. The real boon, however, had come in maths and physics. Free from the tyranny of grammar it seemed Ali had a talent for numbers. 'Yes, I do very good,' he said in English. 'Next year I get put in top maths class and sit with Chinese boys.'

'So he's becoming a scholar,' Nasir smirked, rejecting English. 'Soon you'll make money and women will want you. You're a winner, Ali. You're a winner.'

Ali could detect the sarcasm but was unsure how to handle it. 'I thought you wanted me to do well?'

'Everybody wants Ali to do well. And they want him to come over to their house and rub it in their faces.'

'Is that why you have been avoiding me?'

Nasir smoked his cigarette and looked down at his suit. There was silver spray paint on the cuffs of his trousers that he hadn't bothered to try to remove, presuming that any attempt would be futile anyway. He picked at it now with his fingers. 'Is that what you really want?'

'What?' Ali didn't understand.

'I don't want you coming around here anymore,' Nasir said. His eyes were bloodshot. In spite of the suit, he looked tired and aged – much rougher. His hair had grown into a wild three inch afro and Ali believed he could detect the beginnings of grey.

'But you're my cousin.'

'Ali, go away. Go back to school. I don't want to see you.'

At home Ali talked with his parents. Just like Nasir's, they were in the dark regarding what had gone on with Gavin, and Ali was reluctant to enlighten them. They knew as much as Ali did – that Nasir and Tarabi and Odawaa were washing windows, that they had dropped out. 'They are not cut out for school like you are,' his mother said. 'They arrived here too late, maybe.'

'Why can't someone help them get a real job?' Ali said, looking to his father.

'I was lucky to get one,' his dad said. 'Very lucky. With those boys, I don't know.' He was watching TV while they talked, his mind only half in the conversation. On the screen, a fat white woman was singing to an audience. 'I don't think she will get through to the second round,' his father said absently. 'To be successful, Ali, you have to be skinny. This is something I have learned.'

Ali turned to watch the judging process. His father was right – the fat woman was eliminated. Ali left the room to do his homework, refusing to log on to Facebook – this was something *he* had learned – and buried himself in Pythagoras. Triangles were easy and beautiful, their certainty a tranquil solace. He tried not to think of his cousins.

The following afternoon, Nasir worked it out for himself. His decision to avoid Ali had been an unconscious one to start with – a human reflex. People always talk about taking the noble course and doing the right thing, but they don't talk about how much you'll end up resenting the person you've helped in the aftermath. Yet it was more than that. Beneath him the grass of the park seemed lush and verdant. His vision was speckled with purple dots and he could hear snaps and rustles that he was almost certain were located entirely in his own mind. Odawaa had said something some time ago (Thirty seconds? An hour?) though he wasn't sure what, but even if he'd tried to speak – even if he'd wanted to ask, 'Hey, what?' – at best he could've produced a moaning slur. It was prone like this, settled like a rock in the soil, that he thought he'd figured it. He could hear Ali's slippery English ('Yes, I do very good') and he could see the naïve uniform, the shirt tucked in and the pants pulled high in a way that would never facilitate friends, and the whole thing clicked. He was doing the right thing, and it didn't matter that Ali didn't understand. The world was certainly a fine place. Automobiles move like the sea, and if you rub them the right way, money falls out. He tried to smile, but the muscles in his face did nothing.

MRS THURSTON

Although Mrs Thurston was a cooking teacher by trade, she liked to think she had a knack for photography. She kept her hobby from the Art Department, of course – in part out of fear of criticism, but also because, to her, art teachers seemed to treat the subject with more academic snootiness than good framing, good lighting and a button-push deserved. She did her family portraits each Christmas, and she photographed the particularly lavish culinary spreads of the Hospitality Department for posting on the school's website or – fingers crossed – for publication in the yearbook. But she also liked to photograph the strange. If she saw something intriguing, like a car accident or a pigeon missing a leg, she made every effort to get close and snap it up. These were the photos she printed out and put in her special binder, and they only came out again when she'd had too much to drink and really felt the need to impress (or impose upon) her guests after they'd eaten her food. It was because of this hobby that she always had a camera on or around her, and it had become instinct to pick it up and ship it to wherever she was going, regardless of whether it was the admin block or the toilet. One never knew when lightning would strike, after all, and so it was important to always have the bottle handy to catch it. This was also why, when she heard the screams coming from beyond the room – screams that were asynchronous with the warm light of a Saturday morning in the hospitality block, her students having come in specially to cater a meal for a sporting event – before anything else she moved left to the bench and put her camera in the large front pocket of her apron.

Naturally her students were out the door first. Mrs Thurston was a big woman, as is almost inevitable given her age of sixty and her virtually permanent contiguity to butter and cream, so she was behind her pupils when she turned the corner and found them gaping and unable to act. This was a new experience for most of them, a real-life moment of panic and terror. The abnormality of what they were witnessing had rendered them inert, momentarily jammed. One of their fellow students was being held up against the wall by her throat. She was threshing and kicking and scratching at her assailant, but he seemed impervious to the damage she was inflicting, a giant of a boy with big hands and a dark face set into what Mrs Thurston could only assess was a blind desire to destroy. The girl was at least a foot off the ground. She was screaming out the last of her oxygen, and as she did so her clawing turned to thumping as she attempted to bash her attacker in the ear. It didn't seem like either one of them was aware of the presence of an audience.

Mrs Thurston was the first to act, grabbing one of her paralytic students by the shoulder and turning them. 'Get your phone,' she said. 'Call the police. Do it now.' The kid stared at her. 'Do you understand?' The kid nodded. 'Go!' The cluster of gawkers vanished suddenly, racing back to the cooking room and leaving Thurston to turn her considerable attention to the matter at hand. 'Hey!' she yelled, but the aggressor did nothing. His face was transfixed on the girl, his expression twisted and static as he focused on the act of grinding his hands into her neck. 'Hey!' Thurston shouted again, moving forward now with the cumbersome resolution of a rhino, her girth closing the gap rapidly. She hadn't thought about what she might do if the boy refused to stop. Usually, given normal school routines, a verbal attack was all that was needed. But the boy wasn't really there – something in his mind had broken – and soon the cooking teacher found herself clamped onto the boy's arm (a boy who loomed like an office tower above her) and digging her fingernails into his skin and shouting, 'Let go! Let go now!' And then she pushed forward, ramming him and shaking him, her student's eyes now so large and afraid and animal that they looked as if they might split and burst, and with all her weight and this boy's extremely high centre of gravity – she could smell him now, and she could smell the salt of tears – he toppled sideways, never letting go of the girl, and then all three landed with an ugly thump on the concrete.

It was the sting of the ground that finally broke the boy's psychosis, and panic began to set in as he registered the crushing weight of the cooking teacher on top of him. With Mina, her student, now gasping fresh air, Mrs Thurston began the difficult task of extricating herself from the tangle of the boy's long bony frame. She pushed down on his chest for support, leaning her mass into his and shifting her feet, but the movement was hampered when the boy began to writhe and kick, his dress shoes flailing beneath his short pants as he tried to ruck her off, and as he pulled out from under her Mrs Thurston lost her support and crashed down again, this time clean on the concrete and on her wrist, causing what would later be diagnosed as a fracture to the radius. She let out a brief and rather hoarse grunt, but the adrenaline of her anger helped to stifle the pain. With the boy now up and scampering, his shoes clicking in a bizarre and arrhythmic tap, Mrs Thurston found her footing quicker than she ever would again and began her pursuit, a juggernaut of home economics in a red apron.

It wasn't a long chase, but it ended in a way no one could have predicted. The outdoor thoroughfare in which the boy had chosen to strangle his ex-girlfriend was only a thoroughfare during school hours, when the doors to the Technology Department were open and students could move through and down the stairs and out to the front of the school. On Saturdays, this door was closed and locked, meaning the only way forward was to scale the metal balustrade and chance the one-and-a-half floor drop to the grass below. Unless of course you felt you could reach the tree, but that involved leaping the two-metre gap and clinging to a spiky infirm branch, after which you had to make the climb down. Students had considered this before, standing above the railing at lunchtime and measuring the distance and contemplating what an impact with the branch would actually feel like ('Nah, fuck that – you'd get scratched to shit') but no one had, to this point, either the stones or the incentive to try. However, now there was Mrs Thurston's bulk to contend with, a wide short woman whose wrath seemed to expand into the brick walls on either side of her and cut out all notion of escape, and so the boy in his dress pants and shirt and his soapy dress shoes jumbled his limbs up onto the balustrade and without, it seemed, any real forethought as to the consequences of his actions or any understanding of his own physical limitations, he made the desperate leap.

From Mrs Thurston's point of view, it was like watching an oversized rat in smart-casual attire attempt and then fail to take flight, the boy's body extending its wingspan in the hope of finding the branch before missing it completely. From her vantage, she couldn't see what happened next. She heard a crack and an almost canine yelp, and then nothing. When she finally made it to the railing, she looked over – her wrist now starting to throb – and found the boy suspended and dangling by his shirt, his arms waving uselessly as if he were trying to swim. He'd made it half way to the ground before his ballooning clothing had hooked on a branch, and in many respects he was very lucky that the vertically angled tree limb had caught his clothing rather than his neck.

With her teacher's key Mrs Thurston unlocked the Technology Department and descended the inner stairs, and inside a minute she was standing beneath this huge boy, looking back up at him through the latticed shade of the trees, and he was looking back down. He was breathing heavily. His eyes seemed to look past her. And it was then that she remembered the camera in the pocket of her apron and pulled it out and looked up and established the frame – this boy staring back down at her, right into the lens, his legs caught in the foreground, his arms shorted and useless, blue sky and dappled leaves above it all. She clicked.

The sound of the camera seemed to bring the boy

back. All at once the primal chaos disappeared from his features and he looked lost, unable to comprehend how he'd come to be trapped, incapable of processing the immediacy of the situation. 'I'm sorry,' he said. 'Could you please help me down?'

Mrs Thurston lowered the camera. 'I can't do that,' she said. 'I think it's probably better if you stay where you are.'

'Please.'

'No. I can't. I'm sorry. You're just going to have to wait for the police.' She turned to gather her bearings. She couldn't hear any sirens yet; she wondered how long it would be and whether her students had actually managed to dial the number. She deliberated about Mina, who she'd left coiled and struggling to breathe. She knew she should go back and find her and comfort her, but could she really leave the prisoner, the dangling lunatic in the tree above her? Her wrist was really beginning to hurt now...The sudden tearing sound – like paper being ripped – drew her back, and down came the boy, collapsing onto the grass behind her. He scrambled to his feet and lurched, shirtless and with noticeable blood sheeting on his back, and for a moment she thought he was going to hit her. But then his eyes darted and he was gone, running fast and wild into the bowels of the suburbs, his urgency synonymous with the distant approach of wailing sirens. She looked back at her camera and studied the image. She wondered, through the slipstream of shock, whether a moment like this was really suitable for her special binder.

STELLA

Stella had never wanted to be in school as much as she did that Monday afternoon. Mr Gleeson, being well aware of Stella's penchant for the counsellor's office, and having read the Gershwitz emails regarding the need for understanding and care, simply acknowledged her late arrival with a nod before continuing his lecture on the My Lai massacres. 'Some of you will find this subject disturbing,' he said. But Stella could find nothing disturbing: not here, where students' bags, packed with books and lunches, slumped next to the legs of plastic chairs; where a Shelley quote was stapled to the wall beside her: 'History is a cyclic poem written by time upon the memories of man.' The words meant nothing to her, but they made her sleepy. They were kind and intelligent and they let her rest, unjangling her nerves and cooling the tremor of her hands. The desk beneath her, complete with juvenile graffiti and flipside gum, emanated warm nostalgic safety. Everything overwhelmed her. As Mr Gleeson went on in his unthreatening paternal voice,

Stella's world began to pull in, sheering itself off from anything outside the immediate. No more lime curtains; no more barking dogs. No more web-cams or tattoos or chemically-driven riptides of unbroken consciousness.

Anthony Kirsten.

She'd made fun of him once for having a girl's last name.

He kept guns in his house – he really liked them. He showed them to her once. 'It's about what you can do with them,' he said.

What, like kill people?

'Modifications. The great thing is you can get all the different parts online, you know. So while the gun is technically illegal, all the parts by themselves are not. Then it's just *some assembly required*.'

You're a clever guy.

She smoked when she was around him, because he did and she didn't have to pay, and after a while she felt hollow and could smoke all night without it worrying her; except at around sun-up, when she coughed like she was dying and brought up grey phlegm that looked a little like bits of dead slug in the white basin of his bathroom. But after the expulsion, she always felt like smoking more, like she could keep going. 'You ready for another round?' he'd ask, not talking about cigarettes. He was lying on his bed and looking at the ceiling, his shirt off. His tattooed sleeves made it seem like he was never really naked.

Of course I am; you know I am. But you really need to do something about that ceiling. Do you even know what asbestos is?

'It's fine as long as you don't touch it,' he said. 'Here.'

And she didn't have to pay. That was for guests – frequenters of the property that aroused the barking ire of the Rottweilers; they paid. Damp cash and chit chats. At first he'd told her to stay in the other room. She'd listened through the crack in the door to hard-core colloquialisms and jokes where the punch line was anal rape. From the bedroom she watched them come and go, never talking of Michelangelo. 'Customers,' he said.

But can't you be better than talking like that? – it's pretty fucking offensive.

'That's what I like about you,' he said. 'You want to make me a better person.'

I don't know if that's the reason. But it's all the same: the Earth circumnavigates the sun and that's a year.

And then she was counting the money, and he didn't seem to mind that the guests met her and talked to her, that she was there throughout the whole thing. 'You should take your hoodie off when you're inside,' she told one of them.

'What's the deal with her?'

'Do as she says,' replied Tony. 'She's got manners. Manners are important.'

She'd been in the car with him, speeding along the motorway, when someone up ahead had changed lanes without indicating. 'Fuckers!' he'd snapped, and accelerated, and Stella had gripped the side of the door as Tony pulled up alongside the other vehicle and opened his window and shouted across the wind tunnel of a hundred and ten kmph, his inked right fist waving threats at a total stranger.

I thought you could control your temper; what happened to all that shit about meditation?

'Some people need to learn. They need to know how it is.'

He still hadn't told her about the origin of the scar.

And she hadn't told her mother about him. Why would she? What would she say? And the lies were more fun; they exercised her brain.

'I'd like more time with you,' he said.

Oh yeah?

'You think you could organise that?'

She'd organised everything else. She'd even told her mother about getting a job through Jenny at school.

'Do I know Jenny?' Her mother had asked, careful as always not to intrude on her daughter's independence.

'No. She's in my history class. Her dad organises outreach tutoring. It's all under the table, but it's a good cause, you know – I teach kids English for a few hours after school each day, and then I get paid. It's great.'

'Okay.'

'And don't forget – next Friday I've got my history trip: we leave from school. I'll be away till next week.'

'It seems like a strange time of the year to have trips on.'

'It's for assessment.'

'Okay – Love you, Stelly.'

'I'm not good with words,' said Tony. His shirt was off again. His pectorals flattened as he stretched on his back and the bed springs spoke and Stella found herself on her knees, salinity and meat in her mouth. 'But it's pretty easy to fall in love with you.'

It's weird; on this drug, bad smells good. And love's a tricky word.

'A man has to go a long way to find a girl like you.'

Girl.

Anthony Kirsten was thirty-six and sold meth for a living and was divorced and had a son whom he didn't see. Anthony Kirsten had two Rottweilers that he hadn't named except to call them 'One' and 'Two', and he had a network of tattoos, one of which he'd given himself when he was twenty-three and unable to make bail for a fairly serious assault charge. He'd told Stella about it: the guy deserved it. It was over a woman and sort of over drugs, but it was hard to explain, even in retrospect. 'That's why I got into martial arts,' he said. 'It's about discipline and control.'

So you say.

Anthony Kirsten was thirty-six and calling a seventeen-year-old his girlfriend. And when one of his guests commented, while they were all chatting in the kitchen, that she seemed awfully young, Anthony Kirsten said Stella was twenty-one. The guest looked at Stella who looked at Tony who looked at the guest, and then the guest said, 'Shit, she still looks like a baby,' and then Tony hit him in the face with the heel of his hand. At the time Stella was high and felt the wrong thing: she liked it – she liked the blood pooling into this guy's teeth and his begging for forgiveness and then his desperate pleading to still be allowed as a customer, and she almost loved Tony's response (almost) which was to apologise and say, 'You can't let personal stuff cloud business, yeah,' and then he gave the guy his drugs and sent him on his way.

You're pretty cool for a guy who smells like shit.

Anthony Kirsten was in love.

Anthony Kirsten's brain was wired badly.

Anthony Kirsten's first wife had a restraining order against him and had filed for divorce with bruises still on her face and back.

He wasn't all bad: he tried to control himself; he used martial arts as a way to channel his aggression and he'd gone to courses that taught restraint and deep breathing.

And love helped. He bought Stella things. First it was a necklace; expensive and ugly, she wore it only around him. It wasn't her style, but it was the thought. Then it was a dress. It covered only the essential parts and left her feeling naked, and she could never wear it out, but again it was the... Then it was underwear – black and pink and lace, he got her to model it for him, strung-out and dancing in his derelict bedroom, her skin tinted cosmic green with the glow from the curtains (what time is it?) and he suggested he film her because it would be criminal not to, given how good she looked; and she could tell she looked good, because his erection had cut right through the meth and stood with the lubricity of a stripper's pole in the middle of the room, and so she danced for him as he filmed, pirouetting around it like a totem. And then they did more – snorting, then smoking – a chill across her stippled flesh as the camera lay like a stranger on the bed and recorded and bounced as she did what she was asked – did what she was told – and she never had to pay.

And yes the come-downs were a nightmare: real ones filled with hate sweat and fizzing. But they didn't last, and her mother brought her soup, and she could repress what she needed to if she just squeezed her face into the pillow hard enough. Because the sun always came out again, and one day wound into the next, and she always always always knew she could get more – that all she'd have to do was show up and play: and it wasn't that hard, when she came to consider it all, when she really owned up and faced it, to say I love you – to feed him what he needed. She just had to pretend she was saying it to the drug, that Anthony Kirsten, as nice as he was, with his violence and his stench and his history of arrest, was the drug, because he might as well have been.

'Everything's all the same,' she told him.

'Why are you always saying that?' He was feeding his dogs raw meat and she was in her school uniform, standing in his overgrown garden and hugging herself, waiting for what she wanted. She'd noticed that he liked to make her wait, and while it wasn't in a way that seemed blatant or calculated, she suspected it was nonetheless. There were always small things to do first, pointless domestic errands that he finished at an interminably slow pace.

'Because it's better for you if that's the truth.'

'I don't understand,' he said. But he understood that if he got her high enough, it wouldn't matter.

Bad things taste good when you're like this.

How did she get here? That was easy: she'd made choices. Maybe it was more important to ask why? Why had she come back after the first time, because at that point it wasn't for the drugs. At least, not completely. And it wasn't for this guy's charm or his smell or his choice of décor.

It was the grown up thing to do, she thought. She was naked, her legs open, playing with herself the way women did in porn – porn Tony had directed her to watch as a kind of study guide. 'You gotta moan,' he said. He had the camera trained on her. 'Talk dirty. Believe it.' She did: it was the adult thing to do. Adults make choices. They do things.

They do things.

Stella fucking does things – she's a grown up.

And then it was the drugs and only the drugs. And who gives a fuck about swan plants anyway.

'Now turn around and show me the tattoo,' he said. 'Stay bent right over.'

DANNY

'Blood is kind of like a valve,' he said.

'How do you mean?' Verna swivelled her chair. She crossed her leg and then uncrossed it. She found it difficult to get comfortable. She had trouble following the answers…

…It would've been a struggle to explain things to his parents, so he didn't. He just said he was angry, and that was that. They prodded, of course, and his mother hugged him, and he hugged her back and told her not to worry. 'But I do, Danny. I do.'

'It's okay,' he said. And the nurse in the emergency room removed bits of glass from his knuckles, and his mother was weeping. 'You really don't have to worry. I'm just angry.'

'About what?'

'Sometimes it gets to me, I guess. Like, it invades.' The nurse began the stiches. She was listening but said nothing. Later on – after everything – she would tell her colleagues about this kid, confabulating her perception of him into something weird and sinister. She would even suggest that there was something off about the shadow he cast on the wall, that it was somehow misshapen. 'I'm sorry for making you upset.'

'You're a good boy,' his mother said.

'It'll pass. I'll be fine. It's just growing up, you know.'

There in the emergency room, having been dragged from her evening shift because her son had cut himself and bled all over his English exam, Danny's mother hugged him again, worried about him, loved him. That weekend, his father bought him another camera, a treat to make him happy. He hadn't done anything wrong, after all. And the best way to make anyone happy, according to the codes and conventions of modern culture, is to buy them something, to purchase peace of mind. Danny hugged his father and accepted the gift as he sat in his room, at his desk, at his computer. 'I love you, Dad,' he said.

'I love you too, son,' he replied, jerking a little at the forward rush of sentiment. 'How's the hand? Feeling better?'

'It's fine.' He held up the bandage and rolled his wrist in the light of his desk lamp.

'Have you thought about getting some sun in here? Your mother's convinced your episode was caused by a lack of sun.'

'You know I don't need any light but the light of Jesus.' He smiled to tell his dad it was a joke. Danny had become more certain than ever that the two of them operated in different realities, and that complexity only made his father nervous. It wasn't his father's fault, of course – that's just how things are when the world changes completely each decade.

'Do it for her, yeah – pull the curtains back and let the world in a little. You spend too long at the computer and you'll get clouded. Storm clouds gather, if you know what I mean.'

'Yes, father,' Danny said. 'It's a metaphor – and a fine one at that. I shall heed your advice. And thank you for the camera.'

'It's top of the line – the smallest one they have.' Danny picked up the box and started opening it. 'It's waterproof to a depth of five metres, apparently; and it's light – probably light enough to tape onto the little helicopter you have. Imagine the shots you could get.' His dad seemed eager to have the gift appreciated, to have his level of care acknowledged and reaffirmed.

'It's really thoughtful.' Danny had the camera out now – a tiny black box dwarfed by the palm of his hand, a plate-like wide-lens swallowing its face. The lens stared back up. It was never going to blink. This would see things clearly – vision with enough alacrity to meet the x-axis.

'It shoots in super *super* HD or something.'

'It shoots…' Danny held it between the thumb and forefinger of his good hand and examined it. His dad had backed away into the doorframe, his parental silhouette looming in the light of the hallway.

'You're a smart kid, Danny. Sometimes I forget how smart. And you're getting smarter every day…' Danny looked up at his dad. 'So just take care of yourself.'

In the bathtub Danny lay prostrate and submerged, his eyes open beneath the water, his hair waving gently in the currents generated by his body. He didn't blink. He looked into the eye of the camera, which was taped firmly to the side of the tub, and the camera looked back, unwavering and stoic. He could hear nothing save his heart thudding in his shallow chest. The bath's surface was pale tan. He stayed floating there, not breathing, not moving, for a full three minutes – three minutes until the tan had become a murky darkness and his face stung and his mind had begun to leak away and his nose had started to bleed, a scarlet ribbon escaping and ascending, dispersing. He took a lungful of water and broke the surface.

The violence of his coughing ripped open holes in the universe, horrendous and guttural, the evangelical hack of late-stage emphysema. It vibrated the room and tore a fissure in his diaphragm. He thrashed and gasped and retched the water from his insides. He heaved. The floor beyond the tub fried with the turbulence as he bent up and screamed from his burning throat – screamed for no other reason than to do it – and then laughed, because he was free, the dark smear in his vision clearing into the torpor of real life.

The video was titled *Drowned* – a three-minute segment where nothing moved except the strands of his hair. There was no sound to accompany it. It came with no description.

'How are you feeling, Danny?' The Dean was just checking up. It was a courtesy call more than anything, an appointment designed to be positive and empathetic, but Danny's prior conditioning to the office meant he couldn't shake the feeling that the meeting was disciplinary in nature. He shrugged, unsure whether he wanted to do more. 'You gave everyone quite a scare.' The Dean paused and smiled. He wanted to make the room feel inclusive, but today the presence of files and wall planners and a utilitarian gun stapler somehow prevented it. 'Is there anything you want to talk about?'

'No, not particularly.'

'How's the film work coming? You found a suitable narrative arc yet? Summer's coming up again. It might give you some space to really do something interesting.' On top of the cabinet behind the Dean, the SG105 was gathering dust.

'I'm pretty sceptical about narrative arcs,' Danny said. 'I don't think they do any justice to real life.'

'Oh yeah?' The Dean leaned back in his seat and crossed his right leg over his left. He was evidently intrigued by the statement. 'How so?' He opened his palms briefly, inviting Danny to continue.

'They're constructed to create a neat emotional journey that rarely happens in reality, which makes them false.'

'They might be *constructed*, but they're meant to mirror the kind of struggles people go through. You know, guy bumbling along, a thing happens, he wrestles with it' – the Dean hooked his index fingers together and began pulling them against one another – 'and it either kills him or he beats it.' His fingers released and his palms returned to supplication. 'That happens in life, right?' Danny slumped in his seat and let out what might have been a sigh but could well have been a yawn. '…Right?'

'I don't want to offend you,' Danny said.

'What? No, by all means, go right ahead.'

Danny pulled himself from his slouch to a more formal posture. 'You see it happening because you've been trained to see it happen. Your whole life you've been fed these bullshitty little beginnings, middles and ends where actors who vaguely resemble humans go on a journey – emotional, physical or spiritual – and then learn something about themselves or fall in love or kick the bully in the face, and because you've been so fed on this construct, you look for it in your own life in the hope of giving it some shape and significance. But it doesn't. It doesn't have any.'

'What, my life specifically?' The Dean hadn't wanted to take it personally, but he found it difficult to ignore Danny's choice of pronoun.

'Yours and everyone else's. Narrative is something people throw on after the action to try and make sense of things. It's artificial. Real life, as it's happening, is just a string of tedious experiences with no meaning. If you're lucky, someone might hug you along the way, but more often than not it's boring or awful.'

'Maybe that's why we need uplifting narratives,' said the Dean. He was looking for an avenue to bring back some optimism. 'Even if they are *constructed*, as you say, maybe we need that in order to release some of the things that bother us; we need a universally consumable story so we can all identify and aspire to be something more, or to see ourselves reflected.'

Danny laughed, but it was without the necessary warmth that signals genuine humour. 'So we all need machine-made emotional drivel to fight off the emptiness? We all need to buy in to the same tired shit in order to get up in the morning? And even if you ignore that, you're basically saying that our individual experience – our unique *snowflake* existence,' he sputtered the phrase, 'is actually exactly the same as everyone else's and isn't individual at all, because we're all susceptible to the same shitty lies.'

'Snowflakes might be unique,' the Dean said, 'but they're all still snowflakes – they have that in common.'

'What a gay thing to say.'

The Dean was too engaged to react. The appropriate

244

response would have been to stop and reprimand Danny and remind him who he was talking to, but instead he fought back like this student was a peer, like he was in a bar and someone had challenged his worldview. And so this came out instead: 'You said it first!' At which point Danny stooped to the newly established level and poked out his tongue and blew hard. Wet ersatz flatulence flecked in the Dean's general direction. 'Well we *do* have that in common,' the Dean rallied, refusing to be dominated and ignoring the spittle alighting on his desk. 'The analogy holds. And it doesn't matter if it's snowflakes! It could be grains of sand! No two are alike, right?'

'Look, fuck, I don't know.' Danny was rubbing his thighs and looking at the exit. 'But you're just reinforcing my point. We're all insignificant, inanimate and soulless and the only big thing that's ever going to happen – if you wanna continue with your *sand* thing – will be the tide washing over us, and good or bad there's nothing we can do about it. And I don't want to hear a story about one magical grain that finished up in a bottle and then became part of a Zen garden before being shifted to a golf course.'

'That's actually quite a good stor—'

'No it's not. It's stupid and it's irrelevant.'

'Okay then.' The Dean uncrossed his leg and moved his arms onto his desk, his elbows resting on a pile of reports. 'What's a better story?'

Danny's neck was now unashamedly craned toward the freedom of the door. He started speaking without even looking at the Dean. 'There is no *better* story, there's only a *real* story – a true representation of human life. It starts before you're born and it never really ends, even when you're dead. There are peaks and valleys in the short term, but overall it's just lumpy entropy.'

'Entropy?'

'Winners and losers are a matter for retrospective analysis and don't mean shit.'

'Is there conflict? There's still conflict right?'

'Sure there is. It's unavoidable. But it means as much as anything else.'

Beyond the door, off in the corridor, a student sat waiting for a uniform pass and school receptionists moved in flickers. 'I have to admit, Danny. Danny, look at me.'

'Yes?'

'I have to admit that you're sounding awfully fatalistic – do you know what that means?'

'I've been expanding my vocabulary.'

'I can tell – *entropy?* – Well it sounds to me like you need to acknowledge that you're the master of your own life. You can make things happen if you want them to.' The Dean now used the heel of his right hand as a gavel, emphasising what he believed was the crucial and final point: 'If you want your own narrative to be a worthwhile one, then you have to take charge and do something about it.'

'Don't worry,' Danny replied. 'The planning's already underway.'

HENRY

In the oily darkness party voices merged with music and Henry felt like a log of wood, soaked and bobbing in sea water. He was hot, but there was nothing he could do about it. His head was hanging in his lap and his forearms were rested on his knees. He was sitting on a collapsible chair, staring at his own feet, trying to remain as still as possible in order to counteract the need to throw up. Whose house was this? His shoes were covered in mud. He was sitting in a garden, on what used to be a lawn; between the rain and the trampling surge of guests, it had been all but destroyed. He could feel the rain on his neck. No one else seemed to mind. He heard voices, partial sentences, naked fragments and divorced sub-clauses, laugher without apparent reason: 'Nah nah, man, whatever.' Rain caressing the bush beyond him –

subtropical rain, a hose turned to mist. 'What's wrong with this guy?' Henry remembered walking up a darkened driveway and the yellow light inside a garage; people in black t-shirts fighting over songs. Leila had been there, maybe. Maybe she'd been dancing in a blue dress with floral patterns. Had he seen Ben? Had he smoked a joint in the jags of porch light but never made it to the porch itself? Faces in shadow – expressions hidden. He'd felt himself splinter into bits: part of him was on the trampled lawn, part of him was on the driveway, another part still was standing in a circle taking nuclear drags and coughing and then looking directly into the porch bulb. How long had he stared at it? Long enough to burn solar eclipses into both eyes.

The mud under foot was soapy, his feet sliding with the pressure of his forearms. He felt his stomach shift. An image of calving ice sheets lurched somewhere in his mind; 'Green fever,' someone said. He shut his eyes. More laugher. What was that song? It seemed like something he should know, a song he would normally like, but now its subwoofered bass had found a frequency that his intestines disagreed with. 'You know, if you can get the hertz low enough, you can make someone puke.' Was that here and now or somewhere else? His shoes were making him sick. He shut his eyes, but the feeling of ocean-liner turbulence only multiplied. He was in a single cabin well below deck with no windows, the storm growing. He was atop his desk in the classroom, rolling it forward with his weight.

'Henry!'

His face was hot against the light of the sun; drool on his refill, smearing the pre-ruled lines into turquoise watermarks.

'Henry!'

He was awake. Mrs Vanderbilt was waiting for his attention.

'We can't have this, Henry.'

Everyone in the classroom was looking at him, except Leila, who'd chosen, it appeared, to snub him. 'I'm sorry,' he said. 'I'm finding it hard to focus.'

'I can see that. Would you like to take a moment to get some water and freshen up?'

'I don't know.' It was all he could think to say. His legs felt trapped in iron, welded into the floor beneath his desk, the atmosphere of the class thick and musty. He was having trouble breathing. He looked momentarily at the portrait of Napoleon on the wall of the classroom; the dead emperor appeared to be staring right back at him.

'Well maybe you would prefer to spend the rest of the period in the Dean's corridor?'

'Where's that music coming from?' he asked. It sounded muffled, as if emanating from beyond the room.

'Maybe you just need a good puke,' Ben said, polishing his glasses.

'It's hot in here.'

'You're outside, man. Just have a puke.'

The word triggered something – its meaning connecting with nerve endings in his gut. He leaned forward, his arms slipping off his knees, his feet sliding violently in the mud and darkness. He felt his head meet the gentle floret cluster of a hydrangea, and then the warm violence of his own vomit splashing against the top of his hands. The expulsion felt good. So good that the voices didn't matter: 'Fuckin' sick'; 'Jesus bro, check that shit out': and he went again, forcing red wine and curdled marijuana smoke and his parents' whisky into the bushes. It was like popping his ears, like coming up for air, and then the world had clarity again, a shape to handle, and immediately things began to matter – like the spittle on his cheeks and the taste of death in his mouth and the sticky film of stomach acid and pinot noir that he wore like bridal gloves on each arm. 'Feel better?' someone asked.

'Yeah.' But he was talking into the darkness, into the dense black bush that hemmed in the property. 'Whose party is this?' he asked.

'Whaddya mean?'

'Like, whose house is this?' Henry blinked hard. The scorched circumference of the porch light refused to leave his pupils.

'Does it matter?'

The music was getting louder. Henry turned to face the illuminated world of people, but across the garden he could see only yellow and black – the outdoor lights of the house pouring at him and outlining the moving, perspiring bodies. Smoke fanned through channels; he could smell watery beer and wet earth and sweat and rain, and he could smell himself. He held his arms up in front of him in the pose of an old-movie mummy and a girl with a face he couldn't see moved drastically backward, avoiding his reach as she passed. Then he realised: he couldn't see her because of the angle of the light, which conversely meant that she could see him – all of him: the urine on his jeans and the crud on his face and his burnt-out eyes. They could *all see him*, a plague victim approaching terminus, bleeding from his sockets and circling for a spot to die. He turned and rediscovered the seat and sank back in. The dizziness surged. He touched his wet hair with his hand. He closed his eyes hard and tried to fight, but it was coming all over again, gushing in, and once more he found himself locked into the windowless cabin, the ocean swelling and roiling somewhere beyond the walls.

'Oh Jesus!' Leila's voice. She said it with disgust, physically picking up her desk and moving it to the right.

'Holy shit!' Jason's voice, but it was mixed with others – the whole class was joining in.

'Can you smell that? He's drunk, Mrs V. He's totally drunk!'

Although he could see the vomit on his hands and on his desk, the chunks of food and the red wine – which he didn't even remember drinking – Henry was having a hard time comprehending it, or feeling it, or doing anything about it. He felt as if he'd been sealed in a coffin-sized Tupperware container and submerged in a swimming pool. To knock his hands against the plastic did nothing – reality was a long way up and beyond, unreachable, a murky impressionistic blur of burbling sounds and shifting colours. Something was happening though – he could sense movement that centred around his existence, but he could do little about it. Mrs Vanderbilt was looking him in the eye. She may even have been touching his face and snapping her fingers, but it did nothing: Henry was cocooned.

Henry was on his back and staring at the sun.

Blue sky and sun. Except, he'd looked at it for so long now that it was no longer blue. The colours had dried and become grey. A seagull flew overhead. He could hear the ringing of a bell – three on, one off – and he could hear voices – prepubescent – 'What's he doing…? Hey, what are you doing?' The dizziness had become fatigue; he felt he should answer, but words were soup.

'Are you alright?' A girl's voice. Rain on the back of his neck. Darkness and his shoes.

'I'm fine.' When he lifted his head, blood seemed to

shift and wobble; his skull had all the fine tuning of a blimp filled with fluid.

'No you're not. Let me help you.' Even through the grease of his perception, his slippery quaver, he could tell it was Leila – he could see the floral patterns of her dress and hear the maternal cadence. He was in love with her.

'I'm covered in shit – I wouldn't touch me if I were you.'

'I have a towel. Here.' She handed it to him through the darkness. Life was audible again; sounds had become separated and manageable. He could hear full lines of conversation from behind him and laugher following punch lines; he could make out the treble in the song playing in the garage, and when he pulled his body up, he could see the mess he'd made of his arms and hands. 'Don't worry about getting it dirty,' she said.

'Thank you.' The clean cotton felt safe in his fingers and smelled of memory. He dried his hair and his face and then each arm by turn, the odour of sick coming away with it.

'You should take better care of yourself,' she said.

'I know. I don't know how this happened.'

'Nobody knows how anything happens.' She took the towel from him and tossed it into the darkness behind the hydrangeas he had been resting against. 'Let me help you up,' she said softly, and then took him by the forearms, ignoring the remnant gummy coating on his skin. Henry lifted himself to his feet and turned to face the party. Constellations of talking heads, the porch light, bodies dancing in the garage. He felt better. He could manage this. 'Now follow me' – the voice in his right ear, Leila taking him by the hand and leading him through the people. He saw the rainwater glisten in her ponytail, blinking at him as it moved with the rhythm of her steps. His feet slipped against the muddy lawn, but he held on and followed, and soon she was leading him into the garage and taking him to a couch behind the stereo, and he could see the faces of people he knew – people from class – and they were all smiling. They were having a good time. The sheepshank in his viscera began to unravel. He settled into the couch. It was old and legitimately brown and smelled of cheap felt and cigarettes, and its springs were going, and the material on its arms had worn away or torn – but it was soft, and across from him, on a stool, close enough to touch, Leila Grey was smiling at him and smoking a cigarette. The smoke unfurled around her face and mingled with a bulb hanging from the ceiling.

'Thanks,' he said.

'It's no problem.'

'I didn't know you smoked?'

'I don't.' She took a drag and blew the smoke upward in a hard stream. 'You do.'

'What?' She smiled at him and tapped ash on the concrete floor at her feet. 'It's nice in here,' he said. 'I thought I was fucked.'

'You are,' she replied.

'Whose house is this? I don't even know where I am?'

Leila crossed her legs discreetly and looked beyond him. 'The questions are always the same, and in the end it doesn't really matter.'

'Whaddya mean?'

'Well, it's all the same if you think about it. So let's say it's your house.'

'My house?' Henry felt his face grow warm.

'Yeah, it's your house. Why not?'

Water was beginning to pool at Henry's feet and curl

around the heel of Leila's left sandal. He turned and looked at the dancers behind him; they were still smiling, although water – dirty brown and salty and filtered through mud and sewage – was streaming around their ankles, too. Henry instinctively lifted his feet up onto the couch. Leila did nothing. She smiled, tossed her cigarette into the growing stream of foamy sea water and lit another one from the table beside her. 'Hey, Leila,' he said. 'Where's all this water coming from?'

'I'm not Leila.' She puffed gently, then tried apathetically to blow a smoke ring.

'What?' The water was surging in now and the couch was threatening to float. When he blinked, he saw that the sun had been burned into his retina.

'Don't fight it, Henry. There's nothing you can do.'

MiNA & AHMED

Ahmed woke again during his mug shot. That is to say, he started thinking again. Before the psychogenic blackout smudged his memory, the last thing he truly remembered was staring at Mina's phone and the tumescence of a dense and suffocating hostility. And then nothing.

Coming back into the real world was like driving out of fog. The lights came up and he was looking at a police officer who was looking at a camera and asking him to turn sideways, which Ahmed did automatically, and then he found himself looking at an open door that seemed to lead through to cells of some description. 'You certainly are a tall one. You play basketball?' Ahmed turned to answer the question. 'Keep your head sideways,' the voice said. Ahmed turned back.

'Where am I?' he asked. Someone was moving in the corridor beyond the door.

'You serious?'

'Where's my shirt?'

'Good question. I just take the photos though, mate. Can ya stay still?' Ahmed did as he was told. 'Okay, that about does it.' He looked down at his hands; there were purple rings on his wrists and black ink on his fingers. His back stung. 'Follow me, yeah,' the officer said, so Ahmed did, looking at the squared-off shave line at the nape of the officer's neck. It appeared he'd recently had a haircut.

The two went through the door that Ahmed had been staring into. He was directed to a window made from hard plastic security glass. At its base, near waist height, there was a small slot above a stainless steel countertop. On the other side of the window another policeman sat filing papers, and behind him Ahmed could see other policemen walking back and forward through corridors, chatting with each other. One was holding a coffee and talking breezily about the weekend. 'Going fishing tomorrow,' he said.

'Oh yeah?'

'Okay, let's see what we've got.' It was the officer directly behind the glass. Ahmed couldn't take in the details of his face; they seemed neutered somehow. 'Now I'm going to ask you a few questions and I need you to answer them to the best of your ability, and then I'm going to need you to read this form and sign it.' Ahmed found himself nodding.

'Why am I here?'

'Read the sheet, pal.' The officer slipped the page under the glass. Ahmed tweaked the angle of his head to study the paper. He was reluctant to touch it. The steel countertop scattered the fluorescent lighting and for the first time Ahmed noticed how bright the room was – white walls, white floor. Even the paper was hard to stomach, glaring back at him like an Algerian summer. He tried to read the black type, but the words were small and disconnected, and he wasn't sure which part he was meant to look at. While this was happening the officer had been asking him questions, and to his surprise he'd been answering them, although it didn't feel like his voice, and the officer in the background with the coffee was slurping noisily from the mug – a mug with a New Zealand flag print wrapped around its exterior – and staring at Ahmed, staring right at him. 'Hey!' said the officer with the question sheet. Ahmed looked back. 'I'll repeat the question: have you ever intentionally tried to harm yourself and/or attempted to commit suicide?'

'Hasn't everyone?'

'I'm going to put down a *yes*, then.' The tone was perfunctory. 'Sign at the bottom please.' A ballpoint pen attached to a sturdy chain was slipped through the gap, and Ahmed suddenly found himself signing 'Fuck You' in italics – instinct rather than malice – and then he was taken farther down the corridor and a white door was opened and in he went, a small white room with a long green bench and a toilet and a camera in the top corner, embedded and out of reach.

'Can I have my shirt back?' he asked before the door was closed.

'You didn't come in with one,' the officer said.

And then Ahmed was alone.

Mina, on the other hand, had never had more attention.

In the immediate aftermath of the attack, while her deranged ex-boyfriend was running shirtless and bloody around the neighbourhood, eventually pursued and apprehended with the help of a dog squad, a helicopter, and the assistance of roadside witnesses who had little difficulty identifying the lanky suspect, Mina was propped up against the brick wall where she'd been left. She was crying. She was being hugged and given water. Within an hour she was taken to the hospital with her parents by her side and checked out by a doctor with a gentle bedside manner. She had contusions where Ahmed's hands had been, deepening purple lines that clearly indicated which finger had been where and how determined they'd been to stay. Her father's irate voice was barely dampened by the division of a curtain, his rage spilling across the emergency room as he gesticulated and threshed so that the police officer got the point, and then her mother opened the curtain and told him to go somewhere else – Mina didn't need more of this: she'd had about all she could take of male aggression for the rest of her life. The doctor said she'd be fine – 'Give it a week and you'll be back to splendid.' It didn't look like there was any internal damage, but for safe measure they would have an x-ray done. 'The real thing I'm worried about is up here,' the doctor said, tapping his hair. 'You've been through quite an ordeal, Mina. It's going to take some time for this to sink in.' He looked at Mina's mother, telling her without telling her that her daughter needed love and care and support.

And it did take a while to sink in. In fact, after the initial tears of the attack and the whirlwind of emergency rooms and smiling faces, Mina didn't cry at all, instead experiencing an otherworldly composure that settled in and wrapped her up. Everyone seemed to be moving quickly but her; they frenzied and panicked and moved left and right in endless bobbles and loops, while she simply sat, contented in a cool Zen force-field that she found difficult to explain. 'It's alright,' she told her parents that Sunday. 'I'm fine.'

'You've been through something traumatic,' her mother said. 'You're not thinking straight. I want you to stay home.'

'He's not going to be at school. It's okay.' They hadn't used his name all weekend, skating around the topic, avoiding it like Macbeth, as if the merest mention might summon him from the shadows.

'Still,' her father said, 'we just want you to give it a day.'

So she did.

In the confines of her room Facebook flooded her with a torrent of private 'get well' messages, most of which were skittish and evasive and platitude-heavy. It seemed social media had also self-imposed a ban on his name. Even though everyone knew what had happened (and by the end of Monday the whole school knew who *Mina* was) no one seemed to know how to face it, and so they didn't. Instead they used it, if at all, privately and salaciously, drama on the fringes of their lives that made their own existences seem more valid and less pedestrian – a habit typically solidified in high school and repeated until death. Friendships are either forged or broken in a crucible of a crisis, and Mina was quickly realising that what she had with Veronica and Jason were fickle arrangements of convenience rather than relationships of worth. Maybe she'd known it all along. But sitting alone in her room on the Monday, she also realised that she didn't care all that much. And when Tim texted her asking for the second time why she'd stood him up on Saturday night – why she didn't even have the decency to let him know what was wrong – she felt no compunction about not responding.

Needy men weren't worth the effort. If there was one trait she could define as being the least attractive in a potential mate, it was that.

And yet beyond it all, after the rage of her father and the fear of her mother and the questions of the police; after all the insincere digital kisses and *thinking of you*s and sidewise expressions of secondhand vengeance – *I hope that bastard gets everything he deserves* – she couldn't help but feel an incredible sense of sadness and pity for Ahmed. Because she knew him, and she had broken him, and although she understood that she shouldn't feel responsible, that under no circumstance was there ever a justification for inflicting on anyone what he had inflicted on her, she couldn't hate him or fear him or wish anything bad for him, and she couldn't help but feel like it was directly and absolutely her fault.

'Never think that,' said Verna Gershwitz. The appointment had been made for Mina's early two periods on the Tuesday, her first port of call before form class or any interaction with her fellow students. 'I know it's tempting when something like this happens to feel that you're responsible, but no one has the right to hurt you physically – no one.' Verna said it with force: this point was immutable.

'I know that,' Mina said. With her hair down, the marks of Ahmed's fingers were obscured, however when she moved her head it was like a bead curtain stirring in the breeze and exposing the flickering light of abuse. 'It's just… You know, his dad and everything. He was really fragile, and I was just thinking about me.'

'You've had a tough time,' Verna said. 'But none of this is your fault. None of it. You're too young to have to manage big issues like this.'

Mina scratched her leg and looked at the venetians; they were lowered this morning, open to a third and casting sun in slats on the carpet. 'I'm just worried about him. You should've seen his face... And now he'll have no one.'

'It's bad,' Verna said. 'And it sounds like he's been through a very rough time as well. But you can't think about that. That's not your responsibility.'

'I'm thinking about dropping the charges.'

Verna paused herself for a moment and looked very carefully at the girl in front of her. A pretty girl with something missing in her face. 'I don't think that's a good idea.'

'Why? This is going to destroy him.'

'Do you know what battered woman syndrome is, Mina?'

That day in cooking class Mrs Thurston took Mina aside, out into the corridor and away from the prurient leers of her classmates. 'How are you doing, Mina?' she asked. The cast on her wrist meant she was entitled to six weeks' paid leave, but Mrs Thurston wasn't that kind of teacher.

'I'm okay.'

'Are you sure?'

Mina looked at the thick chalky cast and at the big woman's round eyes, and it was then and only then – in the warm presence of someone truly benevolent and utterly and genuinely concerned – that she began to blubber, going to pieces completely and falling into her arms. Mrs Thurston hugged her back, holding her as if she were her own child, pressing Mina against the warmth of an ample and supportive breast. 'It's okay,' she said. 'Let it out.' She held her there for a long time, feeling the girl's shudders and closing her in like a broken bird, and Mina released everything – the hands on her throat and the myriad pains of pressure and confusion and Ahmed crying next to her in purple light after his father's funeral – then Mrs Thurston held Mina's hand and walked her to the office and sent her home, and she stayed there for the rest of the week.

The only problem was timing, because the end of the year was close and the rigidity of the school assessment system doesn't factor in space for things like the psychological convalescence required after serious daylight assaults, so Mina had to work: English, maths and biology had to be covered, and in order to do so she physically needed the material, and this was an area that Veronica and Jason had consciously cornered, knowing that it was an excuse to see their friend, a valid reason to be allowed into Mina's home and into the sanctity of her trouble. It was their hotline to the action. And it was important, because Jason also had big news. He'd seen him! In the flesh. Just walking around like everything was okay. He'd actually seen *the rapist* – that's what they were calling him now – just walking through the food court. 'It was fuckin' crazy,' he told Veronica.

'Whaddya do?'

'Like, nothing. I was waiting in line at McDonald's and he was right across in a shop.'

'Which shop?'

'Like a jewellery store. He was just checking shit out. He's fuckin' creepy.'

'Probably looking for a ring to put on his next victim. Fuckin' rapist.'

'I know, right.'

'Loser shouldn't be allowed out.'

'Does Mina know he's out?'

Mina did know. She knew all about his release on bail and the temporary restraining order and the date that had been set for the hearing. The police had informed her parents and her parents had informed her, and her dad had been angry until Mina's mother quelled him and reminded him about blowing his top.

'Everyone misses you at school,' Veronica said. She and Jason had been cordially invited in by Mina's father and now they were lingering in her bedroom – a place neither had ever been before. Jason was staring at a poster of a cat and a small plastic statuette of a pink flamingo beside Mina's computer; boys in girls' bedrooms are always ungainly. 'Everyone's thinking of you.'

'Really,' Mina said, making no real effort to sound enthusiastic. 'That's nice of them.' It was the Thursday following the attack and the bruises were beginning to fade, but they were still there, still smudged lightly upon her neck, and she could sense that the two intruders in her bedroom desperately wanted to study them. 'Do you have the work I need?'

'Yeah.' Veronica removed a plastic sheath from her bag and handed it to Mina. It contained an exemplar essay for *Lord of the Flies* and three years' worth of old maths and biology exams. She flicked through it and put it on her bed where Jason picked it up and examined the contents.

'Oh yeah,' he said, finding the exemplar. 'The fat kid gets a rock in the face at the end. It's really funny.'

'You still look really pretty,' Veronica said.

'What does that have to do with anything?'

'Nothing, I was just complimenting you.'

'She's right,' Jason said. 'You still look hot.'

Mina looked at the open door to her room and

wondered when they were going to leave. Empty praise no longer had the same effect.

'You know Jason saw him,' Veronica blurted. 'At the mall. Did you know he was out? Like, are they even allowed to do that?'

Jason took this as his cue and jumped in: 'Yeah, he was just walking around, like looking at things – he's fuckin' scary.'

'God you're lucky. You were so right to leave him when you did.'

'And now he's just walking around. Like, what if he rapes someone else?'

'What?' The word wafted over Mina like a toxic cloud. She suddenly felt a dizzy kind of anger.

'I mean, what if he does it to someone else.' Veronica, covering for the slip.

'You said "rape".'

'Did I? Sorry, I—'

'He didn't rape me. Jesus Christ, is that what everybody thinks?' Mina was looking hard at the two of them now, but they were struggling to look back.

'Hey, Mina – ignore him, he's an idiot. You know that.' Veronica swung herself to Jason and hit him hard in the arm. 'Fucking idiot.' Back to Mina: 'Nobody thinks that. We're just worried about you. Like, maybe you should come out this weekend, you know – have some fun and try to forget about it. Have you heard from Tim?'

Mina had returned her attention to the door. 'Thanks for the work,' she said. 'I think you guys should go now.'

'It could be fun – like, we'll doll you up and wear dresses and party…'

'I can drive,' Jason added.

'Look, I don't want to!' Mina shouted. 'And I want

you to go. So fuck off.'

'Jesus, fine!'

Mina turned her face to the wall and said nothing more while Jason and Veronica left the room and left the house and climbed into Jason's car.

'She didn't have to be a bitch about it,' Veronica said as Jason started the engine.

'I know, right.'

'That cunt really fucked her up. I hope he fucking gets what he deserves.'

'Fucking rapist.'

The engine rolled over and the car pulled away, and from the window of her room Mina saw it leave and hoped she would never see it again. Because it was a funny thing, she'd decided. And it was hard to explain to herself, because any way she said it, it sounded like the worst thing in the world: it sounded so bad that she would never tell anyone. She didn't love him, of course, and she never would again, and having broken down and really felt the trauma, she even hated him now – hating him to the degree that one should hate another after being attacked and choked and having their life squeezed away. And he would've killed her, she knew that. He would have pushed it all the way through. But now she was awake, and she was clear. She was an adult. And this was the bad part, the thing that she would always know but never verbalise: Ahmed had literally strangled some sense into her.

The trade off, though, was the loss of sense in Ahmed, almost as if clarity had jumped host bodies, or as if there were only a finite amount of the stuff to go around. When it came time to make a statement, to lay out what actually happened on that Saturday morning, Ahmed struggled. By this point he'd been told what happened – that he had choked his ex against a wall before fleeing on foot – but his memory of it was still fractured at best. He was asked to start at the beginning, so he said that when he was fourteen years old he met a girl named Mina. He was asked to skip a little – like, three years or so – so he told them about his father in the hospital, how he'd said it was important to take every chance and to truly and authentically live. 'Yeah, look Ahmed,' said the officer behind the table. 'We all want to get through this, okay, so can we stick to what happened Saturday.'

Saturday.

On Saturday it had been warm and Ahmed had worn pants that were too small.

On Saturday he had been happy, because Mina wanted to see him – and the sky was blue and being outside was good. And his mother would be getting a job at a supermarket and everything was going to be okay.

'We need to skip a little,' said the officer.

And then I read the messages. You've never seen messages like this – her phone. But she still loves me, you know, and that's the hard part.

'Look, we've got here that you assaulted her on the school grounds, you strangled her, and then, when you were confronted by witnesses, they tried to stop you, and you fought back, fracturing the arm of one of them. At that point you fled the scene. Is that what happened?'

'I can't say, but if that's what they've said then that's probably what happened.'

'What do you remember?'

'I remember colours. I remember the brick and the sunlight. But I'll sign this, yeah?'

'Are you sure you fully understand what's been

266

alleged here?'

His mother drove him home. She didn't speak. As the houses passed the window Ahmed pressed his face against the glass. When the car pulled in to its modest driveway, his mother didn't get out, her hands clasping the steering wheel as if for ballast, and when Ahmed finally moved, opening his door, she barked at him: 'No!'

'What?' he said.

'You heard the police; you are not to see that girl! This is no more. You will stay here.'

'Mum?'

'You will stay here!' She was still looking ahead, looking out at the overgrown lawn of her depressed little house, and crying.

'It's okay.'

'I can't lose you, too. You are a good boy.'

'It's okay,' he said again. 'Now come inside.' He started unfurling himself from the passenger seat.

'You are a good boy!' She needed to say it, to scream it until it sounded like someone else's opinion. As Ahmed opened her door for her and unclicked her seatbelt, she looked up at him, pleading for his agreement. 'A good boy. It's the others. They made you do it!'

Ahmed nodded as he took his mother by the arm and helped her out. 'Yes,' he said. 'They did.'

That night Ahmed could hear his mother sobbing through the walls. He wondered if she was asleep, if her tears were somnambular, her dreams replaying the losses and torments of her waking life over and over. Just like Mina, in the aftermath of the event itself, he'd entered into a state of unnatural calm. The rage he'd felt had been displaced, and in the darkness of his bedroom – his spartan corner of solitude – he lay fully clothed above his sheets, his spindly legs dangling from the end, and watched it float above him. It took on shapes and colours, formed faces: it became *the others*. It became Veronica and Jason; it became a furry metaphor for a penis. It shifted and merged and mutated into teachers and assemblies and jokes at his expense. It was the words of a text, a name – *Tim* – that had no shape or system, until Tim became every face and every smirk and every external threat. As long as Ahmed kept it above him, he would be okay – if he could keep it distant, side-stepping its sharp edges and razor barbs, then he would remain free and clear: he would see the world as it needed to be seen.

His mother continued to sob. Very quietly, Ahmed got up and left.

He didn't need alcohol anymore. In the pond-like stillness of the suburban night, he shattered the front window of a Honda with a brick. The sharp crunch and crumble of the safety glass sent ripples into the darkness. It felt good, and unlike the other times, where he'd woken with a vague notion of guilt, he knew this one was free. It was free like all attacks on *the others* would be.

In the days following, the concept dug its talons into Ahmed's mind. It went with him everywhere, and if he stayed still for too long – if he remained stationary for any serious period – it caught him and left a wound, a dint of disgust and fire that he couldn't escape. So he kept moving. He left the house early and walked the streets. He lingered at intersections where stoned Somali dropouts washed windows for change. He caught trains around the city and stared at the passengers. But *the others* were always there, always pulling at him: they were in uniforms in the seat across the aisle, boys heading to a private school and making jokes about Asians; they were old men at bus stations, staring at him as if he were diseased; they were young mothers pushing prams, dropping their eyes when he tried to smile and picking up the pace to avoid his reach. When he was forced into stillness at the end of the day and found himself lying wide-eyed and looking up into the heart of the coagulating miasma, he thought of her. He used her to fight it. All he had to do was concentrate and think of her face, the smile she gave him in the split second before a kiss. Because it wasn't Mina who did this. She was just a victim. He knew who the real perpetrators were. And the more he thought about it, the more he knew that she knew too, that although his phone had been confiscated and that there was no way he could talk to her, if he could have, then she would have agreed. It was *their* fault, not hers. He was sorry, of course.

I really am. I didn't mean it. I would never hurt you – *will* never hurt you again.

I understand, Ahmed. The world is a hard place. The water was boiling, you know.

Yes, and *they* were boiling it.

And we were just frogs.

He held on to her smile until he dreamt with it and night turned to day.

At the mall he stood in the jewellery store and stared into the locked glass cases. An infinity engagement ring. He could see the silver and diamond glint against the cool iridescence of her skin. He was already thinking of things he could say: 'The ring is amazing, but it's only a cheap token compared to...' He considered smashing the case with his fist and fleeing, running straight to her house with a bleeding hand, the ring wet in his palm: he would skid onto his knees at her door and propose before the police dragged him away. 'Can I help you with something, sir?'

The voice of a man who knew Ahmed couldn't be helped.

'Just looking.'

The mall was full of them. It was the place they all came to bray and fuck and spend, and now he was surrounded and regretting his decision to walk in instead of past. Then across the food court Ahmed spotted Jason waiting in line at McDonald's. Normally, he would've had the urge to shy away – to duck his frame for some kind of cover and scuttle into invisibility. But things had changed. The craving to sprint over and grab him by the neck and smash his face into the cash register, to work it down until it was a bloody slab of broken teeth and pulpy cartilage... Jason was not looking, but Ahmed's hands were already damp with the promise, and then another voice: 'Are you sure I can't help you, sir?'

'Fuck off.'

Then Ahmed was gone.

That night he did something he shouldn't have. He knew it was wrong, but *the others*... As hard as he tried to focus on her, to let her envelop and protect him, the evil panoply returned, gnawing its way through the shield and consuming him. It was every face now – everyone he'd ever known – and everything. It was an entire school of jeering blackness, glass and knives and the baying of wolves; it was the white walls of the prison cell and the stark light of the sun; his mother's relentless crying and the jungle seething in his chest. And in the vortex of it all, he saw her, afraid and naked and being pulled in every direction, quartered by the violation of foreign hands and alien mouths; they sucked and bit at her and he saw her face in a way he fully recognised but did not understand: nostrils flared and bubbling mucus, the skin of her neck tearing and warping, her jaw distended, her eyes bloated and ready to pop: he heard her scream – a raw violent howl – and he had to go. She was in pain and they were killing her, and he was the only one who could help.

At approximately eleven p.m. Mina was still wide awake. She sat at her computer, Facebook closed, a Word document open, typing a practice essay. The language was coming easily because she had a lot to say. With Piggy's death Golding was making a statement about the savage in all of us. The soft duvet of civilization we cling to camouflages what we really are; take it away and our true natures are revealed. We are violent and we are selfish, and any good in us – intelligence and empathy and sensitivity – will be crushed under the rock of ignorance soon enough.

Ahmed's breath steamed against the glass – a hot relief. She was alive, safe in her room. He rested his forehead against the external sill and inhaled deeply. For now, it was okay. He looked again. The room was soft around her, the light of the desk lamp pooling a warm circle. This was the only place he trusted, but even here he knew they could get to her, that it wouldn't be a haven forever. They were always moving: they could find their way in through the smallest cracks, and if they could get to him, then they could get to her. He wished he'd smashed the jewellery case and brought her the ring; he wished he could knock and say something – to tell her what he was planning, to tell her that he loved her and what he was going to do for her, but he knew she wouldn't understand. The logic of sacrifice is something only the soul can comprehend. He needed to clear a path for her, beat them back. He needed to give himself up entirely, to relinquish his being for something higher and truly noble – and that is what his father would never have understood. To live a life of meaning you can't flutter in the absurd: you have to pick a god, find your deity, then give everything. That is the only sure way for love and truth to win.

So it was on a Monday – a hot one at the end of the academic year – that Ahmed placed a kitchen knife and a hammer in his father's old briefcase and began the slow walk to school.

TOM & DAVE

The air in the Midway House was hot and dry and the plaster in the walls was almost breathable; beyond the broken windows the harbour wrinkled against the heat. A breeze picked up briefly, stirring the bamboo in a way that sounded like momentary rain. Tom blew smoke and watched it cling to airborne dust. Tastes like justice, Tom said.

What?

Everything tastes like justice.

Just give it here. Dave inhaled and let the smoke hang in the cavern of his mouth.

You know what an ugly word is?

What? The cave collapsed and the smoke dissipated.

Toke.

Yeah…? I'm kinda hot.

Yeah?

Kinda wanna take my shirt off.

Please don't.

Why not? It's just you and me.

Exactly, it's just you and me. Frankly I'd find it weird… Justice…Toke.

Is this a faggot thing?

That's an ugly word, too.

Faggot.

Justice… But no, I just don't wanna have to spend my high staring at your stupid chest.

You don't have to stare at it.

Yeah, but it's right there, like under your face. It's hard enough looking at that.

Justice… Fuck, now I'm doing it.

And imagine if someone walks in.

No one's gonna walk in.

Imagine if someone walks in and you're standing there burning your nipples with your lighter and I'm watching.

No one's gonna walk in.

I still don't want you to do it.

Fine, but you're the one that made that weird.

Justice. Justice.

Stop it.

Tom took the spliff and took his turn; Dave flapped the bottom of his school shirt to cool himself. See, Tom said. You can just use it as a fan. The breeze blew again and rustled the bamboo. You know, it's fucking remarkable that you can be so perceptive about some things and so wildly off with other shit.

What? Me?

Yeah.

Whaddya mean?

You remember back in Year 11 when those guys

followed us home on the bus.

Nah.

We were kinda stoned. Remember? We were at the bus station and these Polynesian guys all watched us get on the bus, then they all got on too – like seven or eight of them – and even though the bus was empty they sat completely around us, like in front and behind.

Fai usi!

Yeah, fuckin' fai usi.

Yeah, and that's like all they said. I fuckin' remember! And right before we hit our stop I got you up and walked to the front and then hit the stop bell like *just* before the stop and we took off.

You sprinted – like, you *really* ran – and I just sort of lagged, but like I saw them all start to get off, but some of them didn't, so like your weird movement confused their ranks and half of them were still on the bus when it pulled away.

Dave stepped left and right, dodging an invisible attack. You gotta be onto that shit man.

Well that's kinda the thing – like I wasn't onto it at all. Like that whole ride – because we didn't talk at all – I was just sort of sitting there thinking everything's fine. And like there was part of me going, 'Nah, they're not gonna mug us – it's racist to even think that. They're just some guys on a bus.'

They were totally going to mug us. They were gonna beat the shit out of us and take our stuff. Fai fucking usi!

Yeah, like it seems obvious. We live in a predominately white neighbourhood.

Pre-dom-in-ate-ly. Justice.

And they were sitting all over us, and then half of them actually did get off at our stop. I agree. But even as it was happening I pretended it wasn't, like I was wilfully ignoring all these factors.

Factors.

Justice... But you didn't. You knew straight away. Your perception was tuned.

You know why I knew? Dave said, dancing to an inaudible beat.

Because your parents are racists and mine aren't.

What?

STELLA

She didn't go to school on the Friday. It was cloudy. She changed out of her uniform in a public toilet and caught the bus straight to his place where the dogs no longer barked at her arrival. 'They know your smell,' he said. He was leaning in the door frame at the front of the house and cradling a coffee, nursing it like it mattered. 'So do I. I could smell you coming. You wearing underpants today?'

Charming.

'I've cleared the weekend,' he said. 'Just got to run a few things down first and then we're good to go.' She stood beneath him on the front step, waiting for his bulk to let her in.

'How long's that going to take?'

He shrugged. 'As long as it takes. No kiss?' He bent down to her: sobriety was when bad things tasted bad and she just had to get through it. She pushed her dry lips into the wire stubble of his cheek.

Against the kind of flat light only Auckland can produce, they drove. Stella had her foot up on the open passenger window, looking past her laces and into the side-mirror at the landscape evaporating behind her. She wore the sunglasses he'd bought her, but the big amber lenses did little to brighten the emptiness of receding state houses and streets with no trees. Tony drove with the music up too loud to talk, though there was little for her to say. He stopped outside a high wooden fence and got out and disappeared, the car still running, the stereo still up. Stella stared at a hedge, then herself in the rear-view, lifting her sunglasses to inspect the dark swales forming under her eyes. Nothing makeup couldn't cover. And then Tony was back.

He bought them food at a drive-thru and ate it as he drove, hoeing into a burger that spilled sauce onto his hands and shirt. 'Fuck!' When he swore it was like a bark. He dropped the paper bag and his drink from the window at an intersection, then said something else.

'What?'

He turned down the music. 'Ever notice it's just niggers and white trash that wanna wash your window?'

How astute.

The music went back up.

They stopped in a back-alley car park. Behind a barbed wire fence threads of the motorway overlapped and intersected. Stella had barely registered that they'd driven into the city. He turned the car off and the music died and he got out without saying anything. If he wanted her to follow, she presumed he would say something. She listened to the metallic yawn of passing buses and watched sparrows land on a parking girder. She drifted into something close to a daydream. He emerged again holding one side of a very large box, a shop assistant in a blue uniform carrying the other end. The assistant looked almost her age. Attractive and clean, he was part of a world that Stella no longer occupied, full of video games and curfews. When the assistant saw her looking at him, he looked away, blushing; a boy who still plays with toys.

The box took up the whole back seat, making it impossible to see out the rear window. 'Top of the line,' Tony said. She could smell him: age and decay. The hair on his arms looked like blackened steel wool. 'Why waste your life watching an inferior image, you know. Imagine how good you'll look on that.' The music returned before there was any chance for a reply.

Another house. This time Tony used the back entrance, cutting across a lawn and beneath the empty skeleton of a steel washing line. Stella waited. She went to check the glove-box with idle hands but found it locked.

'What have you got in there?' she asked. He tapped his nose. The scar on his cheek seemed to twitch. 'It's a gun, right? I bet it's a gun.'

'So curious,' he said. 'Little birds should keep their noses out of mouse traps.'

Birds have beaks.

The car pulled up outside a sex shop. They were in the city again and rush hour traffic was beginning to surge. He'd parked in a clearway. 'Move the car if someone tries to tow it, all right. But don't fuckin' scratch it.' The door closed and he disappeared before she could tell him she didn't know how to drive – that he'd never asked. In the front window of the store the display mannequin was wearing familiar pink and black underwear and holding a leather riding crop. Stella looked at the model from the enclosure of the car; its neon red wig was only a shade off the hue of her own. Its blinkless gaze focused on the passing traffic; its pupils didn't move.

Tony was back at the car against the blaring horn of a bus. He was giving the driver the finger and as Stella turned she saw the faces of the passengers staring back at her like gawping pod people. 'Fucking idiot,' Tony said, slamming his door and throwing a bag into the back seat next to the TV. 'City's fucking full of them.'

'That another customer?' Stella asked, nodding toward the vice shop.

'Sure,' he said.

'How much longer are we going to be doing this?'

'We're done.'

Good, because I'm fucking sick of you.

But she had to keep waiting when they returned to his house. 'First things first,' he said, and he dragged the TV into his living room and began the trial of setting it up, shoving the older one aside and filling the floor with Styrofoam and bubble-wrap and torn pieces of cardboard. And then it didn't work and he kicked a hole in his own wall and Stella wrapped her legs into herself on the leather couch and tried to stay out of his way, but she couldn't help herself.

'You can put together a gun off the internet but you can't do this.' He turned to look at her and said nothing, and immediately she regretted it; there were sweat lines in his singlet and his chest had the gentle heave of someone nearing meltdown. 'Maybe you should take a break?' – Although she tried to cover it, her voice had the timbre of fear. He seemed to notice it. He closed his eyes and stretched out his arms and stood above the litter and stray cords and tried to rediscover equilibrium.

'Sorry,' he said when he opened up again. 'I'm losing

my shit. I didn't mean to scare you.'

'It's okay.' She attempted to smile.

'No it's not. I scared you.' He breathed deeply again, puffing out his brutal chest and letting it fall slowly. 'I should get you something. You've been a good girl.'

She winced at the phrase.

→ Stella was coming up hard when he finally got the TV going. The pill he'd given her had dropped on her eyelids and clenched her jaw and flushed her body, and now she rubbed the film of perspiration skirting her arms against the cool of the leather, a cat preening and stretching. Her skin felt humid, an internal sprinkler misting her insides, and the cigarette tasted full for the first time that day – though she kept losing its focus, drifting instead to the image of herself staring back at herself staring back at herself. Tony had hooked up the camera to the TV, and she was looking into the curled features of her own being in a warm sepia light. Can I put music on? she said – can we listen to my stuff?

'Sure. Hey that stuff's really working on you, huh...'

She found herself nodding, sizzling, her eyelids like Slinkys against the pendulum of her head as the movement gathered a life of its own, and she heard him laughing somewhere, the syllables soft and damp and distant. She hooked her phone to the stereo and played music that coated her in syrup. 'You should put on some makeup,' a voice said. She did what she was told, floating into the bathroom and examining the colours of her own face. Even the stark light of the halogen lamp above the mirror had lost its edges. She found it difficult to see herself all at once. My pupils, she said, as if the phrase were enough on its own. When the nausea struck, she sat on the toilet, then pulled herself around and vomited into it. The act of expulsion, something that should have shaken and hurt her, was utterly agreeable – a meadow of lurching and clearing. The acidity of her stomach was pleasant, and she understood that everything was okay: that her eye make-up was a unique shade of turquoise, that her palms carried stars in them, that it was all the same satin blanket, rippling and caressing the universe. And when she tried to think of the day and something deep in the back of her mind asked her to consider the tone of what was now the past, she couldn't. It was gone.

There's only the present, she said, extending herself across the couch. That's all there is.

'What about the past and the future?' he said.

If you can't touch them they don't exist.

He was coming up now, too. He was fiddling with the camera. He'd set up both TVs side by side: Stella on one, lounging in real-time, the anonymous bodies of a porno writhing on the other. She watched flesh move through blurry eyes, unable to discern where one person ended and another began. He was speaking to her; she noticed the hair on his arms, a fur really, above the tattoos: it was familiar. Everything was familiar.

Ten in the evening: she was naked and couldn't recall removing her clothes. He'd been directing her to do things and she'd been doing them – saying things that he wanted her to say. The camera had been running the whole time, hours of footage of Stella that she couldn't remember but had little volition to; the present was where she lay, teetering on a temporal waterfall in a synthetic raft. The drug was still coming in waves, washing over her, then pulling back: Elysian fields followed by sand; panglossian sunlight chased by shadow. Her memory was heavy, filtered through dense yellow impressions of an inconsistent immediate; hours were compressed and seconds extended. When he gave her more she was swallowed up again.

How long can this keep going?

'Your brain's only got so much in it, then we switch drugs.'

Oh.

At some point he said he loved her and she said it back and then followed it with a whole river of glorious words she didn't know she had. 'You're the best,' he said. And then it was well into the middle of the night and the waves were washing again and he lined up white powder using a knife and gave her wine and told her the edge would be gone soon – that they were entering a new space.

Can I have a blanket?

'I'd prefer you didn't.'

She drank the wine and he lined up more and soon she was talking. Talking streams; talking whole oceans, talking like you know; like, you just exist in this space between things – the little black areas between the comics, or the space between each cut that isn't actually a space – like when the screen flicks from the close up of the guy to the close up of the girl, like you're the space between them – you don't even exist. Except you're real, you know – like more real than anyone: those tattoos and the way you flip at people, and those fucking dogs – *real, right…?* And she was aware she was being gagged and tied up and pressed into the couch, but she didn't mind (the present version didn't) and she was aware that on this stuff, sometimes you like it rough, that bad can flip to good, that bad *is* good sometimes, and she was aware too of the camera, looking back at her from the coffee table; and she stared into it, and in the background, on all fifty-five high-definition inches, she could see herself as a bent fleshy shape, red marks swelling where the rough skin of his palms had made contact with her body, his own arms and chest a reticulate sheath of red and blue ink, the sweat of his forehead dripping into the small of her back: she was aware of all of it.

When the gag came off and he lined up more, she smoked and said things she'd memorised through pornographic osmosis, and then the gag went back on. His hand was bigger than the whole side of her face; she could taste his palm; and when she tried to bite at his toe, he shifted and told her she was a slut.

There was a break around dawn – Saturday was snaking through the lime curtains. They smoked meth on the edge of his bed. She found herself doing star-jumps in snotty light. This is all I need, she said. This moment. We could run things, you know that? – You an' me.

'Yeah?'

We could take over! We've got the guns, we've got the drugs. It's ours, you know.

She straddled him on the bed and took more from the pipe. The blood was rushing to her head; an aggressive warmth: a warmth of impenetrability that made her want to cut herself open and bleed onto his chest and into his mouth. She slapped him.

'The fuck was that for?'

I want to swap blood – I want to trickle it all over you.

Like a demented samurai he collected the knife from the bedside table and cut a small line in his chest, a surgical incision from which dark blood immediately started to ooze. His teeth were gritted – 'Now you.' – He handed her the blade. She inspected it, held it up to the light, ran its edge gently across the top of her nipple, then turned it upside down and pointed it into his chest. All she needed to do was lean forward and the tip would push into his skin, into the bone of his ribs and maybe his heart.

Trust me?

'Completely.'

Maybe you shouldn't.

She removed the blade and lifted it to her shoulder and paused. She took three deep breaths and cut, then screeched – a theatrical explosion that had the dogs barking on the lawn outside. The blood started to come. He pushed himself up onto his elbows and licked at the cut before she forced him back down and sucked at his chest…

…It was midday and she lay hogtied on his leather couch. 'You're a lippy bitch.' He said it monotonously – 'A lippy bitch' – like it meant nothing. The knife was dangling in his right hand and he was moving back and forth in front of the TV, which she was on, playing live, interrupted only by the momentary flicker of his legs moving past the camera, his penis dangling like a weapon in repose.

Yeah, well fuck you.

'Say it again,' he said.

Fuck you, you smelly cunt!

He held the pipe to her mouth and she took another hit. 'You like that shit, huh? Who's a dirty crack whore?'

She was no longer sure this was a game. As the afternoon sun moved behind the curtain she found it harder to join any dots, losing the thread of her thoughts to interstitial space. The shape of the room seemed to have changed, seemed to have become another room entirely. She barely noticed that he'd left – disappeared from view – and suddenly she was alone in relative silence. The old TV was off and black, a void where life used to be, and its absence suddenly made her afraid, as if the porn actors that had formerly inhabited the screen could somehow bear witness. She could see herself lying prone on the new TV – a second unreal self that twitched its feet when she did but could do nothing for her. She heard a wooden drawer open in another room and the sound of plastic bric-a-brac being sorted rapidly. She thought she could hear a lawn mower and a car passing and a voice, but when she closed her eyes she couldn't picture the world they belonged to.

'Check this out.' He was back. His naked rear-end obscured the TV, black hair pluming out of his crack and blossoming onto his lower back. He was fiddling with something… and then he revealed what he'd done with a swoop of his arms, like a magician asking the audience to appreciate a body sawn in two. She saw herself again on the screen, though the dimensions were different, and it took time for her to register – dots had to find other dots. 'We're streaming,' he said. 'Stella-cam is up.' Her doppelgänger had shifted to the top left of the screen, and when she moved her head, there seemed to be a delay – a shuttle. She wondered if something happened in that space – if there were essential parts lost or gained – and amidst misfiring synapses and an amnesia that came and went like sudden rain, she was failing to grasp anything wider than the room. His laptop had been connected to the TV, its webcam turning Stella into pixels for mass consumption.

Untie me, you fuck!

'You want more?'

Of course I do – you know I do; I hate you.

'Then work for it.' A distance between here and there and then and now; a gap between present moments.

'When viewers tip you, I'll give you hits.' He stood over her and untied her and she had the urge to hit him or stab him or cut off his cock, but his bulk seemed too dense to hurt; and if she had more, then the gaps might close; things might reassemble and become a straight line again, so she stretched her arms and looked up at him and told him she needed one to start – a down payment – and that she'd work it off, and he smiled, but Stella found it difficult to register the tone of his face or the meaning in his eyes or the reason for anything. But she knew – *she fucking knew* – that the taste she was after, a mix of gasoline and plastic and synthetic adrenaline, would wreck her jaw and tense her body and give her the focus to do what needed to be done, and now he was typing things to viewers (to faceless masturbating comments) and laughing, and she'd say What? What is it? And he'd tell her – maybe – and she'd do something to herself, rub this or fuck that, and eventually it would start all over, all over. 'You're getting lubricant on my couch' – the stuff dried and became tacky on her skin and caused her to stick to the leather. The image of her twin: maybe I should call her something else, like, Stella's somewhere else right now, like she's here, but up there, the lagging sex doll – like, you know she only wants one thing and if she does this she'll get it, right? 'Hey, this guy says he knows you?'

What? Fuck him. He doesn't know shit.

'Says he goes to your school.'

Whatever. Fucking liar.

'You're making money – you know that. These cunts love you.'

Stella doesn't have to pay....

...She didn't notice dusk because the curtains had never opened; she wanted her phone, wanted to check the time and the date; she wanted to stand up and sit down, but she did neither, resting instead on her knees and staring at the television. He'd left, she thought. He'd gone somewhere – To feed the dogs? She wasn't sure if he was outside, whether his car was still in the driveway. Momentarily, she wanted a shower, but the forethought of heat and water seemed like it might kill her, so she simply remained, half sprung forward, the HD glow colouring her forehead… He'd plugged the camera into the TV again before he'd left and now the whole night was playing back; Stella was watching an alternate version of herself lie on the couch, watching her face sink into blankness. She was saying things to him, small words and half sentences, her head dropping; she was pulling off her clothes and falling sprawled and backward; there was a voice directing her – directing the girl on screen: she couldn't join the two, then and now; she wasn't this stripped and dripping stranger and she wasn't sitting watching it. And if someone had seen her at this moment, if they'd walked in off the street and observed Stella like an animal in a zoo, they would've noted how still she was, transfixed, a broken Narcissus unable to compute the disconnect, unable to choose or decide or know what choice meant. Hours evaporated where her only twitch was for a cigarette that was lit and then left and the re-ignition of a pipe that had already burnt though.

He was there and he wasn't. Headlights against the curtains. Asbestos in the roof. She was in the bedroom – tied up properly this time, tied up and gagged and left to stare at the TV he'd dragged in there, a cord running out to a camera beneath the closed locked door. She felt the swelling and dropping of her lids, her teeth working reflexively against the leather strap in her mouth. He'd given her something else – she couldn't recall what – but it made her body tingle enough for her to know it was still there, that she was still the owner of the shell lying roped to a bedpost. Pills dissolved inside her: clouds sped over fields and shadows moved as ghosts – noiseless wind stirring long grass. There were voices from the other room and two bodies on the TV – a woman in a black dress with black hair, and him, pouring wine. With her eyes closed she saw the sun; she heard moans, muffled sentences; when she opened them again she saw Tony, the woman in black pulling off his pants. Caterpillars dying; butterflies eaten by cats. There was no way to tell anymore; her teeth bit into the gag.

'You see what happens?' He pulled the gag down and vomit spilled out onto her chest. She hadn't known it was there. 'Fuck! Come on – stay with me.' Even through the kaleidoscope she could tell what he was offering, the pipe pressed against her lips, its round glass edges clinking on her teeth. 'That's what happens when you stray from me. I take it away, and I hurt you. That's what love is… You need more.'

She was in the shower. The sound was like a hail storm, and when she turned off the faucet, it remained, pelting the inside of her skull and laughing. She left without drying and found him masturbating in the living room. Something had changed again. She had the feeling an extra wall had been put in somewhere and that the window had moved. 'It's black and white,' he said. She took what he offered her, took it and smoked and swallowed. 'You know what I'm capable of.'

Is it day or night?

'So you wanna know about the scar, yeah?' (Is it day or night? ('Because I'll tell you about it – I'll tell you

289

everything you need to know and then you'll understand how important trust is.') I think I want to go home. I can't sleep. I feel like I'm burning in a pan. When I close my eyes they don't close ('It's a statement – it says there's no grey, there's only black and white'). And ('Do you understand?') I think I've snapped something, like ('Because you can't leave now; you have to stay. You have to be with me') the connections have severed ('and don't fucking cry about it, because it's done. You made your choice.') and I can't, I mean ('because you know what I can do to you – you know what evidence I have against you') what's actually going on? ('I can take all this shit and fucking ruin you. I fucking own you...') I want to go home.)))I want to go home.)))))I want to go home.))))))))

But Stella wasn't going home. Instead she was locked to the bed as Anthony Kirsten told her about his scar, his tattooed mass swinging a blade to make a point, and when she blinked, he moved, crawling up next to her and pressing the scar into her face, its pink tissue quivering as he smoked cigarette after cigarette and ashed on her stomach and burnt the top of her thighs with loose embers. 'It's about making a point,' he said. 'That's why I *did this to myself* – I did it because I loved her and she fucked me, because there's no fucking middle. And if I want to be jealous I'll be fucking jealous, and I'll fucking dig this right in.'

Her memory of what happened next became like everything else: she saw it through an over-exposed lens, washed out and dented. He'd jabbed the knife into his own pectoral, working the tip in like he was removing shrapnel, digging and jerking until a chunk of flesh had been removed and blood was gushing down his front and onto the bed and he was sounding inhuman groans into his own open wound. 'This is love and trust,' he grunted. 'This is fucking everything.' The bulb above his head glowed like a dirty halo, the gore almost black against his skin, but Stella couldn't take it in, couldn't understand: against the barrage of everything else, the smashed thoughts and fatigue and the madness that had come on slowly, leaking at first, then pouring, she could do nothing. She could not stay and she could not leave, and she could not think of either. 'I have to kill you if try to go.' He was wrapping his shoulder with a towel on the far side of the bedroom, coiling it into a bandolier to soak up the blood. She had no idea how he'd moved there so quickly. 'And I'll kill anything that gets in the way of you. I love you.'

And it went on.

And when the sun came up again – although it was hard to say how long it had been there – and Anthony Kirsten was lying on the bed watching re-runs of the immediate past and Stella was standing by the curtain, preparing herself – daring even – to look out, and trying, as best she could, not to think about the places on her body that hurt, that had been ripped and stretched and invaded, and every time she ducked her head away from the curtain, from the latency of another world, she saw it again replaying inexorably on the TV, and Anthony Kirsten's chest, crusted with blood, rose and fell, and when her body hit the curtain again, falling just slightly against it, a crack of light jutting through and illustrating the smoke, thick and foggy, and then she turned and opened the curtain and unhooked the window and put her head out, she pushed it into the open reality of the outside and saw everything she needed. The clarity was religious and certain. Beyond his lawn she saw the footpath and trees and houses; she saw a blue sky that wasn't covered in blood and lampposts that weren't smeared with lube. She saw clothing and safety and life-giving colours, and she didn't see Anthony Kirsten. 'Fucking close that shit!' he barked. She didn't. She took a deep breath of suburban air, but it was too much for lungs that had been treated like an exhaust pipe, and the coughing fit came quickly. She had to pull herself inside and squat down on the floor and expel the surplus tar. He didn't help her. Instead, he repeated the command, and with her throat clogged and her body convulsing, she found herself reaching up and backward and trying to do as he'd asked. 'Can you do that shit in the bathroom? Fuck.' She heard him wheeze. On the screen Stella's body was being stabbed with a sex toy; her eyes, blank and half shut, suggested no window and no soul.

She washed her face in the basin and tried not to look at herself. Just go. It was the only clear thought. Just leave. She found her bag in the living room, her school uniform still tucked and folded in the bottom. Her other clothes were gone; she didn't know where and she didn't want to look.

'I have to go,' she said. She tried to make it clear, to use the wave of lucidity for composure and movement. She was standing in front of him in her school shirt and skirt and holding her bag. He pulled himself up on his elbows and did another hit and paused the video in a way that blurred Stella's face across the screen.

'Oh yeah. Where you going?'

'School. I've got a test.'

He laughed at this in a way that hurt him, and he had to clutch his shoulder and cough. 'You've got a test? It's fucking Sunday.'

'It's Monday,' she said, trying to find a tone that

didn't seem confrontational.

'The fuck it is.'

'It's fucking *Monday*. Check your phone.'

He did, jumping up and rummaging until he found it under a pile of clothes. He looked at it quizzically, like an orangutan, his brow scrunched and his face gleaming dumbly off its light. 'Did you fucking reset the date? Did you fuck with my phone?!'

But she'd already started moving to the door, adopting the brisk pace of someone with business to get to and speaking as she went, as if the direction of her words linked to where she wanted to be. 'Of course I didn't. Get some fucking sleep. You're a fucking psycho.'

'You better not fucking leave!' His voice chased her as she entered the hallway and put her hand on the front door. 'You know what'll happen if you lie to me!' And then she was outside, standing on his front step and the sky was open above her and the dogs stirred in the lawn grass. She started the walk to the gate, one foot in front of the other, her shoes safe on hard ground. 'Don't fucking lie to me!' His presence carried over the grass, but it was getting smaller, swallowed by a new reality of noise and light, and when she turned for the last time he was standing naked in the frame of the door. His eyes were wide and his face wretched and he was pointing at her, his arm stretched and taut, his dick dangling beneath a mat of black pubic hair. The blood crusted on his torso cracked as his body moved.

'Go to sleep, Tony. You don't know what the fuck you're talking about.'

'You know what I have on you. I fucking love you!' She felt this final phrase frying against the back of her neck, sautéing her skin, but the meaning was already evanescing. She was through the gate and up the road and blocking it out, directing her face to freedom and heading for anywhere. It didn't matter. When the bus arrived, she got on. The driver smiled at her. She paid the fare. She sat down and looked at verdant trees and passing cars, at the tight curls of an elderly woman's head three seats up from her. Stella had been awake now for well over seventy-two hours. She'd eaten nothing. Her arteries felt like they were pumping in reverse. In this state, she found it impossible to process what had just happened, to take stock of anything outside the impressions of light and texture that existed in front of her. Things like breaking down – regret and remorse and fear – and matters like the horror and psychosis and mutilation and rape: they would have to wait. They would come later. The only thing she wanted now was shelter: salubrious, earnest, genuine shelter, and so she went to school (a choice her body rote-responded to) and she checked her timetable, and she walked into History with Mr Gleeson where she sat down at the back. Sun was coming through the windows and pooling on the far side of the classroom. A voice somewhere distant said something about a watershed in public opinion, a crucial moment that galvanized voters. Stella stretched out her arms and let her face rest on the desk top. Her body loosened, the oil cooking in her spine began to cool, and all of a sudden she wanted to sleep, yawning deep and hard and full, wanting to let go of everything, wanting her consciousness to crumble away, and when the lockdown bell started to ring, she barely even noticed.

TOM & DAVE

With a broken piece of floorboard, Dave was attempting to corral a spider into a hole in the wall of the Midway House. The bamboo outside had ceased to rustle. Tom stood at the window, looking out at the view. The house is breathing, he said.

What?

If you stand here you can feel the house breathing.

Dave left the spider and stood by Tom, his head twitching and unfocused. The fuck are you talking about?

You're not calm enough.

What?

Calm down. Pay attention.

Dave stood still.

You feel it?

Feel what?

The house is breathing. Feel the air currents. The walls are like lungs, creaking in and out.

…

You feel it?

Nah.

Fuck it then… I'm sorry I said Steve and Judy were racists, by the way.

Who?

Your parents.

Andrew and *Sarah*.

Whatever.

You fucking *know* them.

It doesn't matter… Wanna hear my idea?

Not really.

Because I insulted your parents?

Sort of.

Think about this, right. Think about the last time you were happy – like dumb fucking happy. Like how long did the happiness last? I'm betting it probably wasn't longer than an hour. And I've noticed—

You've *noticed*.

I've noticed that that shit is happening less and less. Like it used to happen all the time. You know, you're a kid and you go to the park and you're happy, or you go to McDonald's, or you're watching a movie. All that stuff made you like dumb happy. Now, I'm like, yay I got an Xbox game or yay I'm gonna get high, but that's about it.

Depressing.

But that's the thing. Like, you have to think about it in the long term. Think about evolution.

Do I have to?

Happiness wasn't meant to be a long term thing. Like, if you wandered around dumb-happy all the time you'd get fucking killed. You'd try to pat tigers or you'd wander off and try to make friends with a tribe that likes to skull-fuck corpses and wear its enemy's skin.

They'd be fun to party with. Skull-fuck!

Don't side-track me. But like you'd never bother to hunt for anything or find shelter or anything.

You'd be like those dudes in the special needs unit; they're always fuckin' happy.

Yeah, and they get fucked with and made fun of and they'll need minders for the rest of their lives. That just illustrates my point.

Illustrates. Justice.

Happiness is the thing that's supposed to come at the end of it all. You search for food, you find shelter, you find a mate – all that stuff – and then you get to be happy: you get it for like an hour at the end of a week, and then it goes, because it has to. Like you have to find more food and try not to die. And when you win that fight again, it comes back.

Yeah, but it's not like that now.

That's my point. It's not.

So? Just be happy. No one's going to skin you and you're not retarded.

You're not thinking about it, Tom said, lighting a smoke. How long did it take to evolve from cavemen to now?

Fuck knows. And I'm not looking it up.

A long fucking time. Like a long long time. But then think about how long we've been able to order cheeseburgers and jerk off to internet porn. Like, we've had millions of years to develop happiness as a reward, like a short term one. It's a short-term evolutionary response to winning.

Good sentence.

But now we're all winners, all the time.

You're not a fucking winner.

Compared to a caveman, I am. Compared to your

grandparents and all their shit about fighting for a better world and world wars and stuff, I fuckin' absolutely am.

You know my great granddad was at Gallipoli?

And he was a loser.

Fuck off.

People shot at him for no reason. But they don't shoot at you, which makes you a winner. We're winners and we didn't have to do anything, which is why we're bored all the time. And why we're losers.

Don't confuse me.

Like the only battle we've got left to fight is boredom, and we don't fight that – we just try to ignore it. It's like every time you wank, or play Xbox, or your mum gives you the money to buy some pants and you buy the pants and you're like, yay, I have new pants now. You're a fucking loser. I'm a fucking loser. It's just the way it is.

So whadda we do?

I dunno. Shoot people. Stab people. Start a war. Accept it. Like, learn to love the boredom.

Love the boredom, Dave said.

Justice… Tom said. Can you feel it? It's happening again.

What?

The house is breathing.

ALi & NASiR

Ali was born in the Horn of Africa, the Cradle of Civilization, but he no longer lived there. He lived in New Zealand, with his parents, and he went to school every day. He was never late. He wore his uniform well. When he was seven years old he witnessed a man have his left leg and right arm amputated with a machete, but he didn't think about that anymore. People only have space for so many memories, and that one was being pushed out, slowly subsumed by the green of subtropical grass, by algebraic formulae, and by the naked dancing women of first world media. It was everything his parents had wanted: their son was on his way. When they'd saved up enough money for a new TV, Ali translated what the salesman was saying so his father knew what was going on: 'He said this one is the lowest one in the barrel.'

'Barrel?'

'It's an idiom. It means it's bad. But I think he's trying to upsell us.'

'What did he say about that one?'

'That it has the knees of a bee.'

'Is that good or bad?'

And when the family bought their first car, it was Ali who read the contract and then talked to the insurance company. 'I don't think we need full cover, dad. Third party is enough.'

'What's the difference?'

'If you get full cover then you're planning on hitting someone. If you get third party, you're only planning on someone hitting you.'

'Good boy.'

Ali's improving English was feeding into all kinds of new areas of academic success. In Science he was becoming increasingly adept at manipulating the lab equipment, finding the whole thing easy once he understood the teacher's instructions. In the final days of Term 3 he was spoiled for choice when it came to selecting lab partners; when other students discovered he wasn't quite as hapless as he'd initially seemed, his precision during assessment-based titration experiments became highly sought after. In the end Ali chose a classmate in whose high-waisted pants and quiet disposition he felt an unshakable confidence. Similarly, Mathematics had become a paradise of easy symbols and logical certainty, and he didn't understand why nobody got it: In $(X + 4)(X - 1) = X^2 + 3X - 4$ it was totally fine to swap the X for an elephant or a racecar or a severed human head – it was just an emblem for the unknown. His teacher even congratulated him on his ability to differentiate between the mode, the mean, and the median during the unit on statistical probability. 'How is it that only Ali managed to get this right?' He asked the class. 'What's the statistical probability of that, guys? Come on. It should be very low.' And Ali noticed that when he was being commended for his efforts – when a teacher was lauding his prowess – the other students, like Gavin and his peers, simply looked away, finding a spot somewhere out the window, a seat or a garbage bin or a square in the sky, and acknowledged nothing. Perhaps they were deep in reflection about their own lack of success; perhaps it was a snub; either way, it didn't matter to him anymore.

But Ali's *pièce de résistance* was achieved, against all odds, in Social Studies. Mr Gleeson had asked his students to prepare a report on the country of their choice, and so Ali picked the state of his birth, assuming this would give him an advantage based on his pre-existing knowledge. Studiously and with an eye toward his own organisation, Ali sat down at the computer as soon as he got home and prepared to write, heading up with the title: 'Somalia.' But that was as far as he got. The cursor sat blinking at him, the glowing white void a mirror to his realisation: he knew nothing significant about his homeland. He knew its colours, he knew some of its food, but outside a smear of mental dust and pseudo-redolent memories, there was only blank space.

'Dad,' he said. 'I don't know anything about Somalia.'

His father was watching TV, comfortable on the secondhand couch and with his feet balanced and happy on a rickety coffee table. 'Why would you want to?'

'Because I lived there. Because I have to write a report on it.'

'A report?' His father was watching a show where a toothy middle-aged man introduced home videos of Americans falling off trampolines, but he turned to face his son. 'Which part are you reporting on?'

'What do you mean?'

'Are you going to focus on our illustrious shorelines and our rich cultural heritage, or are you going to focus on our economic failures and near-total corruption?'

'I don't know… Maybe the second ones?'

'Okay, then you need to do some reading.'

'Can't you just tell me?'

'I don't know everything, Ali.' His father turned back to the screen to see a man let go of his golf club on the follow through. It cartwheeled several times in the air before landing in a water hazard. 'I think I would like to take up golf,' his father said. 'How many golf courses does Somalia have? Find that out for me, Ali.'

After sitting at his computer and rechecking the results with variants on his search, Ali had the answer. There were none. Once upon a time, there had apparently been a nine-hole course located on the grounds of the US embassy, but that, Ali figured, was almost certainly gone now. New Zealand, comparatively, had 393 courses. He went to tell his father.

'Fascinating,' his father said. A child on the screen behind him had miscalculated a backflip. 'Why do you think there are none?'

The answer seemed obvious. 'Because Somalis don't play golf.'

'But why don't they play golf?'

'Because there are no golf courses.'

His father let out a measured breath and switched off the TV. 'You're going in circles, Ali. Think about it. Do you think golf courses are cheap?'

'No. They are probably very expensive.'

'So why don't Somalis play golf?'

Ali had everything he needed.

Over the following week he read everything he could about his homeland, and the more he discovered, the more perplexed he became. While what he read should have made him angry – and, in some respects, did – he was overcome by a morbid fascination with how awful his birthplace seemed in print, as well as gaining a bourgeoning appreciation for the fact that his father was sitting in the living room laughing at the TV.

Having rearranged the appropriate words to make the sentences with information into sentences that he had written, and having run it past his ESOL teacher first, Ali handed his work in to Mr Gleeson. At over three pages and more than 1000 words, it carefully detailed his home state's poverty, war and corruption. It was titled: 'Why Somalis Don't Play Golf.'

His report card reflected his efforts, and when Ali ran home from school on the final day of Term 3, cutting across the neighbourhood links and stamping though the bunkers simply because he could, he handed his parents the pre-opened envelope and let them absorb it. They struggled, as always, but when they asked Ali to translate it for them, he refused. 'This is a present,' he said. 'But you only get the present when you unlock it.'

And then it was the holidays – two weeks of wet free time during which Ali found himself unmoored…

Nasir was also thinking of Somalia, but where Ali had been digging for facts, Nasir had tumbled comfortably backward into hallucinatory conflations. His version was all romantic memory: mauve sunsets and dusty roads and AK47s worn like jewellery. Measured in real time, he'd had about as much experience with the country as his cousin, having left at age ten before beginning the stilted process of foreign refugee camps and resettlement. A case could be made that neither one of the boys had even been alive during their time in Somalia – if living can be taken not as sentience but as self-awareness, a nervous consciousness of one's own existence. Because under the age of ten (and for many people it's even later) one simply isn't. Things happen, bodies react; you are led places and you do things, but you have no complex idea of yourself: life is a colour-wheel of random experiences and smells and pains and laughter. It's not until you become self-conscious, until you genuinely think of yourself as a human being stuck in the machinery, until you worry about things like having food on your face, that you start to form the kinds of memories that develop who you are. For Ali, at fourteen, this process had only just begun. For Nasir, at sixteen, arguably his entire sense of self had been chiselled and defined by a universe that didn't include his homeland. Instead, he was his school; he was Odawaa and Tarabi; he was the green fields on which he'd wagged classes to play soccer and the cigarettes he'd smoked and the paint he'd inhaled. Somalia was only a dream, a vestigial imprint at best. Except, he couldn't see it that way – he didn't want to. It was a matter of self-preservation, and so he slid into fantasy. He was going home.

He let it slip one afternoon in the park. A cold spring gale was blowing across the playing fields, the nearby skate park was damp and uninhabited, and the ground they sat on soaked through their pants. The smell of the paint came and went with the wind and the cheap rustle of the plastic bag. Odawaa was eating grass – chewing it – in order to stimulate his taste buds, its bitter cud preferable to aerosol and propellant, and Tarabi was leaning against a tree and could easily have been mistaken for dead. Nasir was still wearing his suit, though it was looking shabbier by the day: paint adhered to every cuff and dirt had fastened to every bend. He was holding a windscreen wiper, aiming down its rubber edge as if it were a gun and sighting a jogger passing in the distance. He imagined the recoil and then the stumbling misstep of his latent victim…There was a very real futility about washing windows in the rain, but it wasn't just the weather that was making the group's enterprise untenable. His cousins were getting slower and becoming careless, bumping into cars instead of swooping around them, ignoring the stones that had lodged in their brushes, even becoming irate when drivers didn't pay. After Tarabi spat on a car, the police had been called, and Nasir found himself talking to an officer who knew him – the same community constable who had arrived at his home following the incident at school. He'd moved the boys on, telling them that if it happened again, there would be a fine involved, that what they were doing amounted to disorderly behaviour – he could arrest them if he really wanted to. But in spite of the warning, and maybe even because of it, Nasir dragged his team back the following day. He'd carved out a niche and he was happy in it. Except now anger licked him every time a driver didn't pay, and the wind buffeted his body and flapped the edges of his suit, and the surface water hissed irritably under the wheels of hermetically sealed cars. There was a ringing in his ears that he couldn't explain, that grew throughout the day, and when a white woman looked at him like he was excrement – a look he used to ignore – and then turned on her water jets and windscreen wipers in order to deter him, as if he were bird shit that could be cleared automatically with the pull of a lever, he couldn't control himself. Knowing that the kind of woman who outsourced human communication to the washing functions on her car was never going to do anything about it, he reached out and grabbed at one of the wipers, bent it and snapped it off. Fuck the bitch, he thought. Horns went as the driver stalled, and then started again, pulling away *sans* one wiper and unable to fathom what had taken place. But that was it for the day. Assuming an inevitable police presence, Nasir collected his colleagues and retreated to the park and huffed paint and thought about a landscape with less humidity.

'I'm going home,' he said.

Odawaa spat grass from his mouth but said nothing; Tarabi drooled. Nasir felt the wiper in his palms and very suddenly wanted to use it as a cane with which to beat his paralytic cousins.

'Did you hear me?'

'I don't think he can walk yet,' Odawaa finally said, nodding at Tarabi.

'No, I am going *home*. I am going to Somalia.'

'Oh,' Odawaa said. 'Okay...' The remnants of what he'd been chewing had adhered to his chin, stuck in the spit and stubble. 'Will you be going by car or by train?' When he smiled, Nasir could see the green mulch wedged in the gaps of his teeth. 'Or you could pray to Allah and flap your arms very hard, and if you're lucky and God is willing, you will soon be on your way.'

This time Nasir couldn't stop himself; blood was pumping in his eyeballs; his head was throbbing; purple smudges swam in his vision.

It was nearly a week later that Ali found himself talking to his wayward cousin. He'd discovered Nasir under the tree behind the Christian Science bookstore. It was drizzling again and the skate park next to the playing fields was abandoned and covered in graffiti. Having spent the first week of his holidays alone and inside, Ali had used his time reading and searching the internet. His ESOL teacher had given him two books to take away. One appeared to be about a seagull; the other was about a boy who'd survived a plane crash and then had to learn to live in the wild. Ali had enjoyed both. It turned out the book about seagulls wasn't really about seagulls, and although he was struggling to make a literal connection, he felt the flock had something to do with school. He felt the same about the boy in the wild, however he was not yet entirely certain how - the deconstruction of extended metaphors was still a slippery process. It was while ensconced in the final pages, just as the protagonist was truly learning to exist on his own, that Odawaa – a scabbing wound on the side of his face – had come knocking and told Ali he needed to go see his cousin.

'Odawaa says you hit him?'

'Yes. He is good for nothing.' Nasir was still holding the wiper blade he'd used as a cane.

'He's your family.'

'Ali! Ali! Leader of Islam. How is school my young cousin?'

Ali was still standing as Nasir spoke. Odawaa had said he was in trouble, and now Ali understood, looking down at the hunched bundle against the trunk of a wet tree, hair like wire, eyes gone to hell, a blue suit wrinkled against his frame and covered in paint. There was a tattered plastic bag between his legs.

'What's in that?'

Nasir crumpled the plastic in his hands and thought about inhaling. 'Want some?'

'What is it?'

'Somalia.'

'What?' Ali shuffled and looked around, but there was nothing much to see. 'You know you really hurt Odawaa.'

'Leader of Islam. You should come with me.' Nasir smiled. There was a silver coating on his teeth. 'Somalia needs a good Leader of Islam.'

'I don't know what you're talking about.'

'I am leaving soon. Did you know that, Ali? I am going home.'

'That is a good idea,' Ali said. Odawaa had indicated that Nasir had been frequenting his own house less and less, opting for full nights in the park rather than the security of a bedroom. 'You need to see your parents. I am sure they are worried about you.'

'They are idiots. They should not have come here.'

'Everyone is worried about you…' Nasir used the silence that followed as a chance to inhale, sealing the plastic bag around his mouth and breathing in. The presence of his cousin began to fade, his limits becoming soft and black. 'Nasir!'

'You should come with me, cousin. We will have guns. We will drive fast cars and kill the enemy.' Nasir's fantasy stretched out before him: the field at his feet became a dusty highway lined with stone buildings, and the highway led to a hot sea and golden sun. Arid land and acacia trees. Across wind-driven sand dunes there are no intersections, no traffic lights and no white women to stare at you. No need to beg for their change.

'Nasir!'

When *tangambili* beats back the monsoons, there are no English verbs to conjugate and no pale men in uniform to tell you to move on. 'Cousin, we will sweat all day and swim at dusk and catch fish.' Nasir's head was lolling, slumping left, lurching on its spine as it made an arc down into his chest.

'I would not swim there, Nasir. Not on the coast.'

'Why not, cousin? – the water is fine: like silk.' He could feel it against his chest as he waded in.

'It is polluted. Foreigners dumped toxic waste on the beaches.'

Nasir heard his cousin's voice next to him in the waves; beyond him, the wreckage of a rusting oil tanker leaned like a warped trophy, abounding with a power he *felt* but could not put into words. 'That is not true, Ali. The leader of Islam does not lie. You know this water is pure.'

'No, it is true – I read it. They paid money to dump millions of tons of it on our beaches, and then the tsunami pulled it all open. Now people who swim get sick. They bleed on the inside.'

'You read it?' Nasir could sense the pressure of a wave somewhere across the Indian Ocean, but he refused to let it ruin his swim. 'Lies, Ali. You are reading lies. Reading is not knowing... Come with me and I will show you.'

'Even if I did want to go, how would we get there? You have no money.'

But Nasir was already gone. Saliva was spooling from the edge of his mouth; Ali watched it stretch like elastic and meet the fabric of his cousin's pants. And so Ali couldn't really understand what Nasir said next; his lips were moving too slowly, the muscles in his face too lethargic to form anything cogent. But Nasir understood it – he knew, with absolute certainty, what it was he was saying: he was born in the Horn of Africa, the Cradle of

Civilization, and now, lying down in the grass, everything was becoming clear. He knew how to get home. He would make them do it. He would force it.

TOM & DAVE

What? Dave said.

I didn't say anything.

Yeah, you did.

The sun of the afternoon had found a gap in the bamboo and was pouring through the door of the Midway House. It washed the room in a white fog of dust and smoke. Tom squinted into it. You're imagining things, he said.

You sure?

Maybe… Maybe someone's outside…

Dave checked the door that led to the bamboo, checked the window looking out to the harbour. There's no one here, he said.

Then maybe I did say something. Maybe I said a whole lot.

Stop it.

What?

I'm not in the mood to be fucked with.

I'm not fucking with you.

Well stop it anyway.

Are you worried you won't understand what's going on?

I *don't* understand what going on. I don't want you making it worse.

Nobody understands…That's kinda just the way it is. And nothing really makes any sense.

Dave looked into the same light Tom had been staring into and squeezed his eyes closed. That's bright.

Justice…Like, what have we been doing? How long have we been here?

Fuck…? Dave backed away from the sun and held his hands against his eyes. Are we going back to school?

If you stare into the light for long enough it's like your eyes stop registering colour.

You're going to mess up your sight doing that.

You remember that party a few months ago? Tom asked.

Which one?

The big one, with the garden – I don't remember whose place it was. Henry puked all over himself. There was a garage. The one where Xavier punched a guy in the face.

Yeah.

You know why he did it?

Xavier? Nah. You know what happened after though?

What?

Like a few weeks later Xavier was walking home from the gym—

His arms are getting way too big for his head.

I know – he looks like a cartoon. But he was walking home, down his street, and this random car passes him and like skids to a stop and three guys jump out.

Actually I do know about this.

Fucking *justice* right. Did you get the full story?

Dunno.

So this is like a total chance thing that these guys spotted him at all. They like charged up to him and two of the guys grabbed him and held him down, and the third guy is the dude he punched at the party. So the guy he punched just returns the whole thing. Like with Xavier pinned there he just smacks him a few times in the face, and then they gap it and just leave him there. He was off school for about a week.

Guess he didn't want to show off the bruises.

Would you?

Probably not. But that's the thing, Tom said. You know why Xavier hit him in the first place? – Like why he hit him at the party...?

Dave shrugged, tried to find a cigarette.

This is the thing that doesn't make any sense, Tom said. Like any way you try to sort it out in your head, it doesn't work. And the bit that fucks me up about it all is that it's just one example that I know about, so if you think about it, there's probably a whole lot of stuff out there like this, like endless examples of things not connecting. Like, way too much of human existence and what goes on is irrational, retarded nonsense.

You're losing me. Maybe you should stop looking at the sun.

And you want things to be sensible, you know. Like, you want to at least understand why people do the shit they do.

Dude: Xavier...

So Xavier's at the party and some guy's messing with him.

Messing with him?

Just like making fun of him, calling him shit and picking on him.

I bet it was about the size of his head.

And so Xavier's getting angrier and angrier about it, but the guy who's fucking with him has a whole load of mates standing around, so he can't really do anything. But he's also getting drunker, so his courage is starting to swell and he's really starting to think about hitting him.

And the guy that's picking on him is the guy that beat the shit out of him?

No, different guy – completely different guy – I'm getting to that. Don't interrupt. So by this point Xavier's probably feeling all his rage in his biceps and stuff and he's hardening himself to what he pretty much knows he has to do, and then eventually, after some final hassle, it all tips over and he goes to hit this cunt.

Cunt…

But here's the bit where everything sort of breaks down and logic just like disappears.

What happened? Did the other guy jump in and try to break it up and get smacked? Like collateral damage.

Nah. That's way too coherent.

Then what?

Got a smoke?

Sure, here, Jesus – you always fucking do this. Finish the story.

So as Xavier lurks up to the guy – the one who's been hassling him – and his arms are up and his chest is all puffed to shit, the guy's mates like immediately jump up and get in between and say like, hey, don't punch this guy. If you wanna start some shit, hit *that* guy, and they point over at this dude drinking beer in the corner of the garden who's had absolutely nothing to do with any of this – like Xavier's never even seen him before or spoken to him or anything. And for some reason – fuck knows what – Xavier seems to think this is a good idea, like it's an appropriate solution to the situation, and so he walks straight over to this guy who's just holding his beer and having a conversation with someone and then hits him in the face.

…I don't get it.

That's what I'm saying. It doesn't make any sense.

This guy had nothing to do with anything?

Nothing. He wasn't even close enough to call a bystander.

What'd he do after Xavier hit him?

He just stood there. Like I don't even think he dropped his beer. He just looked at Xavier like he had no idea what was going on, and then Xavier threatened him or something and walked off… And then a few weeks later…you know the rest.

Man… I find that story really fucking unsatisfying. Like I almost wish you hadn't told me.

I know, right.

The gap of sunlight retreated suddenly from the room, its source once again shielded by the wall of bamboo.

I mean, like…

I know, Tom said. He squinted, trying to rinse the sun from his retina.

315

DANNY

'The key,' he said into the camera, 'is to override your natural impulse to let go.' He reached back and took hold of the fence, the yellow sign indicating its electrification nestled in the top corner of the frame, and then the fence started clicking, sharp snaps less than half a second apart – snick-snick-snick-snick – like a high frequency arthritic joint, like an ankle cracking rapidly in the cold. His neck muscles tensed, tendons straightening against the surge; his eyes drew back in his head and twitched and flickered. As the wire hammered nails of voltage into his nervous system, there was no way he could stop himself from belching a pattern of grunts. The effect was a kind of semi-human alarm, his face distorted as he convulsed a grotesquely perfect and entirely involuntary rhythm: garge-garge-garge on top of the treble-heavy clicks. But the most noticeable thing about the video before it cut to black, its noise bridging into the darkness as he released the fence and hit the ground and wailed, was the fact that half way through, he definitely managed to smile.

Titled *The Power of the Human Mind*, the single-shot video lasted only twenty-four seconds. Later on, after everything, news stations would play it endlessly, the sound off while reporters' voices burbled across its surface and tried to dissect and analyse the boy's psychology.

Danny's peers, however, had no such trouble, and once uploaded the video was an immediate hit. Where future events would reveal levels to the work, forcing the viewer into an up-close examination of the eyes – the locked black pupils as he stared out through the screen and into something deep and uncomfortable – first viewings by uncomplicated sixteen-year-olds frequently missed any significant emotional resonance. The shit was funny.

'Dude, check this – he fucking electrocutes himself!' And then the video was shared, passed on, watched on phones and in bedrooms and in the school computer labs, and one kid after another lapsed into hysterics, watched it again, paused it, watched it again – 'Dude, pause it right there! – Fuck that's funny.'

'Guy's a fucking comic genius.'

'Yeah, but he's fucked though.'

'Whaddaya mean?'

'I mean he's fucking crazy, like legit fucking crazy. You know about the—'

Everybody knew.

Having lost his bearings so publically during the exam, Danny's in-real-life pariah status had increased exponentially, and without the aid of a furry animal to facilitate interaction, other students really saw no need to talk to him at all. It didn't help that the story of his meltdown had been churned so violently through rumour and hearsay. Although the moment itself had been thoroughly public, it was actually only the three or four students sitting closest to him that had borne the true reality of it all before the white-haired invigilator funnelled him away, sequestering the blood and melancholy in an empty office. At best, other students in the exam had seen a flash of white and red – a pink smear – and those back farther still had only seen neck napes and confusion. But the damage had been done. In the scheme of things, it might have been better had someone produced a phone and hit record, because then there would have been objective fact: Danny covered in his own blood – conceivably, it could have been a nose bleed, nothing more. Instead the truth, bad enough on its own, had been twisted and bloated: he'd been cutting himself throughout the exam, getting off on it, and when he stood up at the end, the erection was…; he'd killed his own pet – bit it right open, blood all over his face – and then squeezed its guts between his answer sheets. 'Tina saw the body.'

'Fuck off, no way.'

'She did! He left the thing on his seat. Mr Andrews had to pick it up before anyone saw.'

'Jesus.'

'I know, right – fucking serial killer. Who does that to a small animal?'

Danny had the same question, but there was no way he could get an answer; there was no DNA evidence, no stray hairs to send to a lab, no finger prints to feed into a database; in terms of motive, it could have been anyone who'd ever tossed a pie at him, called him a faggot or stared at him sideways, and so the list was long, and so it might as well have been everyone. Sitting at the back of his classrooms or alone on a bench at lunch, it didn't really matter: they were all guilty. Yet this wasn't something he wanted to share or explore or delve into, and when Mrs Gershwitz asked him how he was and whether he was still bringing his pet to school, he evaded the question and tried to move the conversation forward. Endings were the important thing – when closing off a narrative, it was vital to leave with a boom. 'I'm not sure I follow,' said Verna.

'You've got to think of it as a kind of purification, a purge – that's the end point. When the blood starts to pour, when the explosion happens, that's the release. Then the audience is liberated, and they'll thank you for it. They need it.'

'Things don't have to end that way.'

'Yes, they do – in lieu of love, that's the only clean way for things to end.'

'Look, Danny, I'm not really sure what you're talking about.'

'I'm talking about everything. Art. Life. All that stuff.'

'And who's the audience?'

'I'm aiming high. Why limit myself?'

Verna looked at the boy in front of her: gone were the comical hand movements and satirical edge; he no longer leaned in a way that was calculated to amuse. Instead he sat perfectly still, his vision fixed, rebuking a point somewhere between them. His tie hung pendulously, weighed down by a small black box that had been clipped to the widest section of its face. 'What's that?' she asked, looking for some way to steer the conversation beyond abstract morbidity.

Danny pinched the tie between two fingers and let the camera dangle. He'd left it off for the session, unwilling to record the guidance counsellor without her permission. 'This?'

'Yeah.'

'It's a hotline to truth.'

'Like a talisman?'

'Yeah, sort of – when I caress it the right way it lets me see into everything. Like a superpower.'

'Are you into comics and superheroes? I don't think we've ever discussed it.'

Danny let go of the tie; the camera swung back and bounced against his chest. The stiches in his hand had yet to come out. 'I like Spiderman.'

'You like the idea of being masked, maybe being something more than you are?'

'I'm perfectly comfortable with who I am.'

'I'm sorry, I—'

'But I like the whole concept, you know. Like it's smart and dumb at the same time.'

Verna rapidly scraped through fragmented knowledge of an unfamiliar genre. Red and blue? He uses webs, right? 'What do you mean?'

'Don't get me wrong, slinging between skyscrapers and doing backflips has its appeal and all, although if I could do that myself I certainly wouldn't wear a mask. I mean, you'd want people to know it was you.'

'But isn't the point that—'

'I just like the way Stan Lee would've come up with it.'

'Who's Stan L—'

'Like I can imagine him jerking off into his hand and whipping the semen against a wall. When it stretches and sticks, he's like, 'Ah! Genius!' After that it writes itself.'

'Semen?'

'Spiderman's like this easy symbol for a horny adolescent male; you know, hide your face while you cover the city in jizz. He's Super-Freud. And he can feel good about it too, because he's doing it for justice, and it doesn't matter that the city officials and the police don't really understand, because he knows deep down that if he sprays the entire metropolitan area with his gunk then he'll kind of own it – it'll be his.'

'Danny, I—'

'But, like I said, he also sort of knows what he's doing is a bit dirty and wrong, so he covers his face. It's puberty all over.'

'You really think that's what it's about?'

'Meh – Maybe. There's a lot of sticky, stringy white shit in it. Most people like to approach their issues with symbolism. It's easier than facing everything as it actually is.'

'…Does Spiderman finish with an explosion?'

'Probably, I don't know. I don't read it. But I'm being really rude – I haven't asked about you. How's the literotica coming?'

'Look, Danny, do you want to talk about the exam?' she asked. They'd skipped the topic once already and her frustration with his unwillingness to discuss it was starting to show.

Danny smiled. 'You're struggling with endings I bet.'

'We're going to have to countenance it eventually. Keeping it buried could be really detrimental.'

'Because where do you go with it, right? They meet, they fuck, and then what?'

'Danny.'

'Because the fucking's really the ending – like the whole story's the climax. I guess you could have the lovers fall asleep together and then the motel catches fire and they can burn to death in their bed. That's romantic.'

'Why are you avoiding this, Danny?'

'I'm not avoiding it. I know what I'm doing... And you've got to admit that death is better than any alternative there. I mean, what else are they supposed to do? Recover from the throes of passion and decide to raise a family together? Where's the purge?'

'I'm just worried, Danny. If this has happened once, what's to say it's not going to happen again?'

'The power of the human mind, Mrs Gershwitz. It's all about careful construction. And you know, people want to identify with their characters, but only up to a point. And I think deep down all audiences want their characters to die – that way they don't have to carry them around afterwards.'

'How do you know that something won't trigger it again? You can be glib with me, but I think you know this is important.'

'It's very important.'

'So what steps are you taking?'

Danny leaned forward to let his tie hang, the weight of the camera pulling it straight and tranquilising its movement. He blinked at the venetians.

Most of the steps had been taken already, because when all's said and done, the planning was really the important part. He knew how to manufacture the purge. The little camera on his tie would capture it all: the walking into school, the trip to the Dean's office, the initial strike – because a crowd was imperative: he had to bring everyone together – and then the grand finale of colour and fire…. That was the liberation. And it would be an easy edit. Single shot, the visual signature of the FPS generation, no need for music: the action itself would determine the tempo. And that would be that.

The difficult part should have been the explosives, but that had already been solved with some basic web-searching and a little bit of moxie. It had even been fun. Because of all the people inside the school, all the bullies and all the bullied, all the teachers and caretakers and lunch ladies, the most starved for conversation were the Science technicians. Having completed degrees in the relevant fields, they knew everything one could know about chemicals and reactions and how to melt bodies, but they didn't have teaching degrees and so never talked to actual students. Nor did they converse with the other Science teachers except to take requests; they were told that an experiment would be taking place in B17 – could they please restock the hydrochloric acid. So they did, between periods, when no one was looking, and then they scuttled back to the cluttered tin room at the back of the Science block and kept silent vigil over things students generally didn't want anyway.

As such, Danny found it easy: he asked them questions; he flattered them. 'Wow, you guys really have the power here, huh. They should give you a bigger office.' And he asked them what they had in stock – how many litres of chlorine they kept, whether they ever secretly took home the potassium nitrate and manufactured extra special fireworks. 'We're too responsible for that,' one of them said, punching in the code to the door in a way that was routine and instinctual and in full view.

'But imagine what you could do? Guy Fawkes is just around the corner. You guys could start your own black market business.'

'Boy's got a point,' said the other.

'How much could you make out of what the school has in here?'

'Enough,' said the first with poorly concealed pride.

'How much is enough?'

'Enough to cause pretty significant damage.'

Two days later, during lunch, when the technicians were buying bakery food and the Science faculty was in a meeting about low-ability learners, Danny punched in the appropriate door code and entered the room and lifted what he needed, including a whole sack of KNO_3 (there were four more of them anyway, so who would notice?) and simply walked out. He lumbered through the school with it and no one said anything. He crossed the field, lugging it in both arms, then squeezed it though the metal bars of the gate, jumped over and went home.

Everything else was easy to come by, and when his father asked him why he had so many matches and tennis balls and why he needed the sandpaper, he said he was making a model. 'What of?'

'A narrative,' he replied, slicing open the curvilinear division between the felt with a craft knife.

His father paused for a moment, his body stuck, as always, in the doorframe. 'Is *narrative* a concrete noun or abstract noun?'

Danny put down the knife and tennis ball and turned from his desk. 'Why do you ask?'

'Well…' He rubbed his chin for a moment. 'Are you making a model out of something that *visually exists*, or are you trying to *represent* something?'

'Good question, father. Maybe both. I'm not sure yet. I guess I won't really know until it's done.'

'Well, keep at it then.'

He did.

In the days before Guy Fawkes, Danny found himself alone outside the mall at night. With a bag of tennis balls he'd climbed from his bedroom window and drifted into the streets; houses had become outlet stores, and then car yards, and soon he was standing in the empty parking lot – a concrete sprawl for testing – his black hoodie pulled around his face, his bag at his feet, his tiny sable camera clipped to his chest like a name badge. He talked to himself as he worked, mumbling instructions and listing details: 'Test one commencing: moderate packing; high launch angle.' With the felt of the first ball in his palm he steadied himself and threw it deep into the night, losing its yellow momentarily in the darkness above the roadside street lights. It re-entered and thocked meekly against the parking surface, bouncing only once before sputtering into a roll and coming to rest against a kerb. Nothing happened. 'Test one, negative on high launch angle.' He collected the ball and shifted it to the side. Precision was important.

'Test two commencing: high packing; high launch angle.' Again the ball vanished into the night, and again it hit the ground with an uninspiring thock. Between the first and second bounce Danny had the sinking notion that the whole thing was a bust, but then it connected with the pavement again and the felt seemed to catch fire – a bright languid flame yawning from the interior – and as it lumbered into a roll it began to hiss and fizz and crackle, and then it exploded, popping into a flash of orange. 'Test two, positive on high launch angle: moderate deflagration.' He jogged to collect the debris; white smoke sifted across the plane of the car park. The ball had been torn open and scorched. Pleasing result, although not enough to blow off a limb.

'Test three: extreme packing with the addition of incendiary fluids; high angle launch.' Up it went, a deep enough throw to give him the time to pull the draw strings of his hood tight around his face, and then it hit, but this time the impact was muted by the immediate glow of the flame, and before the second bounce the ball erupted, not with a pop but with a boom that seemed elemental and pure, and Danny could feel the shockwave kicking back at him. He had the sense that he'd broken the parking lot, that the structure itself had shifted, and then everything was silent except the ringing in his ears.

He wouldn't need another test. This was enough to blow a garbage bin sideways, burn a hole in a wall, peel off a body part. It was enough to force a purge and manufacture screams, to seal off the kind of ending that viewers would remember.

With the lights of a security car pulling in to the far end of the lot, Danny collected his bag of unexploded munitions and fled into the suburbs. Things were ready. All he had to do was pick the day and go.

Back in his room, at his computer – the desk lamp puddling amber across his hands – he re-read comments on his videos. His *Drowned* piece had received mixed reviews: 'The fuck is this?' wrote one viewer. 'You need help,' wrote another. 'Good way to give yourself brain damage.' What they remember most is what confuses them. 'What's the point in this? Kept expecting something to happen.' You have to see the bigger picture – force it all into a timeline… *The Power of the Human Mind* had already been tagged as inappropriate, compelling people to sign in and confirm their age to see it. 'Guy, you're a fucking moron.' Just a geek at the carnival. 'What next? You gonna hammer shit into your body?' I'm going to make you remember, and think; I'm going to have tee-shirts printed. 'I don't see the point? You doing this for attention?' It's a matter of perspective: I'm doing this for you, not for me. Because in the scheme of things, I don't hate anyone. But *something* has to happen. It just *has to*. And I want to share it when it does. I want you to be together on this one. 'Do you just ignore the consequences, Danny? Do you just pretend that the aftermath isn't going to exist, that the world will cease to be? Have you thought about any of that?' Of course I have. I've thought about it a lot. *Till love and fame to nothingness do sink*. In the end it's not going to matter, right? 'Have you thought about your parents?' I'll write them a note; but you have to understand that sacrifice is selfish. Martyrs hog all the fame and leave everyone else crying. 'No one's going to cry for you. They're going to hate you.' And it will bring them together. Peace be upon them.

'I think Jesus was selfish,' Danny said. 'He just wanted to be remembered – blah blah blah, look at my religious blood.'

Verna stirred. 'Wow, Danny, sometimes you say these things – you just drop them like bombs – and I'm not sure where you're coming from or why you're saying them.'

'Bleeding everywhere for people. The cross was a podium, you know. Up on a hill so people could watch his sacrifice and appreciate it in full view.'

'I don't understand how you can see it from that perspective.'

'Not exactly a humble way to die.'

'I don't think it was his choice.'

'Of course it was his choice. It was his choice all the way through. But if he really wanted to bring people together, then he wouldn't have worried about the people closest to him hating him. He should've done something terrible and then offered himself up for the punishment.

Hate gels people way more than love. And then his sacrifice would've been truly good.'

'Danny, you just…'

You just have to prepare and plan and go with it – there is no room for doubt – and in the end it is what it is.

'You're a nice woman, Mrs Gershwitz – like really lovely. And I want you to know that. You're good at your job, too, and don't let anyone tell you otherwise.'

On a fine morning that promised the preheat of summer, Danny kissed his mother goodbye, told her he loved her, and told his father he wouldn't need a lift, that he'd be bussing in. 'You sure?' he asked.

'Absolutely. Your parenting skills are sound.'

Alone in the house he made final preparations, clipped his camera to his tie, layered his school bag with tennis balls designed to explode on impact. He left his parents a note to find on his bed – it was short – and soon he was walking, and cars were passing him on the street, and the blue sky seemed like an oath. He stopped at a park and sat near the playground – plastic slides, a seesaw, high-tension powerlines seething current. He listened to birds; he stared at the grass without ever seeing it.

He waited. This was happening. The purge.

This is it.

It's happening.

TOM & DAVE

What class are we supposed to be in now? Dave asked.

English, I think. Blasco. Tom looked into the harbour.

You wanna go back? You ready?

Fuck…

Yes or no?

How many cigarettes have we got?

None.

Beyond the window the day was beginning to look pale.

MONDAY

We all live in the future, in a hybrid of images and technology where everything is mass-produced and everything is individualised. In every respect, the world is more diverse now than ever before; culture and technology overlap, entertainment blends seamlessly with information just as propaganda disguises itself as fact. Seven billion ideologies compete for attention – or even simply validation – and when they move through the phantasmagoria of modern life they gain complexity, reduce complexity, become fragmented, evolve, deform, mutate, swell. Truth has never been slipperier; niches have never been more defined. It's an age of paradox, and it's frightening and comforting, horrible and wonderful all at once. But more than ever, and maybe this is as close to certainty as we can get, it's impossible to hold it all in a single look or a lone unique equation. It's too unwieldy, too differentiated. And so all we can do is CLING to our perceptions – the observations and insights and feelings of one person at a time in one place and in one single moment. Only there does honesty exist. There is no collective feeling; there is no zeitgeist – these things are miasmas, abstract constructs, wishful illusions. Instead we experience only the present moment of an individual human, an ape standing bare against a reality of light and sound and sensation.

And so it was that in the snow-globe of his mind and in his very own matchless present, Nasir knew more clearly than anything what it was he had to do. At this instant in the universe and in the Earth's elliptical lurch around the sun, while a hot Monday lunchtime was whirling in the grounds of a school he no longer attended, he was ready. Because he didn't need ticket money and he didn't need to scale the airport fence and claw at the undercarriage of a 747. He could *force* it. All he had to do was walk back onto the property and start destroying things, hurting people. He'd done it before. And he had no qualms about picking a victim and going to town on them, because *they deserved it*: it was structural. He was on his way.

During period five he strolled onto the premises with a harrow size cricket bat. He'd found it discarded at the park, picked it up, learned to swing it hard enough to make the air rush and cut. Now it was his weapon resting on his shoulder, and class was back in session and the place just wasn't ready, *so* unready that the man getting back into a courier van in the front car park nodded at him like this was normal, and because Nasir was feeling it, he nodded back.

When he attacked the automated doors guarding the main office, they broke apart with a single strike, glass falling like a crying face. He beat on the reception desk and threatened the secretary and took out her computer with a clean swipe that cracked the monitor. The noise brought senior managers to their office windows, and one even opened a door and said, 'Hey!' like it meant something, as if that was enough to stop what was going to happen next. The face of the secretary went bloodless and chalky as she reeled backwards. Nasir loved it. He continued to move. It was all so easy.

He stalked the grounds and no one tried to stop him. Why would they? This was something they weren't prepared to deal with. But a bell was ringing – three on, one off – and with its unfamiliarity he knew it was for him. His bell. And when a senior student he'd never talked to and didn't recognise crossed the courtyard and made his way to the drinking fountain, an idiot of a kid for not understanding the wrath that was befalling the school, Nasir attacked, beating him hard from behind and fracturing bone, watching him hit the ground and reach for the pain. Someone was screaming. He set fire to a bin, lighting the paper and plastic wrappers, really taking his time to make sure the thing was aflame before he kicked it into a roll, its burning contents billowing free, fluttering, singed chip packets smouldering in warm breeze.

He smashed in the door of a classroom and found *that* kid – what was his name again? – and whaled on his racist frame, used the cricket bat to hack hard against arms that were trying to cover his face while he was trapped in the awkwardness of his desk, dug into his ribs until they cracked. Because *fuck him* – he deserved it before, deserved it now. No need to feel guilty. The rest of the class watched and did nothing, too jolted for cognitive function. The teacher remained bonded to the floor at the front, the marker in her hand still pressed against the whiteboard and stranded halfway through the formation of a letter. And then Nasir left the room with an icy swagger, because *that* is how to educate.

There were shouts now and he could see someone run across his path and into the shadows. Three on, one off. The curtains on the classes were closed tight; the cowards were hiding, like moles in the dark.... He blew out the glass of a classroom window just to do it – just for effect – and when he saw a dean emerge from the admin block, a white man in a suit edging closer and closer, his hands raised, his mouth saying something that Nasir didn't care to listen to, Nasir smiled and let his weapon hang, let the guy believe that everything was okay, that it was over now, and when he got close enough – when this suit thought he was in control – up came the bat to break more bone. This was the structure, and Nasir was smashing it, and the digital yelp of police sirens meant that other people were in pain and that he was winning; soon he would drop his bat and raise his own hands and greet them with a smile and a joke about a midget with a fourteen-inch penis, and of course they would handcuff him and bash his upper body against the bonnet of the car. 'Mogadishu,' he would say. 'One way. Let my parents know I am going home.' But this wasn't happening, and it wouldn't happen, because when the lockdown bell incepted its treble grind that afternoon, Nasir was not on school grounds. And even though his body was physically present in the park one suburb over, resting limply against the base of a tree, he wasn't really there either, and at the rate he was going – on his current descending trajectory – he would struggle to truly be anywhere ever again.

Time, perception and intersecting threads: Stephanie

Baker could no longer support her own weight: her hip had become a fire, and when she looked down to see the blood and her own sick, she gave way. 'Steph, I don't know if you should be lying down like that…' Her partner was playing games on his computer.

'I think I need help.'

'Just a second. I need to save my progress.'

She could see sunlight above trees; shifting her body, she ached, and in the courtyard students were standing over her, shadowed outlines, a Year 10 face right down next to her own. She could no longer hear the bell. With her head pressed against the concrete she shifted her eyes to the granulations in its surface: she could see ants moving.

'I think we should go out to dinner,' her partner said. He was wearing a tuxedo.

'I don't think I can move…'

'Look, you don't have to be like this.' He seemed angry; he was straightening his bowtie in the mirror as she lay on the carpet of their living room. 'Why is it always like this with you? If you don't want to go, just say so.'

She was moving beyond her body, looking back in through a window from the outside and watching the blood spread into the carpet. It would be hell to get out. She may even have to replace it.

She was staring at ants. And then nothing.

It was about this time that Mr Blasco had crawled over to check on Brayden; the boy was in shock. His complexion, speckled with glass, gave no hint of emotion, and when Blasco clicked his fingers and waved his hand across his line of sight, the eyes didn't bother to follow. The rest of the students had managed to flatten themselves against the wall that buffered them from the outside – from whatever was out there producing screams and smoke. Akaash remained on his stomach; he couldn't help but watch as Penelope whimpered, and with each second-long break in the bell he could hear her choked blubbers. He wanted to shush her, to shut her up, but he could not make a sound, just as Wendy could no longer operate the buttons on her phone, her fingers suddenly dumb, unable to respond to the question mark her boyfriend had sent or to manipulate their way into a call. At the front of the class, in the corner near Blasco's desk, Sean had crouched; although obscured by angle, he could still read what had been written up on the board during a lesson that now seemed distant, a memory of a memory: 'Willy Loman: A victim of his own propaganda.'

The lockdown bell continued to whine and sing and clang, three on, one off...

An hour earlier, during the melee of lunchtime and between all the pre-organised activities and pick-up games of handball, two Year 12 students slipped easily from the school grounds, skirting the boundary and pulling through a broken wire fence and a hedge and a neighbouring property. They cut up the road toward the Midway House, darting behind trees, through patched shade, and in a curtain of stealth they drew around the rear of a bus shelter instead of the front, and so they didn't see Ahmed and he didn't see them... Except he might not have seen them even if they'd stepped by casually, even if they'd sat right down next to him and said hello and started playing with his face, because Ahmed, like Nasir, was somewhere else. Sure, he was sitting there, literally present, wearing those same short pants, his father's briefcase beside him on the seat; he was breathing in and out and his feet were planted on the concrete beneath him, but at that moment he saw nothing – not the sky or the trees or the houses or the 247 bus to the city centre that pulled up and sat with open doors until the driver became irritated by the inertia and ground away. And then Ahmed had sat in a cloud of fumes he could not smell, his skin tinged yellow by the glow of the giant ad for sunglasses on the inner wall of the shelter. 'Summer's Here!' The ad said. 'Be Full-Time Fabulous.'

It had broken during the walk. Inside the briefcase the hammer and knife had been swinging with his momentum, the weight of clarity, and he'd been thinking of her and knowing exactly what it was he had to do: the example that needed to be made. In the warm light of the day he'd noticed sparrows bathing in a birdbath on a front lawn, and he'd run his hand across the top of a wire fence; he'd been thinking of her – dark eyes looking up at him – and as he approached the back of the school, cutting along the path, he'd recognised the bushes under which they'd made love, beneath which they'd struggled against discovery, and something triggered or opened, an image breached the surface, and for the first time he could remember it all: his hands up on her throat pulling at her skin, the pressure of his thumbs on her windpipe, her feet kicking against his body and the tears burning in her cheeks. And he saw himself, his own dark reflection, bitter shadow on the brick, pointed shoulder blades like the nascent wings of a demon. He watched his darkness fill the spaces of her life, his reptilian hate sucking her into the void. God and the devil had nothing to do with this – he was the possession and madness and pain all in one. *He* was the nightmare. And as this all became clear, the psychogenic haze finally lifting, he could no longer move, his footsteps slowing to nothing.

The back of the school loomed above him, but he was not going in. The catatonia was fully fledged. He didn't notice the movement of his peers behind the shelter; didn't notice the bus or the driver or the monoxide wake. The briefcase sat beside him, but if he had chosen to look at it then, he would have struggled to remember what was in it or what he had been planning or, for that matter, why he was even there. Life is like that. A choice is only a choice until it's not one. Only the lockdown bell, which sounded out across the fields an hour later and was clearly audible from the bottom of the school, carried the necessary dissonance to break the spell. Ahmed heard it ring, its edges invading his despair, and he looked up when he registered the faint outline of a scream, and then he stood for what could have been an explosion. He moved to the bars of the boundary fence and clutched them and looked in, and a whole new kind of worry began to take over.

Like the wave was taking over, because as Henry lay on his back in the school's central courtyard, his head bleeding openly and his brain beginning to engorge, he was drifting into the first damp stages of a coma. The tsunami was here; there was nowhere he could hide and there was nothing he could do. Time; threads; movement.

Danny riding his own wave.

In the morning before the chaos and the final movement of his narrative, he waited alone in a park. It was coming to him with all the psychedelic Technicolor of a spiritual vision, a thick and juicy fog that consumed his being entirely. His bag was resting against the leg of a picnic table; he'd been careful not to jangle it on the walk, well aware that if a single match rubbed against the sandpaper – if it even *dared* to graze it – the chain reaction would blow a grave-sized hole in the pavement. Death-sized. The high-tension lines stretched above him, slicing the coastline and channelling raw energy to the city; in his meditative state he could hear their perma-hum, a high-voltage sizzle that radiated houses and trees and tarmac. His latency was searing black holes and burning open new dimensions; in this mood, he could melt the world. Because clarity was what was needed – the kind that blocks out past and future in favour of the electric flex of *here* and *now*. It was the only way to commit spectacle. He zoned in on the beating of his own heart. He switched the camera on – his objective lens and definite record – and began the walk, his backpack in his left hand, his right hand dry and ready.

Danny was at the gates. The digital sign above him flashed with recent student achievement: Congratulations Girls' Hockey – First in Western Division; Herbert Xu – Mathex Winner; Charlotte Jones – Auckland Barista Finalist; Danny – Blood Is The Catharsis; Danny – *This Is How It Ends*…. He rested his bag at the base of the sign and dropped to his knees and felt the heat of the concrete. The school beyond him had become quiet; period five had begun. Could he feel the vibrations? Was there any sense of a pre-tremor before the quake? The moment seemed molten, and if drivers passing the school had cared to look, they would have seen a boy – normal looking, for all intents and purposes – in what seemed to be a position of prayer, his forehead squeezed against the footpath, his palms flat, seeking something greater than himself, and at that point Danny really was praying, not to Jesus or Allah, but to himself, to the vital sense of narcissism and personal significance required to fuel what was going to happen next.

But here's the funny thing: when he got up and walked in and stood in the open-air corridor between the hospitality block and the school hall, the mood was somehow wrong. It had been punctured, deflated. The electrical surge that had been pummelling his central nervous system had switched off... because as Danny had passed through the entrance, determined and intense, totally ready for his coda, the automated doors of the front office had slid open and out had strolled an African boy, younger than Danny – a boy Danny recognised – and he'd smiled a big stupid smile, a truly unaffected and totally genuine smile. 'Buddy!' he'd said. And suddenly Danny's whole face had felt erroneous, tight and awful and fraudulent, a face that was not his own. 'Buddy! Buddy,' the kid had said.

'What?'

'How is Buddy?'

The camera had caught the boy's grin, toothy and earnest; it had seized on his tucked-in shirt and indomitable goodwill. 'I guess he's good,' Danny had replied, his bag hanging weirdly in his left hand. It had become heavy and awkward, the way a problem is.

'Asymptote,' the boy had said, although his accent was fast and thick and made the word unintelligible. 'Asymptote.'

'Yeah...'

'Yes. Asymptote. Forever. Okay, goodbye. Goodbye, Buddy.' Then Ali had waved at Danny's bag and the memory of a guinea pig he didn't know was dead and moved off into the grounds, and with that, Danny, who had moments earlier been prepared to blow a crisp hole in the side of reality, was unsure what to do. The unexpected juxtaposition had been a bomb all of its own...

He wandered to the front of the hall and stared vacantly across at the cooking classes, his bag lolling at his side. Through the window he could see Mina wearing a hairnet and making what appeared to be crêpes. He felt thirsty. His mouth was dry. Across the courtyard he could see Henry sitting on a bench, out of class; in the distance, from some neighbouring property, he could hear the trilling grumble of a lawnmower. The whole ambience was pictorial and subtle; it had the feeling of a memory even as he was experiencing it, a sort of nostalgia for the present itself, and so the internal voice of reason and common sense – the one that had been beaten and supressed by anger and overthinking – came to him with crystalline precision for the first time in weeks. The fuck are you doing? It said. What's your problem? Cheer up.

What?

Cheer up. This isn't you. What are you even trying to do?

I want spectacle. I want a purge…

What, so you're going to hurt people?

Danny wasn't sure. I guess not.

Of course you're not. You're not a fuck.

I'm not a fuck.

And then Danny had decided. He'd come far enough – the edge is all you need to get to; it's where character is developed, and then it's about having the sack and the smarts to pull short. Get to the edge and admire the view, but if you jump off, you've wasted it. Something eased inside him, his spine realigning against the self-imposed stress, the muscles in his arms loosening. And then he felt depressed. Because he'd worked so hard – and people needed to see something. *He* needed to see something. What you need is a girlfriend, the voice said. You're kind of a loser. You need to give this shit up.

Fuck you. For that I'm going to bomb the cricket pitch.

Your mum will hate you.

She'll understand.

They'll kick you out of school.

Then we're settled.

And then Danny was smiling – because this was the compromise he was after, and as he moved off toward the school field, entirely committed to recording the destruction of an unoccupied slab of concrete and artificial grass as a means of facilitating his expulsion, Anthony Kirsten and his DIY sniper rifle began firing rounds from the roof of the admin building, and in its own poisonous way, this was fate.

ANTHONY KiRSTEN

Having watched Stella exit through his front gate, Tony Kirsten – divorcee, ex-convict, drug dealer and chronic self-mutilator – graduated to an entirely new level of broken, a doctoral thesis in derangement. The symptoms of congenitally misconnected wires had now been exacerbated by a methamphetamine psychosis that increased his threshold for pain, stripped away residual empathy, and heightened his feelings of paranoia and persecution, and after he walked back inside his house and collected one of his guns – a rifle he'd assembled piecemeal, its muzzle niftily supressed by a silencer crafted from the fuselage of a Maglite torch – he proceeded to stamp naked onto his lawn and shoot both of his dogs. They didn't seem to know it was coming.

The next step was logical. He put on some jeans, duct-taped the wound in his chest without any consideration as to how it would feel coming off, then collected what he believed was a sufficiently large amount of ammo. He fired up one last big hit for the road, a hit that would serve him well and felt like the pristine cut of a cold knife, and got into his vehicle. The bitch couldn't have gone far; and besides, he knew where she was going. So, when he couldn't find her on the street, having looped the neighbourhood twice, he turned his ride and made for the school grounds and drove right in through the gates, the music up loud and the windows down, and he slowed into the staff car park and looked out at what was there: a front office, a digital sign flashing with garbled bullshit, some kid with a backpack, some nigger with a smile. He parked on a kerb and left the car running and walked into the front office, and it was here that his impact on the world around him began to take shape.

Because despite his seal of duct-tape, blood was seeping into his wife-beater. And his eyes were red and his hair was a mess, and his tattoos, simply by existing, inflicted the rest of the connotative damage. But the thing the receptionist noticed first and most overpoweringly was his smell, because things like decay and sweat and smoke and death all circulate faster with air-conditioning. It lingered over the foyer. Without even having spoken, all of this was enough to convince the receptionist and the senior managers (who had immediately begun peering through the panes of their offices) that this man could have no good reason to be in the building, or on the grounds, or anywhere near innocence. His mere presence sullied it; dead seraphim lined the soles of his shoes.

And then he talked – sort of – and although the receptionist could barely understand the staccato jabber that issued forth, she knew this was now a *real* problem. So she didn't answer. Because how do you answer something like that? – Cancerous sludge at the bottom of a sewer pipe reassembled into a run-on sentence of threats and expletives. Except her silence on the matter seemed to adversely affect his mental state, *the bitch wasn't getting to the point*, and he leaned over the desk and dunked her in his odour and breathed very close, and this was the cue for the Assistant Principal, who'd been watching half-risen from his seat, to push through the office door and into the foyer and ask what the guy wanted: 'Excuse me, sir – can I help with anything?' Polite words in a strong voice.

But Anthony Kirsten couldn't be helped. These cunts were giving him nothing. He lunged once and suddenly at the Assistant Principal, a fake-out thrust with his upper body and a raised fist that immediately sent the civil servant wincing backwards and covering his head, and then he was out the door and back to the car. In the ensuing minute a good collection of those working in the front office came out to look, to gawk as this guy retreated to his vehicle. Staring from the safety of the foyer, they watched him get back inside his car. And they were breathing easy. This sort of thing happened every now and then – it was, and is, part and parcel of being frontline at a job that services the general public. Sometimes there's an angry parent, or a kid whose family is gang-connected and has perceived, through adolescent mendacities and Chinese whispers, a slight of some kind. They come in and rub the school down with a show of territorial dominance, and then they leave. And that's what they thought this guy was doing now, making a display, because Kirsten had closed the door of his car and revved the engine hard, and they watched as he jammed the accelerator down and began burning out his back tyres, smoking them into thick, white, noisy plumes that swallowed the rear of the vehicle as it began to spin, a rubber fog billowing up and drifting into the heart of the school. Surely that was it, his urine on the fence of the education system. The car was idling now and still. Surely whatever gripe he'd harboured had been solved with this demonstration.

Now he would go.

But Kirsten was not leaving, and they all saw the rifle come out – the Assistant Principal and the Principal proper, the receptionist and the two year-level deans that had been in the vicinity at the time of the commotion. And as is the case with all violent aberrations from the rhythm of normal life, it took a few seconds for any of them to decode the visual language of the situation and filter it through the required processing centres. 'Is that a gun?'

It was a gun, and Anthony Kirsten appeared to be loading a bullet into it, and then lifting it up and pointing it at the front doors, at them. And when it was fired the gun made no sound – none at all – but as the .30 calibre slug penetrated the glass and collected a smiling portrait of a former Head Girl, the receptionist's screams and the tumult of human panic, the clamour of rushing limbs and a computer monitor being knocked over: these things were audible. Wholly internalised alarms were blaring. The receptionist made a dash down the hall and confined herself in the accounts room, locking it with numb hands and curling up under a table. The Principal scattered back into his office and went for his phone. As one of the deans fell to her stomach and crawled for sanctuary behind a photocopier, the other, colliding with stationery and dropping his coffee, skidded for the back office and did what needed to be done. With Anthony Kirsten moving very deliberately back to the admin block, reloading his rifle as he went, the lockdown bell started to sound: three on, one off.

Three on, one off.

The Dean poked his head into space, looked. In the pause of the alarm he registered the clatter, redirected himself. The intruder wasn't coming in. He'd thrown his bag and gun onto a low hanging eave. There was a flashing image of disembodied legs rising up and disappearing. Kirsten was on the roof.

From the roof he could see things.

Although Henry didn't know it, it was Mrs Gershwitz's scream he'd heard in the moments immediately following the lockdown – a scream truncated at both ends by the bell.   Verna had been between appointments when it began, absently spooning industrial-grade coffee into a Pyrex cup and watching steam rise from the kettle in the kitchen of the student services block. The alarm drew her away from the task and into the corridor. Two kids were sitting and waiting in the chairs across from her office. Both looked up as she passed. She moved through the exit and into the courtyard adjacent the admin building, glanced across at the windows; the sun had made them reflective, and from her distance she could see herself, slightly distorted by the age of the glass, a little warped, a touch elongated. She experienced a moment of clumsy vanity, the type only possible when one glimpses themselves from a distance in a stray reflection – a quick existential flash that freshened her notion of being human, a body floating through an environment just like all the others. Caught in this whim, it took some time for her to catalogue the waving arms in the dim beyond her image – the arms of someone trying to signal her, to shoo her or reproach her or beckon her – and then she heard the crack behind and to the left, timber panels splintering. She turned to inspect it, then rotated once, a full revolution: her stretched reflection, waving arms, and above her, a man with a gun. A man with a gun pointing at her for what she now understood was a second go.

Her scream was tremendous and hysterical. Later, in another moment of self-reflective vanity, this would annoy her just a little bit, because she'd never pegged herself as a screamer, always hoped she would be reserved enough to be in control. She was even under the impression that she might be cool in a way that was effortless and somehow fashionable, a form of Serious Situation Chic. Definitely not a wailing banshee. But that was how it was and she couldn't take it back, and then she was inside and bulwarked behind a filing cabinet, hyperventilating in a way that made the room seem like it was going to implode.

It was this segment of terror that Henry had caught, its trill squashed between the ringing. And when he craned his head, angling to locate its position, the sun streaming against white smoke that seemed out of place but definitely connected to the current goings-on – it was then that the bullet clipped the rear of his skull. It entered just back of his left ear and slid rudely through bone; it exited behind his right – a subsonic bullet he hadn't heard and that Anthony Kirsten had loaded and fired, adjusting for gravity's pull and treating Henry like an ambling deer. The puncture was in and out so fast, had come with so little preamble, that he didn't even feel it. He used his hands to measure a frame against the roof and the sky – an image he suddenly liked, stark lines without movement; black and white.

He was on his back. With the pressure between occipital and parietal lobes building, Henry entered his final dream – a swirl that caught him and rolled him and churned him. A swirl of inevitable and endless tsunami from which he would never recover.

And Anthony Kirsten continued to shoot. Load, fire, reload.

The bell was exactly what he needed. The three second phase gave him focus, then a second's rest, and then focus. A tempo for hunting.

An excellent vantage point.

Plenty of targets. Because Ms Stephanie Baker, first-year science teacher, had made the fatal mistake of confusing the lockdown for a fire drill, and Kirsten understood that this was fair game. But difficult. Because at fourteen years old, the world is hyperactive. There's a lot going on. The sensory explosion of simply being awake is enough to facilitate frenzy, and who could possibly sit still when a bell was blaring and Corban was bleeding and the sun was dancing and white smoke was drifting. And a senior was lying down over there. Run circles and break off a tree branch and shout things for no reason; stand on seats and blurt non sequiturs. If your friend isn't paying attention, slap them in the back of the head and run away and hope they chase you…Which is how it was when Ms Baker's class broke out into the open courtyard of the school: zigzag patterns of ADD, a hectic confusion that Kirsten found difficult to follow and which incensed him – because these little fucks didn't even notice the bullets that clipped the concrete beside them and ricocheted off walls. They just keep laughing and jumping. He sighted them and aimed, countered for the drop and distance, but in the last instant they moved, twitching, jerking, shouting at each other, and there was no way he could predict the distortions and turns their bodies would make. So he aimed for the teacher as she appeared behind them all – a woman in a cream dress and holding her nose. And he got her.

And he reloaded.

And off to his left some kid was peeking through a classroom window, a victim of his own stupidity. And down in front, other kids were crowding around the one he'd already tagged, so he fired for the window and watched it shatter, the idiot reeling back inside the curtain, and the destruction of the window sated Kirsten a little. It made him feel like damage really was being done. Because with a silenced rifle and subsonic ammo, you never really feels you're getting your money's worth: the bullets thup from the muzzle, and if nothing smashes and if no one is killed – if a body doesn't spin sideways – then it's really as if you've fired nothing at all. But the shattering glass grabbed attention, and now the students in the courtyard turned and gawped, and it was then that the ones standing over Henry's bleeding head began to register the danger, began to gambol and jag for the darkness. But others didn't: 'You broke the window!'

'Nah, I didn't.'

'You're in trouble!'

'Shut up!'

And behind it all Stephanie Baker was slipping in and out of consciousness. The bullet had entered her hip and lodged inside her body – blood blossoming, blood in full bloom. In the hours to come she would be rushed to the emergency room and into surgery, where she would dream of fading relationships, digital chainsaws and William Prout.

And Kirsten reloaded.

And Danny was standing over Henry, looking down at him. Looking into open eyes. He could see the sun reflecting off Henry's pupils, and when he gazed off into the school he could see a teacher on her side, and he could see the shattered window of the classroom, bits of glass hanging like stalactites, and then he saw the pitch of dust and chipped concrete as a bullet struck to his right and pinged away, and he turned and looked up and saw the man on the roof reloading a rifle and holding it up and aiming it back in his direction, and then a thwack as a bullet lodged in a picnic table behind him. The man was reloading again.

Beyond the lockdown bell Danny could now hear the wail of police sirens. And then he closed his eyes and he believed that past it all, he could hear the sea, the tide moving in and out, the movement of the Earth through space. He could sense the violent surge of powerlines and the wavelength of a frequency that cleaved open the universe. He began to walk forward. Just one foot in front of the other. The gunman fired again, and he had the surreal sensation of hearing the bullet as it fizzed past his head, and with his free hand he opened his bag and removed a tennis ball, and the man with the gun was reloading again, and then firing again – a whirling slice as it zipped by – and then Danny was beneath the roof, and the man was reloading again, but now he had to stand up and move forward, *because this kid was right underneath him*, and he had to lean over the gutter to see where he was…

As the guy's demented face looked down at Danny – a face defined by its scar and sweat and eyeballs that seemed to have come loose – Danny waved. Although Anthony Kirsten didn't wave back, he did watch patiently as Danny began to swing his bag – slowly at first, looping it around and around in large arcs, and then faster, winding up the momentum as centrifugal forces built against his fingers and his shoulder began to ache. 'Catch!'

he called. He released its weight into a wild lob that rose up and seemed to hover above Kirsten, who jerked his neck to follow it, and with his rifle in one hand he adjusted to catch the sailing package in the other. And he did. It thumped hard into his chest and arm. And then he looked down at the kid who'd thrown him this bag, and for a moment they watched each other. 'Good work,' Danny said. Then Anthony Kirsten took aim with his free hand, and Danny smiled.

DANNY

In the immediate aftermath of the shockwave he found himself on his stomach, sheltering from a rain of body parts and guttering. There was a ringing in his head that was entirely unique. His camera was still recording, clipped to his tie, its lens smeared but functioning.

This would be a work of art.

As he pulled himself from the ground, moving like a drunken fog, he struggled to come to grips with the facts. The blast had ripped the gunman to pieces, mulching him into fragments of organ and bone; a paste that no one would miss. When Danny looked down he discovered he was speckled with debris and a fine film of third-party blood, but he had difficulty registering what that meant. He could no longer hear the lockdown bell or the approaching sirens or the screams from around the school; the universal frequency that had arrived to align and straighten now seemed to have swollen, engulfing him in a liquid delirium. He could see through the hole in the roofing and side-wall of the admin block; he could see bits of someone's face, bits of torso, and off to his right, what appeared to be the lower part of a left leg, torn denim adhering to the calf and a cooked sneaker still on the foot. And so he moved over and picked it up, as if it were driftwood, as if it were something that had washed up on the beach of his life and was worth inspecting, and he removed the blackened shoe and looked at the sockless foot and touched its still-clammy skin, taking note of the coarse black hair on each of the toes. And then there it was! His last remaining tennis ball – the one he'd been holding. It had escaped his grip when the detonation roiled him sideways, and now it was lying against a smashed piece of timber. This was a trophy of some kind.

It could even be worth something.

He reached for it and held it up to the sun.

It exploded in a cut of heat and light and took most of his left fist with it.

And the camera caught everything, the scream and paralysis, the pastel impressions of green Nelson blocks swirling against a backdrop. When the ambulances arrived – jammed in through the swell of police cars and firemen, of crying teachers and lost children – they found Danny staring at the pulp of his forearm, angling it to fully appreciate the charred tissue. He was already considering the interviews that would follow. He saw himself explaining things to nodding journalists, talking in abstract ways about the shape of narratives and the absurd angles of real life. 'It's the end,' he said to one of the paramedics.

'You'll be okay, kid. You're in shock.' The paramedic was busy wrapping a tourniquet and failed to look at the boy's face. 'You'll be just fine.'

'I know,' he said.

For the rest of his life Danny would have only one hand. In the seconds before he blacked out, he decided this was cool.

BAM!

Dave smashed an empty bottle against the wall of the Midway House.

Tom checked his pockets again but found no cigarettes. The bamboo was rustling; the breeze had returned. It's like you're always leading up to something. You know what I mean?

Dave shrugged.

Like you're in this permanent state of trying to get there, Tom said.

What about when you do?

Then you're probably not there.

What the fuck are you talking about? You're *there* when you get there. Why wouldn't you be?

Tom thought for a moment. Maybe… You wanna hear a joke?

Sure.

It's a really good one.

Let's hear it.

Like, it's crazy good. It's got sex and death. I mean, it's really more than a joke because you'll take things from it. It'll teach you things, you know. Your brain might melt a bit.

Just tell it.

And your face'll melt. Like all over the floor. So have a towel ready or something.

Beyond the glassless windows the harbour had become bright again, silver and reflective, the tide pulling out and releasing the beach.

ABOUT THE AUTHOR

Alec Hutchinson is from Auckland, New Zealand. He currently lives and teaches in the United Kingdom.

25342099R00201

Printed in Great Britain
by Amazon